Things in Brown Paper

Donovan Irven

Streisguth | Martin

Philadelphia, Pennsylvania

First Edition, November 2012

Cover Design by

Steven Streisguth

Streisguth.com

Cover Art: *Sunset (Ridgewood, NJ)*, Oil on Wood Panel, by

Kyle McCullough

kylemccullough.blogspot.com

Reprinted with artist's permission

This book is a work of fiction. Though the author was inspired by events and persons throughout his family history, the accounts contained herein have been heavily fictionalized for literary and philosophic purposes. Names have been changed to reflect these alterations. This work is not in any way intended as an accurate biographical record.

Also by Donovan Irven

The Ontological I & Other Essays

Two Days of Dying

CONTENTS

For
Wyola Jean
In Memorium

THINGS
IN
BROWN PAPER

PROLOGUE:

Notes on Successful Suicide

Winston had wanted to leave as soon as he received the letter, but a long autumn rain and his own sense of inertia had delayed him for two days. The rain was an excuse. He bought his train ticket on the third day and waited under a black umbrella at the station while the cloudy mist drifted through the corridors of Baltimore. The sun provided no heat and little light.

The train followed the rain into the west where the dissolving clouds made the stripped fall trees glisten like the skin of reptiles. The ampidaean limbs ratcheted tersely toward the ground, rigid in the damp cool.

Winston had dozed winding through the mounded vistas of Appalachia, and descended at last into the low, rolling plains of the Ohio Valley. People around him rocked gently with the tilt and shift of the train, each rushing toward their destination hopeful and afraid.

On the train, tucked in a brown paper envelope in the pocket of a briefcase beneath seat 14D was the letter, which began, *Reading this won't help you to understand why, only how…*

Sitting in 15D, Winston was exhausted by the extended effort of pretending to be alone. A round and aged woman sat next to him in a lavender blazer and matching hat filled with dry white flowers and a wisp of thin lace. She was staring ahead. The rolls of the train caused her head to nod in a barely perceptible rhythm. She remained purse-lipped. Winston was looking at her in bored curiosity. Through the narrow gaps she allowed at the bottom of her eyes, Winston saw that she saw him seeing her. His face remained fixed and the woman shifted uncomfortably in her seat. Realizing he must have caused her some length of discomfort, Winston felt obligated to engage the woman in some manner of small talk. He must have looked as if he were about to say something, because the woman made a showy attempt to settle into her seat and appear at ease.

"Do you live in Baltimore?" Winston asked.

The woman gave him a short look up and down, "No," she said. "I was visiting my daughter there."

"Really?" said Winston. "I'm on my way to Woodsfield. Well, east of there. Prospect Mills,"

"Do you have family there?" asked the other, shifting back toward the uninterested front of the train car.

"Yes. Well, I used to. I might stay out there."

"Hmm, people are always on the move someplace."

"Yes, ma'am. Yes they are," Winston agreed, trailing off. "Do you ever think about dying ma'am?"

She looked at him sharply through the side of her eye.

"Excuse me," she said. "I'm not *that* old."

"No, ma'am. I'm sorry. I didn't mean…I didn't mean to bother you."

Winston withdrew to the window.

"Oh, honey. I'm sorry," said the other, her façade melting under a maternal glow. "Has someone close to you passed on?"

"I suppose so."

"Oh, dear. There's no end to sorrow in the world. My husband's back home in hospice, so close to the end himself."

"I'm sorry to hear that," Winston wished he was more honest. "I shouldn't bother you with my own problems."

"Well," said the other, "we all got problems. We just have to do right by the Lord is all. It's something, I think, that binds us together. There's lots of ends and beginnings in life. All you can do is do your best in between."

Winston looked back at the woman. Her drawn oval face hoisted a thin smile over a look of disquiet. He wanted to kiss her then. She had partially succeeded in making him feel better, if only by sharing with him the burden of being human.

Instead, he asked, "What's your name?"

"Violet."

Winston shrugged off the coincidence and settled back into his seat, eyes trailing down the windowpane to the briefcase on the floor in front of him.

The two sank into a state of silence, lulled into a mild stupor by the gentle rocking of the train as it glided down into the sprawling valleys. Ahead the sun was dispersing the clouds with fresh sheets of warmth that soaked up the chill, damp air and left behind the tinge of evaporation. The now sparse tree coverage began its slow metamorphosis from glistening black to powdery gray. He had watched the trees running by for sometime before they fell away abruptly, breaking into a wide field cut to stubble by the labor of its owner, when it occurred to Winston that the landscape made so much sense. The rising and falling and growing and cutting of the landscape wherever living things moved often resembled an ordered, aesthetic expression. Like living scratched the surface and found an order underneath. He thought of the samurai and how everything made sense to them. Rigid hierarchy—honor and duty unto death. Dying was an obliging task, not some lonely escape or mere accident.

When the train stopped it seemed to Winston to do so very abruptly and he found himself in an awkward hurry to get off the train. Violet was slowly taking account of herself. Purse. Pockets. Hat. Carry-on. Excruciatingly, it seemed to Winston, she eased out of her seat. People shuffled silently behind her, scratching their noses as she felt steadily ahead with the rubber nub of her cane. Winston just sat in seat 15D with his head in one hand. As the last seven people or so passed the folding door and the smiling attendant, Winston snatched up his briefcase and walked off the train.

Outside on the deck everyone was meeting someone and, despite the hassle of crowds, the wide-open pavilion was suffused with happy airs mingling on the fall breeze. Briefcase in hand, Winston wound his way through the hustle and flow of people, up the shaky iron steps that carried him into the old station house. The door closed behind him, canceling the wind and the crowd and the air rushing out of brake lines. Inside was quiet and musty like a library. The nineteenth century was preserved under glass in tiny miniature. Cast iron steam engines puffed cotton-ball smoke into the air of the lobby's museum displays. A minute frozen couple waved goodbye. In any case, Winston felt the homage he had paid to the past by coming there in that way.

He must have been standing by the display for some time because a tiny man with smallish tank of oxygen slung over his shoulder, approached him.

"Is there something I can help you with?" he asked.

"Oh…no," Winston replied. "I'm sorry, do you work here?"

"Yes, for the last thirty-three years thank you very much," said the man,

"So you can tell where," Winston pause to sift through a bundle of papers in his pocket, withdrawing a scrap that read, "14 Pershing Street is?"

The man smiled and wheezed and said, "That's easy, it's the municipal building downtown. You're just going to leave the station here, walk straight out the main doors here and out to the road, that's going to be Liberty Street. Okay? Then take a left there and walk down, oh, say about a block and a half until you're by the parking lot of the old newspaper building. Should say the *Times* real big on the building. Well, just across Liberty Street there is Pershing. The municipal building is on the right."

After finishing the directions, the man fell into a period of heavy breathing, adjusting the valve on his oxygen. Winston watched him and tried not to be obvious. The man held the stiff plastic tube to his nose with two white fingers that trembled ever so slightly with each deep and rattling breath he took. Between his thumb and forefinger was a spot brown with age and another at his temple that was strained with one blue vein as he caught his breath. When he had recovered, the man smiled and shook his head and said, "Cancer. Got it in my lungs about six months ago."

"I'm sorry. I didn't..."

"No, no. Don't be sorry for me."

An uneven silence ensued with the static of sightseers milling about the station house.

"It's just," said Winston, "I didn't mean to stare."

"You think you're the first to stare at me and my tank? Shit. At least you try to hide it. It's the kids that get to me."

"Kids?"

"Yeah, *they* can really stare a guy down. Unashamed those kids are."

Winston almost chuckled. "The kids' staring offends you?"

"No, not so much offends me as gives me something to regret."

Winston looked away and traded his briefcase with the other hand.

"I never had any kids," said the man. "My own childhood, well, you have better things to do."

"Things," said Winston, "but nothing better."

"Well, you better get to them. Idleness is a thief."

"Were you idle?"

"No," the old man chuckled. "No, I wasn't idle. I was a sergeant."

Winston left the old man smiling and went to the restroom. It was quiet in the tiled lavatory, the air sterile but unmistakably old

10

with the varnish of the wooden stalls and the chill of ice in the urinals. Winston wondered if the old man was responsible for filling the urinals with ice as it melted unevenly beneath a stream of his urine. He shook and zipped his pants and wondered who would replace the ice when the old man had died of his cancer. He washed his hands, splashed water on his face, and looked at himself in the mirror. The letter had read:

This is not the kind of place you ever expect to find something, brother. I certainly didn't. But, if you think maybe you'll find something, you never believe—even in your most depraved dreams—that you'd find what I have found here in Prospect Mills. The thing is not so much in Prospect Mills, for it holds no space and occupies no time, but it is here nonetheless and I feel with each passing day that I was brought here to it. No, brought here for it, for this one final act, and brother, I can tell you because I know that you love me—it is terrible what I must do…

Outside the station the wind had begun with a new intensity that carried cold rain from the northwest. There was nothing yet, just the tingling air that was charged with the potential for weather. A cut of wind disturbed Winston's hair, the collar of his jacket. He adjusted himself, drawing closer to the source of his own heat, then began across the wide, empty yard toward Liberty Street. Passing on the periphery of his vision Winston noticed a woman crying on one of the wrought iron benches that lined the boulevard. Her driver, an aged man in black, stood over her shoulder consoling her with an old-fashioned, white-gloved hand. The woman sobbed and dabbed her thin eyes with a handkerchief she stuffed into her open purse. It was Violet, but Winston wasn't paying that much attention. He turned left down Liberty Street and strode the two blocks to the old newspaper building whose bottom floor, it seemed, was now filled with the offices of junior executives and shrinks with loft apartments in the upper stories. He stood outside the parking lot and watched a truck pull out of the retired printing annex, now a warehouse with stern men operating forklifts. Pershing Street met perpendicularly with the road across from where Winston stood and he waited, glancing at his watch, until traffic cleared. It was 1:43 in the afternoon. He crossed the street to the right corner of Liberty and Pershing and continued down the latter until the tip of an old Romanesque building appeared between the tops of the trees maintained by city ordinance. The municipal building was lofty and marble with smooth plate-glass doors on gold plated hinges and metal detectors installed a few paces behind them. A young officer with his ears sticking out from the side of his head smiled and took Winston's personal possessions: phone, keys, watch, change, briefcase. Winston collected them on the other side of the metal detector returning the guards toothy nod as he did. Signaling that he needn't any directions with a wave of his hand, Winston turned and entered the crass, artificial lights in the hall beyond the metal detectors. The hall was exaggerated for a building that size, whose smallness is revealed in the cramped interior made grand by hulking ornaments. Inside buildings of government, Winston always wandered if there wasn't something peculiar about pale green that made it disproportionately cheaper than other colors. Perhaps it invoked a sense of obedience.

As Winston turned the corner the doors opened on a courtroom from which was drug a man with limbs like wires and lips that sagged over the gaps where his teeth should have been. The man's arms were so thin it looked like the guards had grabbed the arms of an empty shirt in their hands and were surprised to find it resisted them.

"...answer to me! You gotta answer to Jesus!" he shouted as Winston made himself small in a hallway that had suddenly become claustrophobic with tension.

When the commotion had settled, Winston moved on wondering if he'd stared or if anyone would have minded or if he would have stared when he was a child. None of that seemed to matter so much, though it made Winston feel disconcerted as he neared the second to last door on the left side of the corridor. Like most things in the building the door pretended to age and posterity with its neat new roman letters etched in black across the glass that made everything on the other side appear garbled and fuzzy.

HON. EDINA H. GIETZEL
REGISTER OF WILLS

Winston knocked and was answered by a proper woman who looked strained as if she were smoldering in her pin-stripe suit. It was kept very warm in the building. The honorary Ms. Gietzel addressed Winston in a terse but polite manner that resonated with business and authority. She seemed sympathetic in a way reserved for people with power over the possessions of the dead.

"There are a few things for you to sign. I assume you've reviewed the letter?"

Winston looked up from the desk where he had been reading a memo regarding the elimination of casual Fridays.

"I'm sorry?" he said.

"The letter. You've looked it over? We were confident of the identity from evidence found at the scene but want to confirm with you that— "

"Yeah," said Winston, "it's him. Don't worry."

Edina looked across her desk trying to mask her irritation.

"He's still out in Prospect Mills?" Winston softened his tone.

Edina relented and began assembling the appropriate papers as she spoke to Winston in her straight, matter-of-fact tone.

"Yes. Everything essential to the investigation could be done there. But there's no judge or attorneys in Prospect Mills so everything gets registered here. Sign these here and here, please."

Winston took the handful of papers and looked them over briefly as he picked a notebook off the edge of the desk to sign on. Edina watched, adjusted her glasses, and folded her hands on the desk in front over her. She watched Winston apply his signature to the documents in his lap.

"Is there even a bus that goes out to Prospect Mills?" he asked as he wrote.

"Um, yes, at 6:30 and 5:30."

"Working class kind of town, huh?"

"Excuse me?"

"Never mind. I think this is everything Your Honor."

"Please," she said softening, "call me Ms. Geitzel," as Winston handed the papers back across the desk and return the notebook crooked. As she looked over the forms, Edina straightened the notebook and returned the packet to Winston, indicating with one plain nail where he'd neglected to sign. Using his hand to steady the paper, Winston signed and stood to leave.

"If you're finished with me Ms. Gietzel, I'd better go. I'd like to get lunch somewhere in town if you know a good place."

Edina turned red.

"I've already eaten today, thank you Mr. Avrich. I suggest you try *The Manhattan* just a block away on the corner of Grand and Thompkins. It's perfect for dining alone."

She seemed more cheery and so Winston didn't have the heart to tell her he hadn't intended that she join him. Instead, he blushed a little anyway, thanked her kindly for her time and left turning once before he retreated to see the pale smudge of Her Honor Edina Gietzel looking through her office door.

On the return down the corridor the air contracted as Winston approached the man that had been dragged from the courtroom. He was less excitable now, handcuffed to an iron rail. The rail was attached to the floor. The man's posture stooped as he sunk toward the ground to accommodate the restraints placed on him. The overall appearance was one of defeat. Winston slowed nervously. The man looked up from his slump revealing the red beneath his eyes. Winston began to quicken his pace after he had inadvertently made eye contact. His progression down the hall took a step in rapidity before halting altogether, words from behind arresting him in the corridor that now felt minuscule despite the architect's pretension to grandeur.

"I ain't a bad man," said the voice.

Winston couldn't turn around, or didn't. He turned his head enough to look back over his shoulder.

"I never supposed you were."

The man returned his gaze downward.

"But still, I ain't."

Winston continued to walk, collected his things at the front desk, and exited the courthouse. He walked the short distance to *The Manhattan*, which was quaint and quite unlike its namesake. There was no one around. A woman in an apron popped her gum. Another woman in a different style of apron emerged from the kitchen. She approached Winston carrying a tray. She didn't talk much and she brought Winston a glass of water with less ice than he liked. The beer was better and Winston ordered a burger, which seemed a bit overpriced. He sat in solitude and thought of his brother.

...I know no one had understood why I moved out to St. Clairsville, away from the opportunities of the city. But I wanted a different life for myself, and no one usually understands when we want a different life—they're all so use to the ones we have. You have to recognize that wasn't me in Baltimore, in Damascus, in Arlington, or Alexandria. Those old names in a new country and all those people. I just wanted a quiet life. I wanted to fall in love. I wanted to die...

Winston had passed through St. Clairsville on the train. It was a quiet, lazy Appalachian town in the folds of the mountains. Unassuming and tucked away, with a small university full of visiting students and visiting scholars, St. Clairsville had been a place to get away. It was not the East Coast. It was that place where the West was still just ahead and the East was far enough behind not to be threatening and the hills themselves yawned with age and long forgotten memories of an ancient vitality. It was where the trouble had begun.

…I can't tell you that the thing was in St. Clairsville. That wouldn't be right. But to say that it followed me from there—that that's where I caught it—you wouldn't be far off the mark with that description. I think it was in the woods. In the spaces between those mountains. I would go out there at night and find a clearing and just lay in the cradle of those hills until I forgot who or what I was and the desire washed over me to be done with it all except there wasn't anything to be done with anymore. There were just the crickets and a rustling in the underbrush and my mind was fleet like a rabbit across the dells…

Winston ate his burger and thought of a mad flight from a quiet mountain town. To get to Prospect Mills, Winston would have to go back east a little ways. St. Clairsville was large enough for the train, but little Prospect Mills was quainter still and the train was much too formidable a piece of modernity to run careless through the Ohio idyll of Prospect Mills. Just the intimation of rain dusted the window beside Winston as he ate, and thought of the last leg of his trip. He ordered another beer from the quiet waitress. He wondered what the Honorary Ms. Geitzel would have ordered. She probably would get the usual, whatever was usual for her and her smart pantsuit. Winston paid and tipped modestly. The thin rain had been weak but left the outside world refreshed in the pale sun of the finished day. From *The Manhattan* he had got a car, ignoring the bus for a rented blue sedan, and prepared for the final sixty miles into the country.

Even with the internet on his phone, Winston was not familiar with the area and thought it might be good to have some company. He'd made arrangements to meet a driver from the hotel at which his brother had been staying. Hotel was hardly the word,

17

for the place was really an elaborate house of furnished apartments in the old style, and if Winston had not known better he would have suspected an unforeseen bend of time had placed him at leisure in a brothel on the edge of civilized America. The fact that they could offer a driver at all was a real boon. He was happy to provide a car, which would subsequently be at his disposal, as well as being glad to have a chance of a moment's rest. The arrangement was to meet at the train station at four PM, and so Winston returned to *The Manhattan* for another drink before wending his way back to the train station to wait on a bench in the late steel autumn afternoon. There was no one else around. Winston had not been waiting long when a solid man sauntered up to him and said, "Winston Avrich," without indicating in any way that he had intended a question.

"Yes?" replied Winston, looking around.

"There isn't anyone else here."

Winston ceased his looking about. "No," he said. "There isn't. Are you the driver."

"That's me. Paul. Where's the car?"

"Over there," said Winston with a stiff wave of his arm.

"Keys?"

Winston returned Paul's coarse manner by tossing the keys to him without care. Paul snatched them from the air. He gave them half a glance and put them in his pocket.

"Let's go then," Paul said, starting off in the general direction of Winston's rented car.

Soon after he instructed the driver to the address, Winston had begun to doze, but the distance ahead brought to mind the urge to conversation. Besides, when his eyes were closed, Winston returned in consciousness to the letter and the cold black and white of the truth it presented.

When I realize what I mean to do, I am faced with the reality that it is to kill. But to kill whom and for what reason? That is the question I have answered…

The driver was overweight, not obese. He guided the car smoothly away from town along the highway and shortly thereafter exited to a scenic route that was demarcated with a series of rectangular green signs framed with white borders.

"You take many people out to Prospect Mills?" asked Winston, his voice caught in his throat.

"What's that?" asked the driver, drawing to one side of his mouth as he spoke.

"Take many people to Prospect Mills?" Winston said louder, the confined space making him seem louder then he intended.

"Nah," said the other.

"Oh."

The road was black from the rain.

The driver, Paul, said, "You got family out dere or sumpthin'?"

"Yeah," said Winston. "I mean…no, I guess not."

"Eh?" The driver looked uneasy for a moment. He then resumed driving nonplused. Winston sat back and looked out the window.

The scenery had become one of more or less consistently dense forest to one side or the other, either empty side being cleared for some manner of agriculture, or else dedicated to some equine purpose. Winston breathed somewhat heavily. His briefcase sat heavily on the seat beside him. The sun was greatly diminished on the edge of the horizon. The remainder of Winston's journey to Prospect Mills would be the slow transition of the orange dappled dusk disseminated across an autumn night plunged through lavender into the bruised azure darkness. He dozed. A pale moon hung ambiguously above the failing light. The rush of the car disturbed the whirl of motes suspended in the purple studded eve. Dandelions swayed naked in the breeze.

"Strange. What's happened out here. You know anything 'bout that?" asked the driver abruptly.

"Strange?" asked Winston.

"Yeah. Strange," said the other.

"Oh."

"You know anything 'bout that?"

"I think you mean my brother," said Winston.

"Your brother?"

"Yes."

Without too much commotion, the driver brought the car to a stop along the shoulder. "Your brother?" he asked.

"I'm sorry," said Winston. "I don't understand?"

"The fella that burned up?" asked the driver. "That fella's your brother?"

"Yes," said Winston.

"I'ma goin' I think."

Winston stared for a moment. "What?" he asked uncomprehending.

Winston wanted to say something, but nothing came to mind and so he just moved his mouth dumbly up and down in a feigned, minute sort of gesture. The driver shrugged nodding and looked Winston sharply up and down.

"It ain't *that* far of a walk," the driver said, glancing at his watch before exiting the car and walking off in whatever direction led him most rapidly away from Winston and all that concerned him.

Winston, defeated, resigned himself to the rest of the drive. He was shaken by Paul's strange and sudden behavior, the road in the darkening eve appeared damp and sinister. Paul had virtually disappeared into the surrounding dusk, everywhere lay dense with trees and the rounded folds of the plateau's shadows. He sat for a moment in the passengers seat staring after Paul's fleet shadow. When he had momentarily decided not to pursue Paul in any way, Winston exited the vehicle and began his way around to the driver's seat. As he was paused in the car's headlights to check his phone, a minivan stopped, though what make or model it was Winston could never have determined in the overabundant light. The driver was a young woman, attractive and modestly dressed. She wore her scarf loosely over a sweater with a dramatic v-neck.

"You okay?" asked the woman.

"Oh. Yeah, I'm fine," said Winston, still in mild disbelief. "My driver abandoned me here."

The woman looked puzzled. "Your driver?" she asked.

"Yeah, my driver. Paul."

"Your driver, Paul?" said the women, her voice quickening.

"Yeah, Paul," said Winston.

"Just lock your car up and leave it."

Winston tilted his head with a raised eyebrow.

"Please, just get in. I live at the Sheppard's Inn. My grandma runs the hotel," she had said. "Well, it's more like a boarding house I suppose, but it's comfortable and cheap. I mean, it's affordable."

"Will there be a clerk at this hour?" after he said this, Winston wondered himself why he had, or if it merely been a distraction from his awkward climb into the van.

"It'll be fine. My grandma's the owner," the tone of the girl's voice suggested he ask anyone and they would affirm the obvious truths she spoke. Tired, Winston acquiesced. They pulled up in front of the house, towering midtown and with a wrap-around porch, well after six in the evening. The girl, named Emilie, showed Winston to a large, old-fashioned registry, had him sign his name, and gave him a key to a room she said was "up the stairs and down the hallway to the left, the door's on the right. You'll see," and Winston had seen. In the dim greyscale of a silent film, Winston found his way easily up the stairs and along a hallway on his left. There were rooms every three yards or more and the third door he came to carried the plaque inscribed with "3C". The room enveloped him, and Winston lost all memory of the night that followed. He collapsed, face down on the bed and was cast into the repetition of the words: *What I found I dare tell no one. Not even you brother. This fact is the seed of madness…the seed of madness…*

Waking life came suddenly to Winston who awoke on his stomach, his head to one side and still fully clothed from the waist down. His socks drooped empty from his toes to the floor. He had only managed to sleep on the bottom quarter of the bed closest to the door. The room was the room of a house, it lacked that distinct anonymity of a hotel room. Though the walls were essentially bare, and the color palate was a decidedly non-descript and ambiguous tone, the room was lived in. There was a reflection in the mirror that caught the light, and the trim around the baseboards was just barely thicker in two to three inch runs. It was cool, but the window was open and Winston wore no shoes. The window faced the east and the mountains and the sun. Winston blinked, squinted and rose slowly from the mattress to which still clung the blankets from the night before. There was a lavatory attached to the room that was little more than a closet with a toilet and sink installed, though there was ventilation in the ceiling of the small enclosure. Winston washed up in the sink, applied fresh deodorant, brushed his teeth, and wore a clean shirt from his briefcase. Making a few last adjustments in the mirror, Winston turned and went into the hallway and towards the stars. A chorded runner with a dull palate muffled the hardwood floors shifting beneath his steps. At a corner he'd forgotten from the night before, Winston turned to his left and walked along a long banister to the stairs, which seemed much more open in the daylight. An elderly woman in a black dress busied herself with the morning paper and a cup of coffee. She sat easily behind the counter.

"Excuse me, but could I get some directions?"

The woman looked up from her paper. She was small, and wore just a bit of lace around her collar in an old fashion. But she was proud so you almost didn't notice her dated way of dress and she hopped down off her stool and was spry and sharp in her tone.

"Yeah, I'll give ye some directions, and if yer Winston Avrich I got another sumthin' for ye too?"

"I am Winston and I'm going to the coroner's office."

The woman chuckled and waved her hand at Winston, saying, "The undertaker, eh? Out front, through the intersection to the far left corner there." She then produced an envelope which she handed to Winston with a warm grin.

"Thanks," said Winston, turning to go. He stopped and turned to the woman. "I'll be staying another night if that's okay."

"Fine," said the woman without ever looking up. "Tend to your business. I'll have a word with ye t'night is all. Good day, sir!"

Winston left and paused on the sidewalk to look at the envelop he'd been given. He opened it and unfolded the yellow leaf of legal-pad-paper on which was written "Your brother sent me a package of interest. Call the number below this evening. I'm free after 5. – Jeremiah" He folded the note away without reading the number and took a brisk walk across the street. The man behind the counter saw Winston coming through the window. The inside of the office was like any doctor on a small town Main Street. But behind the counter it was clear the front served as a depository of records and that behind the door behind the counter was the dead. The air was stale with the hum of refrigerators. Winston put the papers from Ms. Edina Geitzel at the courthouse on the counter. A very tall, pear shaped man looked down at them. He took them up in a big, flat hand and held them some distance from his face, folding up his wide jaw as he squinted and brought reading glasses out of his plaid breast pocket. Adjusting his glasses made the man's sight markedly better and he read the document

24

with an intermittent pause to verify some information with Winston.

"Well, sir," said Elliot, the big man behind the counter, "your brothers been cremated already, sir."

"Yes, I had thought that would be the case."

"I'm sorry, sir. Sir, we do have his remains in a fine receptacle for you. Unless you'd prefer a marble urn? I don't recommend those, sir. I'd stick with the one we give you."

"It's okay. That will be fine. It's as I expected."

Elliot was about to leave and retrieve the urn when Winston stopped him. Winston hesitated before saying, "I was hoping to see him. It's…it's my brother. You know?"

"Aw, sir, I'm sorry. I don't know, sir. I'm sorry I ain't lost a brother like you. But, sir, I express my deepest condolences. I'll get your brother's remains."

Again, Elliot was about to go when Winston stopped him, saying, "I just hoped, perhaps there'd be some pictures, anything?"

"Sir," Elliot said turning grave, "you don't wanna see, sir. There's wasn't—

"Please," said Winston, "I…I *have* to see him."

Elliot seemed moved. He didn't move. "Okay," he said. "There's pictures in the file. Hold on." Elliot finally left. He was gone only a minute or two and returned to sit the urn on the counter. The polished brass looked out of place on the cheap industrial laminate used for the counter top. It was nice. Elliot had left again, this time in the opposite direction, disappearing into the rows of filing cabinets lining the walls in the anterior of the main floor.

When he returned, Elliot carried with him a folder. He placed the folder beside the urn on the counter and opened it. The contents were upright in Winston's view. In the middle of the folder was an envelope of brown paper closed by a red string.

"The photo's in the envelope. I ain't lookin' at 'em. You go ahead, sir."

Winston picked up the brown paper envelope. He unwound the string from its felted clasp. The flap opened without a sound and the photos hissed against the inside of the envelop as they slide onto the counter. There were several, all from different angles. They displayed a body, or what was left of one. The fire had burned away much of the fatty tissue and the musculature had been dramatically warped and dehydrated. The head was doubled back toward the soles of the feet, its mouth hung open in a ghastly grinning fashion. Little of the skin remained on the blackened skull and what taunt tendons and ligature remained only served to draw tight the features in a morbid exaggeration of glee. The arms and hands were turned up as well and curled back almost touching where the toes would have been had the feet not been utterly annihilated by the heat of the flames. The hands were twisted and tapered where fingers had been. No clothes of any identified kind remained on the blackened corpse. Winston shuffled through the photos a few times and replaced them in the envelope. When it was clear that Elliot was not being attentive, Winston withdrew one photo and hid it in his pocket. He quickly closed the folder and slid it across the counter to Elliot who refocused on Winston and the folder.

"I'm sorry," said Elliot.

"Goodbye," said Winston.

Winston left and went back to the hotel. He felt empty after the encounter with Elliot. He thought about the envelope and the mysterious Jeremiah. Then, he remembered the old woman, certainly his hostess, and thought it would be good to have a word with her as she wished. When he arrived back at the Sheppard's Inn, the woman was not around. He took his brother's remains to his room, trying to forget about them as he locked the door. Then, Winston took up reading in an area intended as a lounge, but which was really more like the owner's tidy living room, large as it was accommodating. There were some magazines, Winston flipped through *Sports Illustrated*. He glanced at the women in the magazines for women, eyeing each as the pages turned. He read half an article in *The Economist*, which had carried his interest until he began to think about his brother's letter. What could his brother have sent to this Jeremiah? Winston suspected that his brother had become deranged.

When I realize what I mean to do…

The tone of the thing made Winston uneasy. The woman returned. She saw Winston and he waved, making an effort to appear to want to speak to her. When she was close enough, Winston said, "I'm sorry, I don't think I got your name."

"No, ya didn't. That's okay. It's Judith. Sometimes people call me Judy, but Judith is fine. Now ya got it?"

"Yes ma'am."

"No. Not ma'am, my God. Just Judith is fine."

"Ok," said Winston.

"You got a minute?"

"Yes," said Winston. "You wanted to talk?"

"Well, we got to know yer brother pretty well 'round here."

"I see."

"I wanted to talk to you 'bout Paul and apologize. He was a little wound up yesterday anyway."

"How so?"

"He had to take his brother, Jessie into court and they repossessed his car for back child-support and put him in jail."

Winston thought about the man in the courthouse and looked down.

"It's sad. But, you know, stuff like that happens all the time 'round here. I don' know what gets into people sometimes."

"Tell me about it."

"Right, your brother. He was an honest man, your brother. Shame. So young. I'm old," Judith laughed at her age. "But I've seen some things. Your brother became interested in a piece a land back East, in the mountains, probly two, two an' a half hours out."

"What?"

"Yeah, St Clairsville's the closest town of any note, the place is in the boonies. If I din' know better I'd bet there's old growth forest on that land."

"So, is that what my brother was interested in? The woods?"

"No. I'm just sayin', it's still wild out there. You understand?"

"Sure."

"Well," Judith gave Winston the eye, "in any case, I'll tell you a bit about what I know happened to your brother, not that you'll understand it."

"Okay." There was a moment of silence. Then, "I appreciate you taking the time to speak with me."

"Don't mention it, honey. It's the least I can do," Judith's smile was warm. "You know, he was troubled. He had an old soul, your brother. I could see it, just the way he walked you know. There was something—heavy—about him. He stayed here for a few months. Got to know Emilie, Paul and Jessie. I own the tavern down the road a bit as well. Your brother went in there for drinks. He was a regular for a time. People are familiar 'round here, you see. Everybody knows everybody. You boys from the city don' quite understand what I mean when I say that. But it's true, anyways. He took to hiking out that way. Gone for days at a time. And you know his books and stuff, what he wrote about all that, what'd he call it? Anthropology. Ethnography or something. Whew, all them *words*, ha! He was plenty smart, your brother was. It's a shame. Anyways, he found these claim stakes that were old, he said back to the Revolutionary War. George Washington's time, you know? Maybe not quite that old. Early 1800s. Anyways, the point is they was old and yer brother found 'em and he got all worked up about it. Started doin' his research. Kept diggin' around out there. Found some more stuff. Found an old mine shaft. I knew about that mind you. I told him so myself, I knowed that was out there. And he asked me all kinds a questions about it. Recorded me on his computer and everything. Don' know where you'll get that stuff, I ain't seen it.

"Anyways, he started stayin' out there a lot. I felt bad chargin' him for the room, he was hardly here. An' when he was, he was, different. Off, distracted, you know? Like he was worried about somethin'. I don' know. I supposed I was worried about him. He told me he was goin' to make a big discovery. Write a story 'bout it. Kind of history or somethin'. I lived out there, I know history, but I left. In the '50s see? After the War. I was young and getting married. But me and my husband separated. Funny, you think, someone my age, getting divorced. I guess it was scandalous. That's what he got in touch with Professor Jeremiah about. He works at the university in St. Clairsville. See, your brother wasn't even in Ohio when all this happened."

"He wasn't?"

"No."

"Where's St. Clairsville?"

"Not Ohio. If you want, Emilie can go out there with you. I know secretly she's curious about what happened to your brother."

"I would like to know what he sent to Jeremiah."

"I'll ask Emilie. But I know he was interested in the Indian, er, Native Americans. I think he said the Algonquins."

"He was always interested in the Native Americans."

"Terrible what we did to the Natives. Things your brother told me. They don' teach you that in school."

"No, they don't."

"Anyways, that's what he went to see Dr. Jeremiah about, and he must've seen him three or four times. 'Bout different things. Them stakes, what Native was there before, when they moved on, all that. He had all kinds a questions, your brother did."

"When do you think I could see Jeremiah?"

"Why don' ya take some rest, enjoy what Prospect Mills has to offer, which I guess ain't much but a hot meal an' a beer. I'll get Emilie to go out to St. Clairsville with ya tomorrow."

Winston thought for a moment.

"Yes, I suppose that's fine," he said. "Tomorrow."

"I don' know what else to tell ya. I can't explain what he done," Judith looked bewildered.

"No," said Winston. "I can't explain it either."

The next day, Emilie rode with him to St. Clairsville, to see Jeremiah, the professor. He had taken the time, after speaking with Judith, to walk the distance to his rental car and drive it the rest of the way to Prospect Mills and was glad for it. The afternoon was pleasant and provided an opportunity to clear his mind, into which the words of his dead brother intruded and recurred throughout.

All of them dead. Basically genocide. I will shine a light on them. Then, everyone will be forced to bear witness…

He drove to Prospect Mills in silence. At the tavern, the only one in town, Winston got a beer and a sandwich, both of which satisfied him. He turned in early. It would have been easy to adjust to the casual tempo of this country existence. Then, he was in the car with Emilie. She had been kind enough to drive and offer pleasant conversation.

"My grandma's ninety-two. She doesn't seem that old does she?"

"No," said Winston. "She doesn't."

"Did she say anything about Paul?"

"She apologized. And said something about his brother going to jail."

"Oh, yeah. It's a shame about Jessie. Are you religious? Paul and Jessie are real religious."

"No, I'm not what anyone would call 'religious'," said Winston.

"Me neither. But Paul is. I guess grandma didn't want to gossip, but I don't mind telling you, Paul's a little crazy and he got things in his head about your brother, you know?"

"No, I guess I don't."

"Paul's not like, regular religious. Like he himself is a little crazy and religion just gets mixed up in all the crazy."

"Yeah," said Winston smiling.

"Well, for him, all your brother's talk about Native Americans and their ancestral lands and legacy and all that spiritual stuff, well, to Paul that was as good as saying the Devil. You know what I mean?"

"I think so," though Winston wasn't quite sure he dd.

"He would talk a lot about a woman. I think she was a woman. An Indian woman. Native American."

She didn't know too much more than that. There had been an element of secrecy surrounding what it was the deceased had been uncovering. Winston knew it was partially academic acumen. Being the first to unveil a big discovery, the publications, and so on. But, the letter gave it a sinister quality.

It took them more than an hour to reach St. Clairsville. The weather was clear and there was access to the university from the highway. They were in the mountains now, and had been for some time. Much of the hillsides were evergreens and St. Clairsville sat in a valley with the river curved around and through its outer suburbs. Winston remembered the train passing through, the skyline dappled with church steeples. Passing through town a Masonic Temple stood prominently on a hillock. Just past that, another rise and a cathedral for the Presbyterians, whose subterranean tunnels had been used in the Underground Railroad.

The college was modern, lacking the historical nicety and curiosity of some of the old churches. Jeremiah was on the second floor of one of the campus' older buildings, with a view of the clock tower in the quad, the trees smartly placed across the lawns, occasionally, a bit of modern art.

Jeremiah stood when Winston and Emilie entered his office. They shook Jeremiah's hand.

"Well," Jeremiah said and stroked his full beard, shot through with steel grey and five or six inches in length. "Your brother sent me some of his belongings, and I'm sure you'd like to have them. They might explain some, who knows."

"Thank you for seeing us, Professor," said Winston.

"Forget it. Call me Jeremiah. Look, I haven't even opened this yet. I suspect, some of it's his research. I can't figure out why else he'd send it to me. If there's any thing of value, I would very much like to make some copies, if that's okay."

"I don't have much interest, I'm not really a scholar."

"I see."

"Let's just see what we've got?"

Jeremiah rose and dug around in a pile of papers and books, haphazardly stacked and off balance. Each move seemed to bring the whole thing nearer to calamity, but Jeremiah showed his experience and produced a box large enough for a briefcase, which was what it contained. In the briefcase was a 13" MacBook, a one-page letter addressed to Jeremiah, a ten gigabyte flash drive, and what appeared to be a sizable bundle of documents wrapped in brown paper.

The letter read:

Jeremiah:

The brown paper contains my research, what I've been able to save. Some of it I burned. You should have this, it's the least I can do. Write a book. You can make my silence speak.

Yours,

The Crucified One

"I suppose he wanted you to have it," Winston said.

Jeremiah just shook his head. "That's Nietzsche, 'the Crucified One.' Nietzsche signed a letter just that way as he went insane in January 1889."

"Nietzsche? My brother killed himself because of Friedrich Nietzsche?"

"Don't be absurd, Winston," said Emilie.

"No, certainly not. But I think it's rather a kind of jab at me. We had talked extensively about Nietzsche and self-overcoming. This final act of renunciation! The Will to Power—even to death! Lets see what he managed to save, shall we?"

"Yes, open it."

The paper was pealed back. The bundle, revealed, consisted of a few layers of papers and a folder, which dominated the lot. They opened it at once.

"They're case studies. Profiles."

"There's names, here's just a list and dates. A lot from the early 1900s, look 191_, 192_, who are some of these people?" asked Emilie.

"Holofernes Harbarger?" said Winston, "Holofernes…"

"Biblical, Greek," said Jeremiah.

Emilie laughed a little, "Tatters. Must be a nickname."

"I think the emphasis is on whatever name the person was most strongly identified with in their community. We had lengthy conversations on this topic; how the community and individual shape one another's identities. A mutually created space—culture right?"

"Sure," said Winston. If that was to be counted as an answer.

"Wait, Harbarger, that's grandma's maiden name! It hadn't struck till just now. Her family's from these parts."

"Here's a bit of a map, and it looks like a sizable piece of property. That'd be prime real estate, wow, right in the middle of nowhere. Pristine."

They began sifting through the papers, reading, piecing together a history of the names that would not be forgotten. A large portion of the research was on Emilie and Judith's family, or at least a branch of it. Another line of question seemed desperate in its concern that the author was linked somehow, fated to join in the tragedy he had outlined from stakes in the ground.

"What had got him started on all this?" asked Emilie. "How did he even come to know about this?"

They surveyed the dated notes. Time was passing, the sun was dimming in descent. They read. The oldest dated notes had a photograph attached. Black and white print. A man, conceal by bandages, sitting on the broad porch of a plantation house, flanked by two daughters. Hound-dogs are at their feet. There is no mother. The notes to which the photo was attached seemed to have little relation to the photo itself. But on the back of the photo was a red asterisk, drawn with heavy strokes.

"That's pre-Civil War, I'd guess sometime 1840s or 1850s. Not earlier than 1830," Jeremiah was fond of speculation.

"What's the notes?" asked Emilie.

The notes were on the oddly named "Tatters".

It was eventually decided that Jeremiah make copies of the documents, and send an organized version of the papers to Winston in the mail. He knew these contained the secret. At last, he would have the hidden knowledge for which his brother had died. He received the package while still at the Sheppard's Inn. For a week, Winston sat in the lounge, by the window or fire, or in his room, like that of a house, and slowly, he reconstructed a past that moved embodied about the hotel, tidying up and keeping an immaculate business. The business of history; providing refuge to wayfarers who have passed by to lay the dead to rest.

PART ONE:

Names Not Forgotten

TATTERS

Tatters was better at chess than anyone on the mountain, which gave him an intellectual edge in just about everything else. Whenever someone would approach him sitting on his porch or giving advice down at his brother's hardware store and say, "Tatters Marks, when the *hell* are you gonna git yourself a new pair'a pants?" Tatters would just reply, "Don't see much wrong with these'ins." And when they inevitably rebuked that, "The whole damn bottoms of them'ins is torn ta *shreds*," Tatters would just shrug and turn back to slowly rocking his chair or explaining the importance of the new hex-socket screws coming out of the Standard Press Steel Co.

"What do them boys over in Philadelphia know that they don't know up in Pittsburgh?"

"I don't know what they know but I know that them hex screws is gonna be the best thing for tool and die work, you mark my word. Now I might not know what I'ma talkin' about, but I'm tellin' you them hex screws will be best in that motor'a yours."

It was true that Tatters was still a young man, and his youth more than anything had unnerved all the old timers that had been beaten in chess by someone who would refuse to even shoot at a buck he didn't think would come in over 175 inches for the Boone and Crockett. And he was famously accurate at estimating the score a set of antlers would get him. All in all, Tatters was a bit of an upstart.

Not that the mountain wasn't full of these and that Tatters was only one of three brothers to come out of the hollow playing flushes, straights, and calling checkmate with a restrained smile. Tatter's older brother Wayne was more clean cut than Tatters, wore better clothes and shaved every other day, but he could drink with the rest of them and hadn't suitably settled down to one woman by the age of 21, like his mother would have liked him to do. The youngest brother, Harold, hadn't warmed up to chasing women yet and was, like most youngest sons, often guilty of being Mama's boy. Of course, it was very easy to be the youngest son and a Mama's boy when your Mama was the one who raised these boys. It was the older sons that lived in the shadow of this woman; the youngest had been born into the sunlight of Mama's mature years.

Mama had been a hard woman when her husband was running around skirt chasing and gambling. She had resented her boys for that, for being boys and for loving their father like they did. There was a daughter too, but in those days having a daughter wasn't the same as having a son, and maybe Mama Clay resented

Margaret for not being a son. If she did, no one ever knew it, and maybe Mama wouldn't let herself know it either. Clay had been Mama's maiden name, and like all good wives she took her husband's name, Marks, but her nature was like the rock of the earth and so her maiden name stuck and she was maiden of the earth all her years; a rock to her family, a mountain woman, and a damn good cook. It wasn't wrong for a woman to cook in those days and Mama Clay was a proud woman of the hearth. Her husband had come over the mountain and into the hollow from Irishtown, a coal-mining shantytown on the next mountain west that sent men and boys into the earth, some never to return. Abraham, who's given name had been Jan, came up fighting in Irishtown, unable to be the patriarch of the name he'd chosen. America was suppose to be a new beginning, and Jan, now Abe, soon to die, was aiming to make it a royal beginning but could never get such a flush on the flop. Or maybe he could never see it through the moonshine in his eyes and the coal that had become a permanent part of his face—inlaid around his elusive smile and branching like carbon marquetery in the crow's feet etched along the ridge of his prominent zygomatic arch.

The story of a man like Tatters is the story of escape though not from prison or even the metaphoric escape of the drink which men like Tatters are known all over to imbibe. A man like that, his story is the escape from his father. The cruelty of parenting is exacted on the parent more than the child. The parent, and at that time the father especially, had to give everything to bring up his boys, the best of him was left down in a mine or stretched on a hot slab in the blast furnace of the mill or factory. Spent and broken by

41

toil, the father was left to see his own mortality in the face of his son's youth and feel the betrayal of losing that labor he had reared to the freedom of the world and a woman's call. The heat between a woman's legs was always more attractive than the heat of the fields at the homestead. It was, after all, the unavoidable gateway to the tragedy.

Abraham had become a tyrant because of hard labor though in spite of his hardness his family loved him. Hell, Tatters loved him best of all and the rebellion Tatters waged was a rebellion for the prize of his father's respect, which he never seemed to earn in the reputed fashion.

Tatters' father had done everything on his own. He came across the sea on his own, learned to correct his tongue to the language on his own, and worked on his own anyway he saw fit, including in the mines, but also hauling timber, raking gravel and quarry work, and making moonshine that could be sold for a fair six dollars a gallon. He had liked to play chess as much as he had liked to fight and was especially fond of fighting over chess and so it was natural that this game was the first competition between Abraham and Tatters. The name Abraham had given Tatters was Irven, after an old man Abe had barely known but who had given the young immigrant refuge when he had come into the mountains from the coast barely a pup, whose patchy beard had still been mixed unevenly with peach-fuzz and whose full, bare lips still spoke like a child. The old man Irvin Russell, Jr. had taught Abraham chess, and Abraham had taught Irven Marks. Abe had no better notion of legacy than that.

Firelight was the light by which the games were conducted, after the day's labor had been seen to and Abe was satisfied that his youngest son was developing a sense of masculine responsibility. Tatters was nine years old and had been playing his father at chess for two years when he waited up one night for Abraham, who never came home. The boy would recall for some time the anxiety of that night, sitting awake after his mother had turned in long ago. The window grew cold in the night, even so late in spring, and young Irven's breath was suffuse across the pane when he exhaled and withdrew again as he inhaled. The next morning, Mama complained that Abe was somewhere drunk.

By the time Abraham had returned home, he was indeed drunk. The night before, however, as Little Irven sat alone, Abraham had had a sobering experience. Abraham had been working in the mines since a month before Tatters was born. He had received an increase of wage in 191_ and at the same time his workday had been shorted. Life seemed good under the United Mine Workers of America. The UMW of A, by Abraham's judgment, was a friend of the working man, which is what he was. These advances made by the UMWA on behalf of the workers were upheld until about 192_ when the agreement began to sour and mine operators were increasingly disavowing the agreement, which led to labor unrest. Word around town was "strike".

Margaret had just been born, and with a baby in swaddling, talk of labor unrest was the last kind of talk Mama wanted to have about the house. Games of chess became fewer and Abe was out of the house, down at the local tavern meeting with his fellow workers, organizing a resistance to management at the mining company. This was the familial holding-pattern throughout Margaret's infancy as the unrest grew and relations between labor and management stagnated before going wholly sour.

By the time Tatters was ten years old he could probably have beaten Abraham at chess. So much had begun to occupy his father that Tatters was never given the chance. Abraham was gone all day in the mines, then gone to the tavern to get drunk, play cards, and talk about the plight of the working class. Tatters stayed at home, digging the earth with his older brother Wayne, and helping his mother around the house. Tatters' labor was milking, this was his biggest chore, though he was responsible for eggs three days a week as well. Their house was small, though it hardly mattered because they were inside only to sleep and eat in the warm months and in the winter sat close together by the stove to keep out the cold. They had a chicken coop, kept pinned in all around with wire, and they had a stable of sorts, lean-to though it was, the structure was sound enough for a dairy cow and ass to sleep under, and would eventually be useful enough for a horse. From time to time the Marks's would raise pigs, but Mama hated their constant wallowing so close to the house, so a season or two would pass before she gave in and allowed Abe to acquire more hogs. Working this way, Tatters felt abandoned. At ten years he was strong and he knew he could have beaten his father at chess, but felt with each passing week and month that Abraham couldn't be bothered with him. The labor movement was a real challenge, one that eclipsed the tiny tactical prowess of his ten year old son.

It went on like that for some time. Mama was not unhappy, Abe still brought home the better part of his pay and the call of social justice is never lost on a woman of merit. But Little Irven was growing impatient with his father and as adolescence began settling into his groin, that old fire of patricide began to burn in his heart. Finally, in April of Irven's twelfth year, a strike was called.

The strike, at that particular time, decimated any time Abe had had in which he was willing to cultivate a relationship with his second eldest son. In a few months, Mama would learn she was with child again, this time with Harry, the youngest. But until her belly grew fat, Mama encouraged Abe on the picket line, baked bread for the laborers, and took them jars of Abe's moonshine to keep off the springtime chill at night.

Irven began to see, in spite of his father, that there was something beyond family, something in the world outside his milking, checking the hens for eggs, and digging furrows with Wayne in the field. Wayne was the oldest and so he did the eldest's share of the work in the field, driving the mule back and forth to till the red and brown earth that got sandy in the lowlands in the shadow of the mountains. Irven, even before he was Tatters, wore the tattered clothes of a hand-me-down son and worked the field with an old pick axe his father had brought over the mountain from Irishtown. He struck minutely at the ground with the axe, whittling tiny furrows across the clearing with his eye fixed on the sifting clay being driven and divided below him, his hands gripping the handle too tight, his blisters more black than white from the dirt caked in the grooves of his hands and the axe. Wayne always had the big picture, driving the mule to and fro, but Irven saw the details of their livelihoods sifting around the pick-axe. From time to time he bent to pick up a shell, whole and white far from the sea. He kept these stranded sea shells in a jar beneath his bed.

On July 1st the strike got a shot in the arm and all activity in the bituminous fields ground to a halt. Some 750 miners were on strike and their names began filling pink slips and black lists and company men made rounds among the scabs and new hires with yellow contracts and threats and warnings about the UMWA. Money stopped coming into the Marks house when Mama's belly was growing fat. Abe was less encouraged on the picket line. As Autumn came full into the nights the moonshine did less to keep the lines full. Thick necked men patrolled with revolvers tucked in their jeans. A sentry became commonplace at the entrance to the mines.

It was cool in September. Irven had been inside for two days due to rain. He had beaten Wayne at chess so badly that the oldest brother had refused to play on the afternoon of the second day. Instead, he went outside despite the damp and did some work around the garden where he could. The next day, digging around the potatoes, Irven saw the white fluff of an oomycete under the warm, wet leaves of the potatoes that had kept in the ground since the last season. He had been hoping to start to dig these out and rotate the over-wintering to another patch, but that day's harvest brought up potatoes shriveled and blackened from blight. Abe hadn't been home in three days. It would be two more before he showed and when he showed he would be drunk and unable to recognize the grotesque stench of death that pervaded his fields and sent his boys scrambling to burn the spore covered leaves of his ruined crop.

Irven had hid all day the day Wayne left home. Something told Irven's stomach what Wayne intended to do. It didn't make sense. Wayne could easily maneuver into a ladler's position at the glass mill, or take up with the quarry hauling gravel and stone for transport. But he didn't try any of those things. It was as if he had never even thought of anything else. So, Irven had hid knowing his father would be home and that the confrontation was inevitable and had in all likelihood already occurred. The day had stretched on indeterminably.

When Abe came home he stormed and raged about the homestead. His boots fell heavily on the wooden floors of their house. Irven watched his father from the stable where he had been needlessly brushing their mule. A barrel of blighted potatoes smoldered in the far corner of their property. Irven stopped brushing. Hair had long ceased to fall from the mule's sagging back. Irven left the stable, went to the side of the house, and crouched down listening. Mama has been making bread inside when Abe came in in a state of great agitation. She paid him no mind as he stomped his boots off all over the main rooms of the house. Finally, as if it were of no significance, Mama asked, "You see Wayne t'day?"

Abe stopped his stomping. He came into the kitchen.

"*Seen* 'im?" Abe said mortified. "I seen that boy. You bet yer ass I *seen* 'im. That bastard son 'a mine's down in the mine. My own flesh a scab! Looked me right in'a eye as he crossed. Right in'a eye! Bastard!"

Mama had just rolled the dough as Abe spoke and spit with anger. "I asked 'im where he's goin' this morin'. So early an all."

47

Abe just stared at Mama.

"You *asked* 'im? You *asked*? You knowed damn well where he was a'goin' woman."

"I din'" said the other.

"You did too know it," without warning Abe had struck out from where he stood and near took Mama off her feet with the back of his hand. Her head snapped away to the side and she took a few forced steps away from her dough as Abe reared back to let her have it once more. She didn't shrink away. She had composed herself and stood square up to Abe, his hand opened and drawn back.

As a rule, Abe did not strike his wife. That fact made this singular moment impress itself all the more on Irven's adolescent consciousness. His parent's stood facing off for the fraction of a second, but that infinitesimal duration lay frozen before Irven's eye for all time. He shrunk rapidly to the ground and pressed the back of head against the side of the house until white spots whirled in the vision of his clenched eyes. He waited for Abe to deliver on his threat of a beating but the blow was never struck and Abe and Mama just kept looking at each other while Abe slowly lowered his hand and Mama eased her posture and came close to comfort again.

"Why don' you do what ol' man Russell done said?"

Abe was silent.

"Why didn' you ever *listen* to that ol' man?"

Abe had been looking at the floor but looked back up to his wife.

"Cause Russell's scared woman."

"What's he scared of? All that money sittin' up in the mountain? Jus' *watiin'* Abe. Waitin' for you an' them kids ta git up there'n git it."

"It ain't that simple. It ain't jus' sittin' an' you knows it."

"I'm talkin' bout the sweat o' yer brow, Abraham Marks."

"You never did marry no lazy man."

Mama Clay was stone in the slanting shafts of sun.

"But I don' wanna go back 'n under the earth again."

Mama Clay stood firm. "It ain't a matter a wantin'."

"I know, woman. I know."

"You know damn well what they's a gonna do ta this place. You *knows it*."

"I reckon they'll be round in a few days."

There was a silence then. The quiet was broken by the minute footsteps of the child Margaret as she shuffled into the kitchen between her parents. Abe got up and left the room. Margaret cooed and shuffled and Mama picked her up. Then the kitchen was empty and Irven still crouched beneath the window with his head pressed hard against the bottom of the sill, his eyes slowly opening to a world from which the air had all gone out. He breathed haltingly and wondered what to do. When he got up to go inside, Mama was sitting on the porch nursing his little sister. Abe was still somewhere in the house.

"Let yer father be."

Irven stopped with his small hand on the doorframe. Mama rocked back and forth in the chair making no effort to hide her nursing habits. Margaret was calm as she sucked the milk. Irven's hand fell from the doorframe.

"Is Wayne gonna be alright Mama?"

"What kind 'a question is that?"

"I don' know."

"You ain't got nothin' to worry on."

"But Mama…"

"Hush now. You listen to yer Mama. Wayne ain't lost ta them mines. He's jus' tryin'a prove hisself. You don' worry 'bout that what ya don' understand jus' yet. You hear me?"

"Yes, Mama."

"Yer a fine boy, Irven. You go wash up an' I'll see you git fed too. We got food in the icebox yet."

Irven didn't say anything in reply, but obeyed his mother and went inside. Passing through the house, Irven went by his parents' room. The door was just slightly ajar and from an angle Irven could see his father seated on the far side of the bed with his back to the door. Irven had been walking through the house with great care, heeding his mother's warning to let his father be. He stopped short outside his parent's bedroom where he could see Abe cradled something in his lap. Holding the object close to himself to shield it from the world, Abe's posture gave Irven the sense that it was he from whom Abe withheld the great secret. Irven stood there holding his breath for some time, hoping his father would shift or turn just enough for him to get a glimpse of the secret sheltered in his father's hands. He withdrew from the door so that Abe wouldn't see him but lingered just close enough to watch as Abe got up from the bed and walked over to the hulking chifforobe and placed a small rectangular box wrapped in brown paper back into one of the small top drawers which were about level with

Abe's breast. Irven darted away as Abe slowly turned and approached the door, which he had not noticed was ajar.

Once inside he and his brother's room, Irven made sure the door latch clicked shut behind him. He went quickly to his low, narrow bed and pulled a small chest from underneath. Working with an unknown haste, Irven collected a few warm clothes from within, threw them haphazardly on himself, and crawled gracelessly out the window. Looking back at the house, he hurried along the perimeter of the yard where the smoldering smell of the lost crops still hung like a ghostly reminder of Irven's isolation. He crept into the inadequate barn, gathered an armful of rope and a buck knife, and exited without a backward glance. With the house hidden on the far side of the barn, Irven ducked into the woods where he used the last light of day to cut a length of rope before wrapping the sheathed buck-knife along with a handkerchief, a pair of socks, and a ball of twine in a square of sackcloth bound up by the length of rope. He'd left enough rope to secure the bundle over his shoulder and, this done, followed the road away from his home and away from the neighbors, deeper into the dark of the Appalachian foothills. A light flickered on and off as it passed between the trees away on the road and Irven assumed this was his brother Wayne returning home to whatever familial drama awaited there. Minutes later, Mama Clay could be heard calling for Irven, her voice fading as Irven pressed to place a greater distance between himself and the civil unrest that pitted his father and brother against the interested of their collective will. He went on and on into the mountains, picking his way along a worn deer trail, until his twelve year old feet ached from their pounding the ground and his knees felt the chill of night coming into them and he at last found his refuge in a hollow amidst a grove of trees and mountain laurel wherein he could safely crawl into a ball and let the sleep he longed for sweep into his soul and steal the troubled consciousness from his eyes, if only for a span of a few hours.

The sun was slow to find its way into the thickness of the mountains so that Irven was never sure exactly how long he had slept in the wilderness that first night. Of course, it was passing slowly into autumn and the less direct ascent of the sun into the noonday sky allowed the cool of the morning to give away slowly to the mild warmth of the after noon. When Irven at last awoke to the rising sun, the shafts of light undeterred by the canopy were sifting at an angle onto the back of his neck. After coming to and taking account of things, he guessed it was ten in the morning and wondered what exactly he would eat that day. He took a bit of jerky from his pocket and chewed it while he thought. There wouldn't be enough jerky to eat for long but he had anticipated tiding himself over on the last shreds of dried meat he carried in his pocket to abide him in his field work. He went around in the woods, up the mountain a ways and back, carried himself farther into the woods for about 2,000 paces and began walking a diameter around an area of what he thought must have been about five acres. He chewed the jerky slowly and marked off the diameter with a broken branch or two, together with a few piles of rocks interspersed among the underbrush.

After he had finished, Irven walked into the middle of the territory he'd surveyed and left the bundle in a dell next to a low shelf of rock and a fallen tree. He chewed the jerky and took the buck-knife and twine from the bundle. Along the way around the woods he had seen a few rabbits and the evidence of other wildlife. He went around again, quietly looking and picking out a few trails here and there and again seeing a rabbit or two moving discreetly out of sight. Birds flitted about but he was careful not to send them in showers from the forest floor to disturb the orange red leaves above them. The air was greenish and yellow and saturated with the hard brown striation of the trees. In a well worn line across a little brook, Irven laid a snare by driving a sharpened stick into the edge of the trail and fastening to this a length of twine made into a slipknot with a tail about a foot long. He laid the snare across the little path using a small forked stick convenient for the purpose. He was quick and left without much fuss and set a few more snares in the wide circle around his bundle.

The day was getting on when he followed the traces of the little brook to a creek which happened to skirt the edge of his territory. On the surveying walk he'd smelled the damp of the water passing between the arms of the trees. Absently, he stripped off his clothes to wash himself in the creek where it pooled among the rocks of the lowlands. He looked around to where the water began to slow and the debris of the forest seemed unusually abundant along the water's flow. Sheltered by outcroppings of rock, a beach of sediments had been deposited against the steep ledge of layered stone and the land had gradually formed itself around the rocks and trees until finally a quaint little watering hole emerged from the unnoticed rotation of the earth. Irven stood waist deep in water and reviewed the environment. He followed the current upstream until the creek slowed and the bank was more even.

On a sloping part of the bank, Irven spotted a piling of wetted wood and mud caked drift too conveniently arranged to be the chance of wind and water. He tore at the dried branches of a thicket of bushes on the side of the creek opposite this dam and waded to and fro until he had braided the torn thicket into a fence about two feet from an opening in the dam with a radius of about four feet all around the hole. He left a gap in line with the hole in the dam and therein submerged another snare that was fastened to the creek bed with forked sticks, mud, and perseverance under the chilly mountain stream. This snare he took extra measures to secure to the creek bottom and he left a gap above the snare, between the line of twine suspended in the waters and a bit of wood which he had laid across his little gate like a parapet over a gateway. This finished, Irven returned to the beach and lay naked in the afternoon sun to dry and warm himself.

Once dry, he put his clothes back on and walked through the woods, eying his snares from a distance and chewing on the last shreds of jerky. There was nothing in the snares. Irven was hungry. With the ache in his stomach he built a modest fire pit and finished the jerky as he used the twine to spin the whittled end of a stick against a log on which he'd used the buck-knife to shave a tiny mound of kindling. The fire grew under the bellows of his lungs and he warmed himself and forgot his hunger and slept.

In sleep Irven forgot that he'd learned all these things from his father and brother. The world of the blighted potatoes and the miner's strike was far away and the stars over head were so near to him. He looked up at the reeling lights projecting their twinkling distance down on him and thought that the blood feud raging back home might never die just as the light from those stars never faded, not even after the explosive death of those stars forever silenced the fusion of atoms in space. No human eye would ever detect that long nuclear death as the light rushed ever onward from the last breath of its source into the dark and absolute zero of space and time, running on and on into the night until it fell at last on the distant histories of humanity as they slept beneath a blanket of these eternal dying suns. The rustle in the thicket was as near as those stars and the owls were in Irven's ear as sure as they perched in the boughs of the oaks and the high bristled tops of pines crowded in throughout the sycamore. There was no distinguishing this manifold behind his closed eyes, and the futile unity of the world weighed heavy on Irven's heart as he thought what was to be done on that second lonesome night on the mountain. A return awaited him. But what return and to where he did not yet know.

He could still hear the distant call of his mother in his ears, subdued under the metronomic hoot of the owls and the periodic swoosh of their deadly descents. He would have to make that return trip, but he must make it without the emptiness with which he left. As he slept it came into his mind that he had come to this mountain to fill himself up. To fill himself with the resistance of the stones and fortify his will against the unrest of his father whose unrest was the unrest of labor and of toil and of the hard cold light of the distant stars that Irven had made so near by his lonely baptism in the creek.

In his mothers voice, now just an echo in his young memory, he heard himself calling out to himself in the night. He was recalled again in dream to the upturned soil of the field and the white fuzz of failed crops and the scab his brother marked on his father's heart. He wanted to forget it all in the wilderness, but the regularity of his various toils had reminded him of the curse of Genesis that demanded the sweat of his brow in exchange for a calm in his belly. His pant legs were in tatters.

The next morning he found rabbits in two of his snares. He broke their necks with his hands and carried them by the scruff to his place in the hollow. He skinned them and dressed them and cooked one while he thought about how to best preserve the other. He was worried about keeping fresh meat in the woods. After he'd eaten, he went around to the creek where a beaver had drown in his submarine snare. Irven was pleased with himself. He laid the beaver aside on the shore and reset the snare and looked about for a place where he might trap some muskrat. The confidence he'd gained made him a little less careful than the previous day as he set his snares and as he walked around checking the others he found a frantic squirrel chewing the twine and its own rear leg alternately. Irven fell on the squirrel, killed it quickly and decided he'd caught lunch. Then, he thought it best to dress the beaver and think on making his way to town where he might turn a profit for his labor.

He had been somewhat sloppy on this second day, his youthfulness already forgetting the earnestness that plagued his stomach the day before. He had been sharp and awake. Now, he began to plan ahead and sink into the haze of anticipation that glazed over the present and brought the uncertain future into a relief just as impermanent as the fog of memory from which it was projected. In any event, Irvin cleaned up his belongings, took account of his approximate location, and headed into town.

The walk wasn't as long as Irven had thought and the town wasn't as big as he had remembered it. The Marks', as a family, didn't go into town very often. In fact, the last time Irven was in town, he was barely old enough to hold a memory in his head. He had clumsily followed his mother about the general store as she gathered some supplies for years worth of clothes. At that time, going into town meant an all day trip. Without his family surrounding him and the jaunt of youth in his step Irven was able to pass the distance in a short time and he found himself in the middle of the small cluster of buildings just as the sun was hastening its descent toward the tessellated crest of piney mountains.

It was the mines more than anything that had formed the center of their life in the hollows. When they moved, it was near the mine's for work and when they next moved it would be away from the mines. The town would remain more or less equidistance from the family and was always just a peripheral event in the minds of much of the older family, even as the terminus of the twentieth century approached.

For Irven, standing in a world of one saloon, one general store, one tannery, a run down blacksmiths hitched up to the ramshackle side of a stable still taking boarders for trade, the train platform wreathed in the slick black of anthracite, this is the World, the way it was to be even if a bunch of big city lawyers could convince the mass of people it wasn't with rows of cookie-cutter houses on loan. It would all have to come from somewhere, especially when it seemed like it didn't have to. That obscure world. Ugly, hidden fruit. The hides left a tinge of blood still on Irven's hands. He went into the general store.

There was a man already at the counter. He seemed to be engaged with the shopkeeper in a genteel sort of argument. They both spoke in the rough way of the country folk but their voices carried the strained effeminacy of one who tries to be polite simply because it's what everybody expects.

"I know them's hide'sas good as anythen' you'll see. Five dollars at least fer the beavers. Maybe two fer the muskrat."

"Sorry Buck, four fer the beaver. I can do two fer them muskrats."

"Take'em! I'm keepin' the beaver. Yer damned lucky I's *got* ta git supplies too. Wouldn't catch me swappin' bills with you in here if'a din' have ta."

There was a brusque exchange between the two and the trader called "Buck" left his bills at the counter while he gathered what supplies he required for the next foray into the forest. Irven kept a little distance between them as he approached the counter and untied his bundle.

The shopkeeper stepped back slightly, a little disgusted.

"These tain't even tanned!"

Irven just stood.

"I can' pay fer these'uns if'n they ain't even finished."

"That beaver's worth five easy," said Irven.

"Boy, I'd give ye *six* if ye jus' 'ad it tanned."

"That the truth?" came a voice over Irven's head. It was Buck. Irven turned around and Buck held out a fold of hides to him. "Sell these'ins and give me them'uns. I'll tan these fer sure," then Buck looked at the shopkeeper and said, "I'll get *six* for this beaver skin, that right? I heard ya quote this feller here *six* for it. I'll tan it up real good and sell it to ya fer six I reckin'."

"Well, I," fumbled the shopkeeper.

"You wouldn' go back on yer *word*?"

"Well, no. I…"

"Good! That settles it. Nice ta do business with ya kid!" Buck smiled a wide smile riddled with gaps and slapped his hand down to collect the bills he's left on the counter.

"Guess, I'll be back after I finished off these here hides," and with that he practically bounded out of the store and across the way to the saloon.

The shopkeeper looked sternly at Irven. Irven put his furs down on the counter. He had been shorted he realized. Buck had left him with only a beaver and a rabbit skin but had made off with Irven's beaver, two squirrels, and a muskrat. The shopkeeper nearly fumed.

"I'll give ya seven for the lot. Take it and git outta here kid."

Irven did, but left behind four dollars for a new shirt and a pair of jeans, some candies, and a little coffee, bundled up together in the burlap. Pleased, Irven knew he would remember this trip into town much more clearly than the last. The sun was still providing ample light and so Irven set off for home, quickening his step so as to make the most out of the remainder of the day.

As it was, night fell and Irven still had a full third of his walk in front of him. He was tired. The course of his journey had criss-crossed the forest and roadways, and it was only when he had left the small outpost of a town that his feet had made a straight trajectory toward a steady destination. But he was none too rushed to get back home. Consciously, he assured himself that waiting another night out would really show old Ma and Pa. That would teach them to take one of their kin for granted. Irven would just hold out one more night and really make his parents sweat back home. They'd be so happy he'd come home. But in his heart, Irven knew better. It was this deep, more primal fear that kept Irven in the field that third night.

Away from the deep of the wood the sun was quick to bring Irven from sleep. He was anxious and slept more lightly than before. It was just creeping into dawn when he sat up, stretched, and stood. The walk was long and that day began to grow hot. As he walked, Irven began to recall the day before. Each footfall was followed by a pang of doubt. He began to worry that he had been badly taken advantage of, that his pelts had been stolen, that he'd received a price less than fair for those that had been left to him. Rubbing the dollar bills folded in his pocket made him feel minutely better. Three soft, felted one dollar bills. He could give them proudly to Mama. How could she be mad then? He was turning into a man. Surely, Abe would be angry with Irven, but he would understand. He would see the three dollars and he'd have to understand. Irven and Abe could argue congenially like the men in the General Store. Abe would see Irven's side. Just as Buck would get his six dollars for the beaver pelt Irven had snared. Irven began to wonder if Buck would actually get that price, or if the storekeeper would just argue with him again. How many times had they had the same argument? How many more times would they?

Irven could see his house drawing near. He ducked away and changed into his new clothes, bundling the old ones up in his burlap. It was thus on the third day that Mama Clay saw Irven come down the road in his new clothes and walk timidly into the yard while Wayne stacked the last of their furniture in the back of the truck riding low from the weight. The rocking chair that had once made the floor chirp with each child's draw on Mama's breast now looked helpless, inverted on top of the mammoth chifforobe, made enormous by its prominent place by the cab of the truck. Wayne didn't notice Irven coming in by the front gate. The oldest brother was busy canvassing the truck bed with a wide canvas tarpaulin. Mama saw her middle son immediately and went out to meet him, heavy but quick as she was with child. She met him half way and took his face in her hands and looked him up and down and kissed his face. She spun him around taking account of every angle of him. She stopped him when he finally faced her and held him still. In an instant she changed over and hit him hard square across the same face once graced by the comfort of her love.

"Dammit!" she spat loudly over the door clapping shut.

Abe stood on the porch. The doorframe shuddered with the force of Abe's exit and the sharp sound of the wood being driven home brought a sudden silence into the clearing. Irven stood rigidly on his own as his mother backed away.

The word "boy" was a roar erupting from his father's mouth, loud and clear and sober. The distance between Irven and his father began to warp and close about him as time lost all significance to Irven in the face of its potential end. Abe had to dig his heel into the dirt to stop his charge as he came upon his son, who had failed to register any flight response in his paralyzed brain. Abe struck a blow to the side of Irven's head that he would have delivered to a grown man. As slow as the warp of time around Irven had become, the speed with which the ground rushed to meet him shattered all inverted measure of that timeless moment when his father leapt to kill him. Irven had blinked and he was on the ground. It seemed at that moment as if the sky was ripped open and God Himself had deigned to rain down upon him a hailstorm of fists made hard by the ores inlaid across their knuckles.

Then, Mama was there screaming "Stop it! Stop it, Abe! You'll kill that boy sure as I'm about to birth another! Stop it! You'll kill that boy!"

And then, the hailstorm stopped. The sun was shining, hot as the blood spattered on Irven's face. A crimson paisley spiraled sloppily across the top left quarter of his new shirt. Wayne approached warily, his will broken not by his father's fists, but by disappointment.

Abe looked down on his beaten son.

"What're you wearin' boy?"

Silence. Irven moved his shaking hand down the side of his body, into his pocket. When he withdrew his hand, it held three flimsy dollar bills out into the air with two trembling fingers. Abe reached down and took the three dollars.

"You bought new clothes?"

Irven nodded.

"The company men come around here while's you was gone. Ya knowed that?"

Irven shook his head.

"You knows who the company men is, huh? The money man? Jus'…jus' be quiet, son. They took the house. It ain't ours no more."

Irven looked. His eyes were wet.

"Get up. Clean yerself up. Put yer old clothes back on. You'll need them'ins later."

Abe didn't help Irven up, the boy arose by his own will. Still unsure on his feet, he left the yard. It was the last time he was to be in that old homestead. He wondered if they would live in the city. He wondered where they would live as he scrubbed the dirt and blood from his skin. His skin ached. He cried under the pressure of the rag and warm water on his arms. He cried under the pressure. Mama came in before he was finished. She held him in an embrace and he shook silently for some time. Then she finished cleaning him up. For some reason, he did not cry as she scrubbed away the dirt.

She was drying him off, the last time Irven ever remembers her doing so, and she said, "You'll have to make do with them tatters. We'll all have to make due with tatters for a while."

She pressed the towel into his arms and turned to leave.

"I haven't seen ye with no clothes for a while. I guess you'll be thinkin' yer a man soon. Just remember son, we all start with nothin'. Never forget son. Don't ever forget them tatters."

Irven just stood there as Mama closed the door.

Abe had driven with Mama Clay in the truck. They went on ahead even before Irven had finished up in the house. When he had finished and come outside, Wayne was hitching the cart up to their old mule. Whatever farming equipment could be loaded was either in the cart or close at hand. Wayne looked at Irven with the sun behind him.

"Yer comin' with me," Wayne said, squinting. "Help me load these, Tatters."

Irven rode in the cart in his old clothes. Wayne walked alongside the mule, only occasionally taking a break in the cart next to his brother. It was during that time that it happened. Like Mohammed's passage to Medina, this departure marked a metamorphosis within. The cart rocked to and fro.

"Wayne."

"Yeah."

"Where we goin'?"

"Down south a ways. A bit west. You know that city down south? St. Clairsville?"

"I reckin'."

"Ain't much of a city I hear, but you know, bigger than the lil' Slabtown outpost. Just miners there."

"Yeah."

"Well, we ain't goin' to the city, but still a lil' southwest a there. Pa said he got claims on some land. Said it was give to 'im by some Old Man Russell. Said Russell helped 'im out when he was a boy. But he said the Old Man was scared a the land. Wouldn't say why. I can't reckin' it."

"Don' figure."

"Yeah, lil' ol' Slabtown. That where you git them fancy clothes?"

"Yeah."

"Pa was gonna kill you."

"He should have."

"I guess you died a bit. The way he done whipped you, *whew* boy. Even I din' git whipped like that fer goin' down in the mines."

"Prolly why I did git whipped."

Wayne didn't say anything else for a while. He got down and walked with the mule for a spell. Behind the cart on a length of rope walked their cow. They traveled away from the towns on the country roads still familiar to carts and horses, mules and buggies. Abe and Mama Clay would have went around them, on more modern highways, new, and smooth under the rubber of their heavy laden truck. Mama would only have to winced under uneven road in the end, as they worked their way back into the mountain, at last off the manicured pavements of an urbanizing center for production. The mule and cart worked slowly toward them, the cow plodding behind. Wayne returned to the cart to say that they would camp over night and meet their parents the next day at whatever new home awaited them.

Tatters would always remember that night spent out with his brother, on the road, in between homes with nothing to go home to behind them and some unknown laid out ahead where whatever home there was would have to be made from nothing, or from what was as good as nothing to the boys who had only ever known a roof over their heads and a fire in the stove. Nothing seemed likely, yet as they talked around the fire they had to admit that anything was possible.

The young brothers slept out under the stars that night, as Tatters had been sleeping out the three nights previous. The fire went low and crackled subtly throughout the long dark, crumbling and white by the time the horizon cracked open above the silver arc of the dawn. They cleaned up camp, cut the mule and cow loose to graze. They ate dried meat and stale bread. As they rounded up the grazing mule and cow and began to hitch up the flat, a rider approached from the same direction they had come by. Seeing the boys moving at leisure, the rider pulled up beside them and hailed with a curt, "Hey, there!"

"Mornin'," Wayne nodded.

"You boys headed down yonder to the Russell tract?"

"Don't know no Russells," Wayne said.

"Hmph. Down where Harbarger was squattin'?"

"Don't know no squatters either."

"Hmph."

There was a pause and the mule shifted against the harness. Tatters took over, and finished hitching her up himself. Wayne took a few steps in the rider's direction, since the man on horseback showed no intention to ride on.

"You boys goin' down yonder, or no?"

"We're headin' that way, yea. But I don't know none 'a them names you's askin' for."

"That's jus' as well. Ride ahead with me a ways an' maybe we'll see if you ain't aheaded where I think you are."

"That's fine. We'll ride along with ya."

"Name's Ezra," said the rider at length.

"I'm Wayne, and that there's my brother, Tatters," Wayne gave a sideways smile at Tatters when he introduced him thus, the understanding that the name was going to stick being reached at once between them.

"Good. Well, if yer all hitched up, let's git a move on."

Ezra led them on, Wayne and Tatters keeping their own pace at first, just so that they could talk outside of the new acquaintance's earshot. Since they found they had nothing useful to say about the situation, they gave in and sped up to join Ezra along the way.

"What bring's you down this way mister?"

"See here, I ain't any older than you'ins is. Ain't no mister. But I gots ta go down here an' see if this claim is right by the law and such. Got word I gots ta see some papers an I aims ta see 'em."

"Oh," said Wayne. "Where's the claim?"

"Tract a land folks 'round here used ta call the Russell tract, but ain't been a Russell in these parts leastways since anyone livin' can remember it. Fer years it's been in use by the Harbarger's though they have no rights to it far as I can tell."

"Then why were they allowed to keep on?" said Tatters, taking a sharp side glance from Wayne.

"Well, they's got there first I reckin'. Most people out these ways jus' want left well enough alone I suppose. So, they leave well enough alone if ye follow my meanin'."

Both brothers followed him well enough and was accustomed to this way of settling things, or at least making it so that there was little to settle. Quiet reigned for a spell while the birds darted and called about the day. The three crossed over some train tracks coming around a bend in the mountains out of the north, and then the road dropped down some and took an arc up northward before cutting back down again, to the southwest into a broad valley wreathed in steeper crests than the boys had seen along the road so far. In fact, the road they traveled took them out of the mountain northways, and went qua circumlocution to a mountainous area south of their first homestead and as far away from the corporate coal fields as Abe knew they could get and still strike into the ground for a tidy profit. The modest possessions of the Marks's came into view ahead. Mama seemed busy with some manner of outdoor cookery. Abe was not immediately present, though he must have seen his sons approaching from where he worked in a thicket of gum trees, for Abe soon strode into the opening, passing Margaret as she frolicked in the grass.

"Hey, there!" said Abe to Ezra as he came forward. When he was within a comfortable distance, Abe nodded to his boys without a word.

"A good mornin' to you, sir," said Ezra, his youth now more apparent to the brothers with whom he traveled.

"It's fair enough," replied Abe, "but I suspect yer comin' along with business for me?"

"Of a sort."

"Out with it then. What is it?"

"This land was in use. You might've heard."

"I heard. I also got the deed to this tract. I knew yer Ol' Russell."

"I see," said Ezra, clearly not expecting what he heard even knowing it was likely true. Skepticism is a pure and unattended vice. "There's a clan a folk livin' yonder, over that hillock at yer back. That's still part a yer land if you got a right to it, but I beg ya ta have a heart in regards them folks."

"Them's the Harbargers I figure," said Abe. "You know of a Holofernes Harbarger? I got word he was squattin' on this land here."

"I daresay he was, sir."

"Was he now? An' where did he git hisself off to then?"

"Sir, that's what I come ta tell you, if'n you got a right ta this land. Holofernes Harbarger is dead."

HOLOFERNES[*] HARBARGER

The pocked copper alembic was hot in the shade of the hollow, filled to rumbling with the acrid steam of fermented corn, wheat, and rye. Holofernes Harbarger stoked the fire gently with an iron rod. As he moved about the embers, his young apprentice, Ezra, looked on, the low flame kindled in his eye. Slowly, with patience cultivated in virtue of inanimation, the clear, strong liquid dripped with calculated persistence from the tip of a coil suspended above a glass gallon jug.

The weather had only permitted Holofernes to work for about two weeks. It was still early in March; the grains stolen away from under his wife's watchful eye and stored in a cache supplemented by a meager offering from Ezra had allowed a jump-start on the work of distilling quality mountain moonshine. If it wasn't for his wife and daughters, Holofernes would make his

---

[*] A biblical name, pronounced: "*Ha-law-fur-knees*"

spirits at home, perhaps in the cellar, but his wife's temperance and the cherub-faced looks of his daughters was enough to persuade him to keep his business out of the house. Not that he was a particularly thoughtful man when it came to his wife and children; in fact, Holofernes was a hard man to love and an even harder man to call a father when you were one of three daughters doomed to his patriarchy.

He had quit the mines well before the reforms were being hailed as the salvation of the working man in 191_. That struggle was more than he care for, preferring instead the solitary struggle any man would face when the burden of solidarity was one they were unwilling to endure. Since 192_ Holofernes had raised his children hauling timber out of the forest on his own. He found work on and off at a glass mill in St. Clairsville, but they furloughed him time and again, and he was more apt to bring money home from hauling timber and making moonshine than he was ladling glass in St. Clairsville, which proved dangerous work. Plus, he was getting on in years for a glass ladler and was tired of calling other men "boss". There were no sons Holofernes called his own, just Ezra, a friend though twenty years Holofernes' younger, but a friend nonetheless and one who could haul timber and was anxious to learn the secret mountain alchemy of the moonshiners.

"Hmph," Ezra watched the yellow tinged liquid drop by drop into the jug. It pooled in a thin sheet across the convex bottom. "We can drink this when it all runs through?"

"No," said Holofernes.

"When?"

"Need distilled another two, three times. Then's good."

"Ah," said Ezra.

"Patient. Jus' wait."

"Yes. Wait."

Ezra was slow picking up on Holofernes ways. At first, Ezra thought Holofernes was just stupid, or maybe one of those simple minds, similar to that of his youngest daughter, Verge, who Holofernes said could fall full into the Devil's grasp in fits that defied his control and understanding. But this belief was a prejudice of Ezra's atheism. Even though Holofernes had not been to school since he was seven or eight years of age, he emerged as quite brilliant once anyone got past his quiet, contemplative, and drunk exterior.

Drink was one of Holofernes great vices, though he had several. Often, it was bad for his business, because Holofernes could drink vast quantities of his own brews as fast as he was able to sell them, being in the habit of drinking even on the way to a sale. Now, it would not be fair to say that Holofernes was perpetually drunk. He experienced long stretches of lucidity and was, by many accounts, a sort of family man. That is, he spent a good amount of time at home and was well aware of all the goings-on within his household. He knew the annoying and undecipherable details of his daughters' lives and guarded them in his way against the evils of the world. There was a strong sense of religion in the house, Holofernes being a Baptist, and it was by this code of conduct that the behavior of each in the house was judged. The severity of Holofernes' interpretation of the Law was in proportion to the quantity of spirits he'd consumed—God ever more the tyrant when liquor guided His hand.

"Holofernes."

"Yeah?"

"You think it'd be an idea ta hop the train out ta town fer a job in the train yard?"

"You gonna jump th' train ta work in 'a train yard?"

"Yep."

"I s'pose that'd work alright. I'd jump off'a that train 'fore it hit th' station."

"I reckon it'd be wise."

"I reckin'."

The trains ran close to where Holofernes had taken up residence. Down in a hollow, opposite side of an upspring of the mountains from the roads going to and fro between the towns and villages, had laid for ages a dilapidating old fort house, built in times, some say, before the Civil War. The final time Holofernes had allowed himself to be furloughed, he knew that he would be unable to afforded the taxes on his current property. Seeing eviction in the future, he uprooted his family to the vacant tract of land grown over and wild from years of neglect. Being a religious man, Holofernes had considered the warnings he'd heard regarding the land and its past. No one had outright warned Holofernes, but when word began to circulate that he might take advantage of the property to solve his current dilemma, talk around the mountain turned to the ominous association the so-called Russell tract had in everyone's collective conscious.

The small mountain was south, and to the north, across a field cultivated into wheat by the Harbarger's, ran the trains. This greatly facilitated the selling of timber by Holofernes, for he could persuade engineers to stop and sell him empty space on the train. He had taken a tremendous risk to wave down the first train he did business with. There had already been arrangements made with a lumberyard who owned a post-truck and could meet the train in the yard to unload the timber. Moonshine was enough to persuade the shift foreman in the train yard to allow the transaction, and it was set that every two weeks Holofernes would have a train stopped just across from his homestead waiting to collect his timber and have the engineer's palm greased with cash, moonshine, or whatever wares the Harbargers happened to have on hand.

Ezra thought he could easily jump the train from such a location. He had been looking for ways to increase his income. His share from the timber venture was fair, though he made nothing to speak of for his help with the moonshine. Holofernes felt he was being generous in teaching the young man his recipe and showing him the hidden process by which he distilled the grains he grew. It was secret work, illegal for one, but also the source of wealth in a land still ripe with voluminous trade. The more his plans panned out, the more attached Holofernes became to the Russell tract and to his young cohort, whose labor was relatively cheap and whose company was one sorely needed by Holofernes. Ezra, on the other hand, was anxious to break away from his dependence upon his would-be-mentor. This was, perhaps, the best explanation for why Ezra looked so keenly upon the completion of this batch of moonshine. Afterward, he would have a full demonstration of the distillation process in his repertoire and would be ready to make his own efforts at the alchemic art.

Another incident had increased the desire to separate in Ezra. Late in February, barely a week prior, a stranger had come calling on the Harbargers, specifically to speak, at some length, with Holofernes. The topic of conversation was clearly the land, however, it was also clear that the stranger staked no claims on the land. The stranger had been an old man, about which everything was grey and hazy. His clothes had been fine at one time, but gave a shabby appearance with creases stressed white and threadbare patches at the elbows and knees. It had been early in the evening when the elderly stranger appeared, as though he had ridden a great distance to be there. The entire grey atmosphere of the man was one of nostalgia and a long forgotten time from which he sought to influence the future.

"Mr. Harbarger, I presume?" he had said with genteel familiarity.

"I'm Harbarger," Holofernes had replied.

"I come to take counsel with you. I wish to talk. About the land."

"You got a claim here?"

"No. I make no claims on the land, sir. It's as good as yours if you'll have it."

"Hmph," Ezra had said.

"It was brought to my attention, Mr. Harbarger—"

"Holofernes."

"Yes, well, Mr. Holofernes, it was brought to my attention that you've made certain arrangements that would indicate your intention to stay on here. You've been here some months or more, is that so?"

"Talk plain ta me. What'dya want here?"

"I'm sorry, please excuse my tone if I've offended you. Can we speak indoors?"

"That's fine. Naomi, git some food fer the gentleman."

The two had gone inside while Naomi busied the girls elsewhere. Ezra had dawdled on the porch, tired from a day felling timber. The horse sweated and steamed in the cool air.

Once at the table in the Harbarger's square kitchen, Holofernes offered the stranger a drink, saying, "I didn' git yer name."

"Yes, ah, no thank you, I'm Wittacre, William Wittacre, III."

"Mr. Wittacre is it. Pleased ta meet ya. I'll be havin' some if'n ya don' mind."

Mr. Wittacre shook his head placidly as Holofernes poured himself an ample tumbler of whiskey, the bottle wrapped in brown paper.

"You know this land's been vacant almost sixty years. It's somethin'."

Holofernes watched the old man as he began what Holofernes surmised was a long speech on whatever it was that brought the old man this far.

"That's almost since the Civil War. And there's two claims on the land that I know of. It was split up by Old Russell's Daddy, and I've come to know that Russell gave half of it outside his family. An immigrant I believe, that was a ward of Russell for some time."

Holofernes nodded and sipped the whiskey neat.

"Neither one of them has ever came forward."

"Why the immigrant?" asked Holofernes.

"Oh, I don't know all the details, but I believe Russell's son was killed in the War. Russell himself was an invalid after the war, though he had no business going to fight it in the first place. A man of his age has no place on the battlefield and he was lucky he didn't lose more than his leg."

Holofernes drained the rest of his glass to that, then poured himself a bit more.

"Don't you think it odd no one has ever made good on their claims?"

Holofernes shrugged. He didn't put much effort into figuring out the reasons why people did the things they did. The faces of others were opaque to him.

"Well, Old Russell himself had come to fear this place. Seemed to think it was cursed."

Holofernes looked up from his drink. "How's that?"

"I don't know. But I can tell you my own family has been brought nearly to ruin after associating ourselves with this land. There was a family house, a great plantation house from the colonial period, and if you went up out of the hollow here around to the road, you can see in the distance the very spot where this house once stood. But it's long since been destroyed by fire, one more in a list of tragedies that has befallen my family for three generations. My great-grandfather was involved in a land dispute with a man over this land, and as I understand it, my great-grandfather was in the wrong on that account. His punishment was great, and he suffered the rest of his life for his pursuit of this grudge."

"Look here," Holofernes cut in, "what's yer family 'istory got ta do with me an' mine? You come all this way ta tell me tall tales an' ghost stories? I ain't got nothin' ta do with you an' yer bloodfeud, or whatever done happened to yer Pappy before the damn War, Civil or otherwise!"

"I'm sorry, I don't mean to waste your time. I just thought the proper context would—"

"Ta *hell* with yer damn contents!" Holofernes forcefully finished his whiskey, putting his glass down with a *clap!*

"I see. Then, just hear this Holofernes Harbarger. I came here and warned you. Do not stay on this land. Good day," and with that, Mr. Wittacre gave the slightest of bows to Holofernes and was gone before Naomi had come in with stew and quick fried bread. Her eyes followed the strange man across their lawn and to his horse, which grazed casually not far from the trail to the road.

"Who was that strange man?"

"No one to take account of, Naomi. No one of account."

Despite these words spoken by Holofernes, Ezra had taken account of the strange incident.

As Mr. Wittacre reached his horse, Ezra had approached him from the porch. Naomi had retreated into the house, where Holofernes remained and so Ezra was alone with Wittacre in the afternoon sun. The horse was listless. Wittacre had his hand on the swells of the saddle as though he would mount when Ezra spoke to him.

"What'd you warn Mr. Harbarger about?"

"Mister, well, yes," Wittacre was tentative.

"You rode a ways, I'd say, to say what you wanted to say."

The rhythm of Ezra's voice made Wittacre reticent. His hand dropped from the swell and he turned to more fully address the other. Ezra stood half slack-kneed, his arms crossed loosely across his midsection.

"I had family 'round these parts."

"You warned Mr. Holofernes about yer family?"

"Not exactly."

"I like plain words"

"The land has a memory, Mr…"

"Ezra. Jus' call me Ezra."

"Yes, well, Ezra, see, the land. The land has a memory, you know?"

"I reckin' I don'. But I heard folks talk that way before."

"Yes, old folks."

"Yep. Old folks."

"I'll be off then," Wittacre took up the slack on the reigns and mounted smoothly, drawing himself full into the saddle, feet easily in the stirrups. He looked down at Ezra.

"Just you take care now? You hear?"

"Yeah. Thank ya kindly."

The horse reared back under Mr. Witttacre's hand, but before he fully turned he paused and said, "That Holofernes, he's got himself *three* daughters?"

"I reckin' he does, but I don't see how it's any uh yers."

"Good day."

Ezra nodded and Wittacre left without another word. His pace was quick along the road and momentarily, he was out of sight.

Holofernes did have three daughters, of which the oldest was Ruth who was very pretty and thick. The first child, Naomi had doted over Ruth for some time and lavished nourishment upon her. So, she ate well and with appetite, filling a curvy adolescent form with vivacity and mirth. She was generally cheery, if matter-of-fact, which could have been surprising considering. She was always considerate of the middle sister, Judith, because Judith had been a project for Ruth and their mother, and often, Ruth loved Judith the way a child loves a favored plaything, the doll one names and dresses up and feigns to be a mother for in concert with her own mother, the ideal form and arché of her scheme. The youngest daughter, Verge, was the ruin of the family in the eyes of Ruth, due, by and large, to Verge's strange affliction, which their father had come to believe was the hand of the Devil himself. Verge had always been odd and was born premature and weak, barely over a year after the birth of Judith. This disrupted the kinship Ruth had invested in Naomi, and added strain on a situation strained enough by the pressures of their father.

Holofernes had always been fond of drink. And he was strictly a Bible man. He like to sing the gospel relaxing on porch in the eve, sipping shine, rocking in his chair. He had the girls singing the gospel as early as they could sing it and the family sang the gospel together and enjoyed it. They were bound to each other, in good and in evil. Ruth was becoming a woman and Judith was precocious and ten when Verge began taking fits. The girl had always been odd and troublesome. She could never drink the proper amount of milk, and her stomach would pain her over the least bit of good food. She preferred bread without butter. She was slower than her sisters to speak, yet without Naomi's doting and Ruth's imagined maternity Verge learned how to speak, but she had no interest in reading. She was a reserved little girl. She would wake up screaming sometimes when the trains would pass by at night. Holofernes frightened her, sometimes even when he wasn't drunk.

Judith was kind to her little sister, but was often annoyed by her. Ruth had little love for Verge. Naomi loved her as a mother does and watched out for, even pitying her weaknesses with little boosts and flatteries she hardly offered the older girls.

The first time it happened, Verge had been playing by herself, away from the sun in the yard under a stand of trees, most prominent of which was a great sycamore Holofernes always said he would cut down but never did, the grand thing stirring a kind of respect in his heart. Verge played by herself fairly often and the shade beneath the tree was a favorite spot of hers to do so.

Cool shade and damp grass on her knees, little dress, with a flower print over her legs, splayed in the grass. Don't get a stain on the print, those flowers don't leave the impossible green of grass on the fabric, soft and cotton. Something was strange, just before that first time. It was like a ringing. A very clear, high ringing, somewhere, was it? Just behind her right ear. Like a bolt from the sky was suddenly thrust into her skull and beamed a sound into her brain that was more real than the real sounds around her. There were birds flitting about, making lilting songs as they do, but now those sounds were filtered through this beam, through this ringing that was somewhere, that had some distinct invisible locality. It subsided suddenly, as it had come. But nothing was right after. The world had shifted. Verge had tilted her head and got up from the shade of the tree.

She walked out into the yard where Naomi was hanging clothes on the line to dry, Ruth rinsed clothes in a big wooden bucket at a little distance from the line and brought the wet clothes to her mother after wringing them as dry as she could. It had been Judith's turn to do the scrubbing and she always took longer than her more practiced elders. Ruth wanted her to be done so Judith might run the clothes to their mother instead of Ruth.

Verge stood some ways away from the working women. She walked in a stilted manner into roughly the center of the yard. Her head was at an awkward angle and she seemed not to be looking where she was going, though her gaze was more or less fixed straight ahead. Then, she fell to the ground, convulsing, her eyes white to look at and staring back into the recesses of her skull. Naomi had seen her walking across the yard but took no mind of her. When she happened to see her daughter collapse in the periphery of sight, she dropped her wash immediately and was off to Verge's side. It took the sisters more time to discern what was going on and even then, they did not immediately go to the younger girl's aid because they were frightened and their mother seemed to hold them at bay with an outstretched hand. The episode seemed to go on indeterminately, time hanging thick in the air, polarized around the fallen girl and her kneeling mother. The sun flickered in the heat, tagged by the ragged edge of a quickly drifting cloud.

Then, Verge was still.

Naomi leaned close, cautious. She placed the back of her hand gently on her daughters cheek. In the sun, Verge was hot and flush. Naomi passed her hand over her face and picked her up. Naomi walked across the yard and into the house cradling Verge in her arms.

Ruth and Judith looked at each other and followed their mother into the house. They found their sister sitting on the couch. She appeared perfectly fine.

"I don' know," said Naomi, coming in from the kitchen. "I come in. Laid her down on the couch. And up she came! Plain as day an' good as new. Like nothin' ever happened!"

Naomi put her hands up in an exasperated gesture and walked away again, leaving the three sisters alone together. A dab of spit was dried white on the left corner of Verge's mouth. Judith took up a corner for her dress and wiped the stain with her hard finger until it was gone. A spot on Verge's chin was red. Her cheeks were still ruddy and flushed.

"Why're you'uns lookin' at me fer?" asked Verge.

"What?" said another.

"Quit lookin' a' me. Stop."

"Okay," said Judith. "What's wrong with ya?"

"Yeah, what's wrong with you?"

"I dinno."

"What?" said another.

"Yeah, speak up," said Ruth.

"I dunno!" Verge said louder, crossing her arms tight across her chest.

All of this had transpired some two years prior to Holofernes ever having heard tell of Mr. Wittacre. The Harbarger's had just moved, their homestead forfeited for taxes, and Verge's fit was another in a string of tragedies that had befallen the clan of late. It wasn't the last Verge was to take ill either.

Holofernes had been off felling timber and setting up his still when Verge had taken sick. He had been felling trees since the day they finished fixing up the old fort-house and clearing the cellar, as Naomi had demanded. Holofernes had wanted to hold off renovating any more and let winter pass in the rooms he'd afforded them. Naomi was to have none of it. The cellar was cleared and jars of food began to line the shelves that went in. The girls where made to work too, both in the house and the fields. Everyone was tired, and they had slept a good deal that winter, harsh that year from mid-December through February with constant snow drifts. They hadn't any animals at that time, so it was stored foods, jarred and pickled and reheated on the wood-burning stove in the kitchen. They spent a lot of time in that room because it was warm and because the rest of the home was little more than their bedrooms. It was enough company for them.

It was when that winter was over and the days grew hot that Verge had her first fit. Holofernes remembers he had gone out to haul some timber up from where it fell the day before, and had taken with him his newly and suspiciously obtained alembic. He had been gathering and had a forest cache of equipment with which to make his shine. That was the final piece, and he hauled the timber with extra vigor. He spent the rest of the afternoon setting up his still. When he had returned in the evening, the mood of the house was strange and Naomi had told him at length what had occurred. Holofernes was suspicious of Verge. He kept a cold eye on her for days. Things went on as usual. A train in the night startled Verge, who came up from sleep with an awful sound in her throat.

Soon after, Holofernes had met Ezra and the two became fast friends. After a time, Holofernes began to let Ezra into the secrets of his moonshining. Ezra had been asking how it was Holofernes was always in possession of such vast quantities of the stuff. Red eyed, Holofernes had swore Ezra to secrecy. The two could turn a tidy profit, hauling timber and making moonshine.

One day, in a dead July heat, Verge stood in the doorway of the kitchen, looked vacantly at Holofernes, and said, in a creaky, head voice against all the usual rhythms of speech, "Helizikinopo," before falling to the ground in a fit of convulsion and some amount of frothy white saliva, thick with mucus issuing from the side of her mouth.

"Christ!" Holofernes had exclaimed and nearly fallen backwards over himself to keep clear of his daughter's writhing form, as if she posed a great danger to himself.

"What did you say?" he cried, now on his knees.

Verge was unresponsive.

"What did you say!" shouted Holofernes louder. "Devil!"

He had gotten drunk that night. He left Verge lying on the floor and went into the woods. Naomi had come inside and found

Verge a few minutes after. She looked in vain for her husband. He was afraid.

In his stupor, he compared himself to Christ in Gethsemane. He was filled with doubt. He filled himself with hard liquor. Visions presented themselves to him as he walked along in the twilight with one eye pressed shut and the other tilted out to make his way forward. It grew dark. Holofernes fell down several times, cursing the same each time he had to lift himself up again. When he arrived home, Naomi went to bed. Holofernes had been wanting to make love all that summer and, more than sex, wanted finally to put the seed of a son in Naomi's belly. Not that Naomi was pregnant, in fact, she seemed to be failing to conceive, and this fact was the simulacrum of his superstitious mistrust of Verge. She had done *something* to Naomi. When his wife had turned her back on him that night, in his drunkenness, this made Holofernes irritable. He drank some water. He cleaned himself up a bit and drank some more shine. Verge left her room to go to the outhouse. Holofernes heard one of his daughters leave. From the window, he could see Verge completing the short distance between the house and the toilet. She opened the door and stepped inside. Holofernes went outside and waited.

When Verge came out from the toilet, her father was standing in her path with his arms crossed. He was swaying slightly in the light from the house.

"What'd you say to me today?"

Verge just stood there, shaking slightly.

Holofernes rushed upon her, taking her shoulders in a firm grasp.

"What did you say!" he was urgent, manic.

Verge could not speak. She let go a stream of urine. In her nightgown, her stance wide in an effort to stand firm against her fathers hands, the piss fell unbroken to the ground to make a sickening sound upon striking the slate flagstone. Holofernes released her abruptly. He stepped back. Verge began to weep. Her father stood dumbstruck, then suddenly took her up by the arm and slung her bodily over his shoulder. She began crying more loudly.

"Shut up!" Holofernes' voice was harsh in the moon light.

He carried Verge upstairs. In the hall outside the master bedroom was a little door and an attic crawlspace little more than a box space under the roof. Holofernes opened the door and threw Verge into the space. The door slammed. Verge whimpered in the darkness. She cried silently to herself. Near morning, she took another fit and soiled herself. For another day she remained. When Holofernes released her, he was drunk again. For the mess in the attic space, Holofernes gave Verge twenty five lashes with his belt. Her back and buttock were raw from the blows. Holofernese beat her in the kitchen while Naomi wept upstairs, and Ruth and Judith sat in their bedroom on the edge of their beds, staring at the cross on the wall. For the next three days, Holofernes was almost never at home.

On the third day after her beating it was almost August and Ruth and Judith had been distant. Verge made overtures of good will. Judith listened.

"What's wrong with me, Judy?"

"I don' know Vergie, but we're gonna take care a ya."

"You promise?"

"I promise, sis."

Verge asked her mother the same question a few days later. Naomi had said, "Ain't nothin' *wrong* with *you*, doll. That Devil's got a hold on you is all. But you a *good* girl, and you'll shake the Devil right off yer back! You'll see!" Naomi smiled and hugged Verge and assured her it would all be alright, but Verge was terrified. She cried at night. Ruth and Judith tried not to hear, but they could.

The place where Holofernes spent these days away from home tending his still was in the mouth of an abandoned mine, deep in the forest on the mountainside, its ancient frame weathered to look like an opening almost natural to the mountain itself. Big, it was tall and wide and Holofernes could easily stand and turn about and tend the still in the entrance. Eventually, Ezra too would be able to stand and turn with Holofernes, the space was adequate. The rest of the mines were a mystery to Holofernes and he, truth be told, was a little spooked by them. Wind made the mountain groan. Never a thought was given to returning to work in such a place. Naomi was ignorant the things were even there, delving deep into the rock.

All of these events had transpired before Mr. Wittacre had ever shown up around the Harbarger's improvised homestead. They had made it through that second winter without too much duress, the winter being much more mild that year than what they had suffered through previously. Verge's fits had become a memory, though she had obviously retreated into a place within herself that no one in the house was allowed to access. Naomi would think she had made some progress with her youngest child only to be shut out the next day, Verge again a mystery for lack of speech, unwillingness to read, and finicky habits of eating. Ruth was becoming a woman; it was more clear to Naomi each day that something would have to be done about Ruth's maternal instincts and swings of emotion. She needed to be allowed to find a man, and that meant she needed to be let beyond the confines of the homestead that had been the main scene of their production for that past year. Holofernes suggested Ezra take Ruth into town, out to a social to meet some boys and girls from town, but Ezra was old enough not to be a child yet too young to be trust with the undisrupted flower of her first born, and so Naomi was very wary of this option. A mother always prefers to accompany her own daughters to town.

Since Ruth was born in wintertime, she retreated indoors each fall and emerged again in spring a new age, 13 the year Mr. Wittacre stopped in on her father. When that stranger had appeared to him, Holofernes reckoned all those odd months to a disconcerting kismet invading his peace. He had gotten settled and these happenings were harbingers of change. He watched Verge with increasing unease. Everything about Ruth mildly disgusted him. Naomi still evaded him, she herself becoming more desperate to conceive again. She had told him this; that she felt a strong desire to become pregnant by him, even so she was unable to bring herself to give him physical pleasure and Holofernes took this as proof she was lying. Everything seemed to him to be thwarting him.

Ezra had the foresight to take more responsibility for the joint-business ventures he had begun with Holofernes. He had been diligently excavating deeper into the mineshaft in order to construct a set of racks upon which they might stack barrels of moonshine two high, maybe three along the wall. A nice set of six barrels, even if not put to use that year, would be a fine boon to their income; Holofernes would reward Ezra for his effort, that could be assured. It used to be when Holofernes would want to be alone, he would tend his still after a morning of cutting wood and the forestry associated with hauling timber. But with Ezra developing a knowledge of the still, Holofernes took to drinking by himself in the wood, his pace at felling trees became pitiful. Once on a two-manned saw, Ezra knocked Holofernes to the ground with a standard thrust, which had thrown Holofernes into a rage. And so, Ezra manned the still, tended to the mineshaft, leaving Holofernes to his own designs in the solitude of the hollow.

One day, Holofernes came to Ezra and this was a fortnight after Wittacre had gone. The older man had a sober look in his eyes, but he still smelled of liquor and didn't seem to Ezra to have a steady gait.

"I'm not sure what ta do."

Ezra was quiet, stoking the fire.

"Ezra."

"Yeah."

"I'm not sure what ta do."

"'Bout what, Holofernes?"

"You know. Them girls."

"Humph."

"You think I ought take Ruth in'a town?"

"I reckin'. Don' know how you figure on gittin' her hitched."

"She can git herself hitched, don' reckin'?"

"Yeah. I reckin'."

"Is that why you're drinkin' out there?"

"What?"

"You know damn well you're drunk more an' sober. Our business'll go ta shit if'n you don' mind."

"*You* know *damn well* I mind," the drunkenness became apparent in Holofernes' eye. Ezra put his hands out and spoke calmly.

"I ain't a sayin' that. All's I'm a sayin' is: act like it."

The older man assumed a defeated stance.

"I know. I needs to git home."

And that's just what he had done.

The next day, Holofernes had come early and sober into the woods and hauled a good share of timber. The night had passed singing the gospel on the porch and in laughter. Life had been good and he had talked more easily with Naomi about Ruth. He did not want to keep his daughter a caged bird. Without a son himself to make work the fields, Holofernes knew his daughters wedding would mean, at worst, one less mouth to feed, but better still, there was always the remote possibility of bringing on a set of hands he could put to work. A man in his early twenties, properly invested in the work, can produce such a quantity of goods Holofernes often regretted he had not taken advantage of his powers when he still possessed them. He could, perhaps, have taken real advantage of the mines that hid his shine from the light.

Sober as he was, he began to take close account when he broke for a while around 11 in the morning. He had put in a good five and a half hours and felt invigorated in the morning sun, filtering through the green that grew more densely as the days wore on. He had had the time to do some sowing early on, and now was a time of water and waiting. His daughters were perfect to tend the gardens, which was all he really had, his "fields" of wheat and barley modest plots at best, and he could spend a few days now and again with the heavier work. Ezra benefited from the food grown there as well, in exchange for his labor. Holofernes had not seen Ezra that day, as his thoughts turned to him. He wondered if perhaps Ezra had not stopped to tend the field. His reverie turned to the expanded opening in the rock. The work showed. See, even the frame of the first level of racks can be determined. It was all laid out nicely. Some labor had been spent in crafting the boards. Perhaps there was somewhere Ezra had set up to plane such even surfaces? Holofernes had not seen Ezra at work in the yard, or around the homestead.

The mountain yawned. Noon approached. Holofernes stood in the deep of the opening, the dark descending into the gullet of the mountain. The incline was not great, but the chill of the air suggested great depth. The alembic made a sound. Embers shifted in the fire. Holofernes quickly left the shaft.

Outside, he saw Ezra approaching from a dell. He hailed his apprentice. The solitude of the mine had made him uneasy. He took a sip of moonshine that was ready to hand. It dripped in steady, measured drops from the coil into the glass. Ezra ducked slightly to enter the opening.

"Where've you been?" asked Holofernes.

"I was seein' 'bout a horse."

"A hoss?"

"An' a cart, yessir."

"What'chu need a hoss an' a car' fer?"

"I'ma takin' you an' Naomi an' the girls to a picnic if'n you have a mind ta go."

Holofernes stood aback. He smiled eventually.

"I reckin' I have a mind fer that."

"We might'n a barn ta raise."

"A barn?"

"Of sorts."

"How ya figger?"

"I figure if'n I git this horse, I'll need a place ta put it."

"I don' know about no barn rasin' but we can shelter yer hoss, mark me on that," Holofernes was pleased with his friend. He took a full swig of shine.

A few days later, Holofernes and Naomi, Ruth, Judith, and Verge, along with Ezra, were all in a cart, drawn by a horse, down the road to the church picnic, maybe three or four miles from their homestead. They may have been the family that lived farthest away, though they knew the McClain's to have a sizeable farm where the land was more even than theirs. The McClain's weren't at the picnic, but everyone else the girls had ever met in their lives was. It was gorgeous all through the morning and ample white clouds kept a pleasant shade drifting across the sixteen or twenty faces that moved in and out of the opened church, mingling as the tiny motes on the breezes ruffling all the skirts and dresses and pleats that bounced from the vital strides of the girls running and playing hop-scotch or jacks, chanting double-dutch rhymes in their carefree way. The boys played catch mostly and had a rowdy undisciplined game of baseball in the wide field. There were a few cowboys and Indians still waging war across the plains, and the older boys watched, playing it cool as they were in the cities, which few of them had ever seen. The parents were in attendance, looking on, playing cards or chess, drinking homemade wines that were sweet and lush with fruits; men traded shine in the recesses of the crowd. A few told tall tales of their hunts and exaggerated their success with trapping. For all the activity, the gathering was quiet. Somebody began picking a banjo, and a guitar was produced as well and they rolled the church piano out to sing the gospel and bluegrass. Someone shouted "Salty Dog!" and they played that. "I'll Fly Away," and "Go Tell It on the Mountain."

Everyone gave the band a taste of their moonshine. An old man sang some songs. He said he had to sing it for his brother and sang "O Death" and everyone was somber for a spell. Then the banjo and guitar picked back up again, a little more fervently than before with the discovery of a fiddler and they all danced circles as the afternoon went on.

Just before the end of the day, Verge took a fit. Naomi had tried to shield her, but a few of the other mothers saw it. Word spread. By the time people were aware, Verge was fine again, but the damage was done. Ruth was mortified. Judith mostly acted as though nothing of note had happened. Holofernes had been drunk for sometime. Shortly after the brief disruption caused by the dissemination of Verge's "condition" or "ailment" among the community, Ezra had made sure Holofernes was in the cart, already dozing and oblivious. In any event, it could have been worse. Ruth had talked to some boys, though she would swear no one would even look at her after Verge's incident. Even so, Ruth knew that boys had noticed her. She was not unaware of the fullness of her body, of the eyes it drew to her and the way sometimes men could not find their words around her, when she gave them a certain look that she did not quite understand. What was it; she thought she looked stupid, pouting her lips in the mirror like she had seen in a rare magazine one of the girls had had at the church picnic. Though she could understand sometimes how those girls could want the men to look at them. It was too much for her. She would turn away from the mirror, occasionally glancing back at it for a moment, and not sensing, in that very turn, the coyness that would so enervate a male who stood instead of the mirror.

It must have been two weeks before it had come out to Holofernes exactly what had happened with Verge at the picnic. He had learned it from a neighbor who lived closer to town and worked as a fireman on the engines that stopped in their way across from the old fort-house down in the hollow. He had asked about how Holoefernes' little girl was doing, "you know, after wha' 'appen an' all."

Holofernes didn't reply. He fell into a gruff silence afterwards. Truth was, he didn't know what to say. None of it made any sense to him, why say something even you yourself can't make sense of? But it got him to thinking about it again, which was something he had been avoiding. He must have drank a mason jar of moonshine sitting on the porch that night. The next days he was pretty sick from it. Naomi shook her head and *tsk*ed.

They had built a respectable stable and were ready to put a pen in for some hogs when Naomi put a stop it, at least for the time being. Holofernes fell into another period of idleness. Ezra was almost fully in control of the still, though Holofernes lorded over the actual moonshine, his thirst for which was strong and hard to quench. Late in August, Holofernes took for a week to sleeping out by the still. After a July of vigorous love making, it was clear that Naomi still was not pregnant. When Verge had fallen in a fit and broken a chair, striking her head upon the table and sitting in a stupor for more than six hours, Holofernes quit the house for the woods. He no longer felled any trees. It had been going on six months since the damned Wittacre had passed by.

It had been three days in the forest when Holofernes had been wakened from drunkenness in the middle of the night, a low, silver moon casting black trees against its descending orb, the sky diluted by light into an unseen thing, misted by stars, muted clouds like heralds to a far off dawn.

Wind made sounds in the trees. It had grown cold, and the mountain groaned, a dull whistle issuing from the shaft. The air gusting over the opening.

Holofernes stared into the hole. His still disappeared into blackness. Perhaps he should get it out of there. He stood up. Recalling he had a lantern stashed with his distillery, he looked for it and for the box of matches Ezra had wisely provided. A few fumbles and he'd found it all and lit the lantern whose flame flickered and flashed in the breeze from the mines. What seemed wide and opened in the daylight seemed small and constrained in the encroaching shadows, stark and palpably black in the lantern light. He moved forward tentatively in the shadows. The light flickered. Holofernes stood at the threshold of the mountain deep. His foot passed into the tunnel. Darkness was about him. There was little the lantern was able to do against the heavy black. Holofernes took a few steps forward. Standing in the glow allowed, he took a beaten tin flask from his pocket an pulled a long hit of whiskey from it. He gasped slightly once he had finished and replaced the flask. Slowly still, he moved deeper into the shaft. There was a minute sound and Holofernes halted again, withdrawing the flask to drink, replaced it again, and inched farther into the space.

The sound that came into Holofernes' ears just then ruffled the loose parts of his clothes, disturbed his greasy hair, and made him stand bolt-straight, the hair on his ears and neck bristling in the sudden dark silence. Moisture dropped from a shelf deeper in the shaft, *kop*. It was irregular, *kop-kop*. The wind picked up again, filtering around Holofernes, *heeliz*...a long, breathy disturbance. Holofernes strained. He was trying to hear, wanting to hear—what was it?

"He-hello?" What was he doing?

Helizikinopo...

"What's that? Who's there?"

Indeterminable vacuum without reply.

"Verge? That you? What you say girl?"

Nothing.

Helizikinopo!

Holofernes let out a sound, inhuman, weak, scared. And he turned and ran. He ran so fast that he hit an outcrop that framed the entrance to the deeper shaft. His nose made a flat, packing sound as it struck the rock. Blood poured from both nostrils. Curses spat from Holofernes' lips and he rose with tears in his eyes, his blood abundant and running and dripping *kop-kop-kop* onto the stone below. Reoriented, he left in haste, one hand pinching his nose as it turned purple and blue beneath the smeared blood still warm across his face. In the entranceway, he emptied his flask, gave it a toss, and took up another jar of shine, wrapped in brown paper, and drained that too. In a stupor, Holofernes made off into the thick of the wood, fell on a neglected bit of timber, and went immediately to sleep stretched awkwardly across the fallen trees. The sleep that took him over was restless and mean; dreams turned his head to and fro, visions arrested his thoughts and held them to dwell in the dark places of the hollow.

The next day, Holofernes was sick again. Nothing pleased his stomach; all liquids quickly returned to his throat. The sunlight accosted him. The beat of his heart was a hammer upon his head. To ease his pain, he drank more. Naomi was worried. The worry of his wife irritated Holofernes. When his headache had gone, he found he was drunk again. Bleary eyed, he took up his shotgun and went out to Ezra who was working in the plot.

"You dug sumthin' up."

"What?" asked Ezra, shielding his brow from the sun.

"In'a mines. You dug it up."

"Yeah. I dug aroun' in them mines."

"Sumthin' I said. You dug sumthin' up."

"Ya gotta move some earth ta do some diggin'."

Holofernes just stared at Ezra.

"You wanna take it easy for a bit?" asked the younger man. "What'chu got that gun for anyhow?"

"I'm gonna git it."

"Git what?"

"I don' know."

"Go sleep it off. Damn, it's barely noon."

"Done past noon."

"Hardly by an hour. Git on inside, git Naomi ta make some coffee. Take rest."

Nothing more passed between the two. Holofernes went off on his own, Ezra watched until the old man was gone. The shotgun worried Ezra. He quit his work and went into the house.

Ruth sat in the kitchen as if she would make bread, but she simply looked over the ingredients instead, casually placing some of the stuff into a bowl at her elbow. Upon seeing her there, Ezra straightened up. Ruth had taken on a crush, the chief subject of which was Ezra, young and dark, thick haired and handsome, the girl would sometimes watch him work and would on occasion take the effort to make Ezra know she watched him work and for what reasons she looked on. For these reasons, Ezra had become embarrassed in Ruth's presence and only less so in Naomi's. As a clever girl, Ruth had taken note of this change. It pleased her. She sat up as Ezra came into the room.

"Howdy, Ezra."

"Afternoon...Ruth."

"What's got yer pants in'a bunch?"

Ezra swallowed. "I'm worried 'bout yer Daddy. He's gone off again an' he's got his gun on him."

Ruth looked nonplused. She shrugged, "I don' know what gits into my Daddy, sides all that drink a'course." Looking down to her ingredients, she looked hurt.

"I'm sure he'll be ok, I jus' want yer Mama ta know where he's gone."

At that time, Naomi walked in, a serendipitous occasion for Ezra. Ruth began measuring flour into the bowl.

"What'd I hear? Holofernes's done gone off?"

"Yessim. With his gun."

"Oh my," Naomi was downcast. "That man'a mine, that man. Ezra, don' treat yer woman this way, if'n when you done settle down ta one." Ruth turned her attention the conversation. Naomi went on, "Go after him, Ezra. Jus' this once. I know he goes off an' he's in his own head you know. But with that gun an' I knows he filled that damn flask again. He's got dem jars wrapped up like ain' nobody ever git their corn from a jar before him."

"I'll follow him if that's what you want."

"Please, jus' go after'im."

Ezra nodded and was off. The whole episode was so dramatic from where Ruth sat that she started to cry.

"Girl, what is wrong with you now?" Patting her eldest's shoulder, Naomi said, "Yer Daddy's gonna be *fine*," reassuring herself by a tone of voice.

Holofernes had made directly for the mine with a purposeful gait and his shotgun firmly in one hand, swinging at his side, back and forth with his stride. Ezra hadn't anticipated such a pace.

Holofernes never broke to light his lantern, cradling the gun to strike a match as he walked, only slowing enough to turn away from the breeze. He paused within the entrance to take a draught of shine, then plunged straightaway into the darkness.

Brusquely he walked on, determined, until he came unexpectedly to a fork in the path. He chose a side and thought he'd choose the same side at every subsequent division so that he'd easily find his way back. He took a drink. A few more, then re-pocketed the flask. Moisture dripped nearby. The air was very cool, if close all around.

Outside, Ezra was calling for Holofernes. All around the woods and the entrance to the mine, Ezra paced and searched about, calling out intermittently in a loud voice, hoping Holofernes was within range.

Holofernes stopped. He had taken more than one fork, how many exactly? There was a voice on the breeze. Distant. Did it come from ahead? Or back where he had come from? He went ahead a few more paces. Then a few more. He began to walk when a stronger breeze stirred up within the tunnel. The mountain made grumblings and the moisture dripped more quickly and dust seemed to rain from fissures in the rock. Holofernes turned. The lantern seemed to flare violently; startled, Holofernes dropped the light. For a moment, a great illumination bathed the shaft and the dark world took on a definition and clarity that shook Holofernes' very being. The rock was dug out with stone rivulets like gravel tides upon the ceiling. Yet even in light the texture of everything was blackly glistening in the flare, slate and grey in a damp cool. The division between this brief conflagrated world and the depths of the mountain extending in either direction was an infinite divide. It struck Holofernes that he could see the light shrinking, retracting under the weight of the stone back into the source of its brilliance, collapsing at last into the last dense shadow of its own defeat. Nothingness. No sight, or touch, the air silent now in the void.

He screamed. He screamed and screamed again and was silent. His breath was labored. He drank. Somewhere, still very far off, he heard his name. Heard a name. *Helizikinopo...*

"Who is that?" he said.

Nothing.

"Who?" asked Holofernes.

Ezra had determined that his quarry had gone into the mines, though the idea was almost inconceivable. It was known to him that Holofernes was superstitious after a sort, and the mountain's belly spooked him as though a nascent evil lay dormant in that forbidden recess. The work demanded to get any good out of it had taken a toll from a younger Holofernes and his first drinks had been to dull a pain he'd had from living. So it was that Holofernes had returned to the place of his lament, now there submerged in darkness. Without a lantern, Ezra did not follow, but instead called after Holofernes in the dark. He heard a scream echoing far off.

Holofernes rubbed his eyes. The whirls he saw were faces, just as, when the light receded, terrible visages chased it back to the wick to snuff the salvation of Holofernes' exit.

"Holofernes," said a voice.

"Here I am," said Holofernes.

"Holofernes."

"Here I am!"

"Holofernes!"

"Who are you!"

A disturbance in the air, *Helizikinopo*, "Why?"

Helizikinopo

Running. Holofernes ran away into the dark. He ran back toward the exit and turned right. Or had he turned left before. He doubled back. He turned.

"Damn, *Damn!*" he cried. The tears came.

Defeated, he sank to the floor and drank. At least the drink he could feel. There was nothing else except the Name. What was it? Had he heard, or was it himself? What had Verge said; she had said it—it was her.

With one hand against the wall, Holofernes gradually made his way back.

After some time passed, Ezra could not cry out any longer. He stopped and sat for a spell by the still. He had a few sips of shine to calm his nerves. To pass the time, he went about looking for other signs of Holofernes, but he knew it was in vain. The old man had gone into the mines.

The gun. He had the gun. Holofernes had nearly forgotten in his panic. He took the shotgun in both hands. In his pocket were extra shells. He turned back, away from the exit he sought.

"You there! Hey!" he called out, his voice rough, strained from his earlier fits.

"Helitzknopo. Healitzanop! Nope! Hey," the moonshine was getting the best of Holofernes, as he saw waking visions in the total black of the mine, visions of nothing but indistinct distractions occasionally a vague feature, an eye, mist. He stumbled. Then he stopped, and stood. There he remained, rooted to the rock for hours, watching, waiting.

He began to grow tired. Keeping sentry in the mine was exhausting him, each passing second of the hour weighted with the anxiety of the stranger lurking in the shadow. The Other that haunted him from the deep, enormous before his mind's eye as the hills themselves were monoliths. Even in the pitch black of the shaft, the moonshine was still bright in Holofernes' eye, and it brought a sleepy haze even there, and with the hours wearing on him, he dozed and the shotgun slipped. Upon striking the ground, the readied weapon discharged with the sound of Armageddon—a clap of awful thunderous doom, a bolt of penetrating terror that turns a heartbeat into the pall of death echoing the perpetual bell left to ring eternally in the ears.

Ezra had himself been dozing. The boom of the shotgun brought him wide awake and he immediately feared suicide.

He called out to his friend, "Holofernes!"

No response.

"Holofernes!"

He had not noticed how far the day had got on. The sun was beginning to set, the air golden and open beyond the mouth of the mineshaft.

There was a sound from the depth. Ezra went forward with caution, he heard the sounds of a man walking, feet dragging, gait uneven, moaning, a ragged tiresome moan threatening to wail. Ezra found Holofernes coming out and tried to help him, but the drunkard waved him away. Insistent, Ezra went to help again.

Enraged, Holofernes took a swing at his young friend, catching him square on the jaw. Sloppily executed, the punch might not have had the same effect on Ezra had he not struck his head on the stone as he fell. As it was, Ezra lay out cold in the opening to the mountain. Holofernes moved on grumbling to himself a secret stolen from the mountain.

Since Verge had been asking all that week, Naomi took some of the dough Ruth rolled and fried it. Sprinkled with a little cinnamon and sugar, the sweet stuff was one of Verge's favorites. Naomi had kept some flour aside as well, and was bringing chicken stock to a boil on the stovetop for dumplings, even if they had no meat on hand. Verge sat at the table, playing Old Maid with Judith.

A stirring in the thicket drew Naomi's attention out the window.

"I wonder if that's Mr. Ezra come home with your father?"

Ruth came out of the other rooms into the kitchen. "I'll see," she said.

Judith said, "I hope he jus' sent Daddy on home."

Momentarily, Ruth was outside and the three other women sat quietly while Naomi stirred the broth.

"Git them dumplin's ready," said Naomi. Judith and Verge kept on playing Old Maid.

Then the door was flung wide open against the wall with a great commotion as Holofernes came through dragging Ruth by the hair behind him.

Naomi made a sound as she turned around, but her husband interjected, "Git out! *Now!*"

Everyone was dumbstruck as Holofernes raged for them to leave the house at once. His commandments issued forth with a terrible gnashing of teeth. His eyes were red and his hair wild. The shotgun was brandished haphazardly, swinging across the breadth of the house with each woman and child in its sights in turn. Eventually the family was made to acquiesce to the will of the father. He herded them outside, one by one, in a single file. They all marched out to the old sycamore tree. The sun was vanishing in the crest of the mountain, a frothy white distilled by light on the undulated horizon. There beneath the sycamore they all stood in a row to face the wrath of religion and drink.

"I'm a'goin' a cleanse this house-*hic*-hold."

The women were silent. Judith began to weep.

"There's…there's a reckonin'. One a yous is put up agin' me! An'…I'll be *damned*—"

He raised the gun and fired. It roared forth his fury above the heads of his daughters. Judith fell.

"Git up," said Holofernes, raising Judith by the arms. "Jus' *one* barrel."

"Please…Holofernes…our babies."

"Shut up. Woman. Git in line there with 'em."

Holofernes raised the shotgun. He took aim.

"Please…"said Naomi.

The shot echoed across the hollow. It reiterated and faded into the dusk, a futile gesture, nothing but the bark of the sycamore was made to bleed in the last rays of the falling sun. Judith and Verge wept openly and clung to each other. Holofernes made to reload.

A scream came from Ruth in a sudden feral gesture and she ran at her father, leaping on him and striking his face with her fists, beating and clawing at his eyes and cheeks and throat. Surprised and off-guard, Holofernes fell at once and Ruth continued her assault on the ground, rolling and punching and kicking her father, fighting like a man would fight and blind to the proprieties foisted upon her as the 'weaker' sex. Holofernes was bloody, his nose re-broken and eye blackened, before he was able to get the upper hand on Ruth. And then he let her have it as he would any adversary, beating her ferociously, hitting her with the butt of the shotgun in the abdomen, back, and buttocks. When she reared up again, he let her have one in the face. That put her back on the ground and silenced her attack.

He was about to reload the gun when Ezra burst from the thick of trees and charged Holofernes, taking the older man down by the waist, and letting him have a bit of his own medicine while they grappled on the ground. Naomi ran and took the gun. The two younger girls were led back into the house. Eventually, Ruth came in, followed by Ezra.

"He took off agin'," said Ezra winded. "How's everbody?"

They all took account of one another. Battered and a little bruised, Ruth was okay considering the evening. Judith and Verge were unscathed, at least where the flesh was concerned. Naomi embraced Ezra. Night fell outside.

A train passed in the night. Verge did not awaken.

In a few days time, buzzards began to circle close to the homestead, off by the train tracks. Ezra went to confirm everyone's fears. Holofernes lay decapitated by the tracks, a jagged wound for a neck, the whole of his blood dried and black across the wood and steel, flecked and spattered on the grass. It was almost September.

VERGE McCLAIN

The marriage of Verge McClain was really one of convenience. Once the Marks clan had arrived in the hollow, it was clear that Ruth would marry Tatters. Not that Ruth was quick to give up on Ezra, but he showed no interest in the girl ten years his junior and when Ruth began (after a long struggle with naiveté) to suspect there were other women warming Ezra's nights, she made a valiant effort to look hurt before subjecting Tatters to the affections of her young heart. He was glad for the attention, getting well on into adolescence himself and wanting more with each day that discovery of another's naked body. The body of Ruth was a bounty of discovery.

Judith had begun a long process of leaving the hollow. Since the death of Holofernes, she had been intent on finding an exit from the place and she shook with nerves whenever a train would pass. She told odd stories about lights on the mountain and an old tree where her father died. It was a way to frighten children at picnics but she spoke with conviction enough to scare some of the men too, who felt the absence of Holofernes through their lack of quality moonshine. Ezra had been wary of taking on the business in full—the fate of Holofernes was a warning sign on the lips of the women of the mountain.

Verge couldn't help but read the letter of conspiracy into the whole affair. It had all unfolded so seamlessly over the course of many years. The Marks' had come into the hollow, took up on the other side of the rise, and built a sturdy house with near five rooms on a ground floor including the kitchen and adjacent dining space. The construction was centered around a stairwell and the better of two weeks had been spent in the laborious digging of a foundation and cellar, complete with a showerhead and concrete floors.

Verge had watched from the doorway as Abe had come into the old fort-house soon after he'd arrived. Her Mama had been talking to the newcomers, and Verge understood that her family would be allowed to stay on the property. Still, in the girl's mind, a violation had taken place that had disrupted the peace she'd found in the wake of her father's death. His absence had rocked her into a lull and she felt that surrender one feels after having been overpowered and resigned to passivity. But with these new people Verge felt new responsibilities looming and was shaken from her suspended freefall to see the ground of her womanhood rushing to meet her. She had stood in the threshold and watched as Abe came into her house, took out a chair from the table and went into the other room, the family room. He placed the chair under the crossbeam and stood on it. He reached up and felt with both hands along the length of the crossbeam where he could. He must have struck upon what he sought, because he fumbled around muttering to himself. Abe removed something from the crossbeam. Something paper, money. It was folded and went into his pocket. Abe walked out of the house, patting Verge on the head, tousling her hair slightly as he passed. She watched him disappear over the rise.

Everyone who could and was willing was digging and a few days after Verge had seen Abe stand on the chair in the house, Abe, Ezra, and Tatters got into the truck and went into St. Clairsville. Wayne stayed digging, pausing to make marks on paper, sending little Margaret scurrying out of his way. Mama Clay helped as she could, but her belly was fat and heavy. Naomi would rub her hands over her own womb, slimmed, though still framed by ample hips, and would watch the other mother. The widowed Harbarger knew she would be a great service to the other, and took care to pay her debt to the Marks' generosity.

In reality, the Marks had nothing to give. Ezra had taken Abe to the woods to show him where a good forestry business could be made, though Abe thought he could get a post-truck that would pick up timber on the road by the Marks' young homestead. The old fort-house had been hidden somewhat, removed from where the world was catching up to the mountains and to the hollow, and the country road that wound up north to Slabtown and the bituminous fields and the company house where Tatter's had been born. The new homestead was built facing this road, still set back a ways; a grove of trees curved to obscure a side of the house, an oak, purposely preserved from clear-cutting, shaded most of the structure from direct view. Under the direction of Ezra, Wayne and Tatter's had cleared the way for a drive from the road to where they believed the side of the house would be.

Abe and Ezra had been getting on well, though Ezra made clear his plans to find work in the city, possibly in the train yard. It was largely because of Ezra's help, and the advantage of the new stable at the Harbarger's, that the Markses were able to get two rooms up before the onset of winter. Inside, they busied themselves with domestic preparations and finished up the niceties of a furnished abode, while the girls on the other side of the rise adjusted to life without their father. Mama Clay had inquired with Ezra about a school in the vicinity and then, upon learning there existed rooms of education in the hollow, took counsel with Naomi about the schooling of their children. Wayne took no interest in this talk, but Tatters inclined to schooling and all three of the Harbarger sisters showed interested, though Judith seemed most likely to succeed. An element of Ruth's character was more boastful than bright and she was primed to be attended by a throng of slack-jawed boys. Verge wanted whatever her sisters did. She still hadn't taken to reading, though she recited the alphabet and could make out Dick and Jane and Spot, throwing a ball, or running.

Ruth had been a big help to Mama Clay, who gave orders to those around her more than she herself saw personally to any task. Sometimes, Verge would accompany Ruth and watch and the girls developed an awe of Mama Clay and the subtly with which the woman directed her household, the amiable way Abe heeded the fullness of her womb. Maternal and guiding, Mama Clay was seen to be an architect of sorts by Verge.

As soon as the weather seemed kind enough, Abe and his wife went to the schoolhouse to see about enrollment and within a week it was arranged for Tatters, Ruth, Judith, and Verge to start out in the two-room schoolhouse two-and-a-half miles down the road. The Marks' made it clear two more would be on the way in a few years, but they were assured the older children were all set to be gone within a season or three. In fact, the school teacher seemed delighted to have pupils enough to go on, and Abe, not being opposed to book learning of any kind, asked the sort of questions someone asks when they have a mind to give you something for a job well done. Parting with surplus vegetables, or a few spare eggs was an easy enough show of appreciation.

Mama Clay had a way with people, and the arrangements for school were easy enough, though Naomi was sure to keep the girls singing their gospel at home. It was in the two-room schoolhouse that the collective youths meet the McClain siblings, of which there were a great number and who, depending on the time of year, were hardly ever all present at school at the same time.

The McClain's had nine children in all, though two would die very young. Another achieved adolescence but was killed in an accident when he was seventeen. The youngest of the nine children was an odd boy and very quiet. He was Verge's age, one of four students in the fourth grade. Verge could have been in the fifth grade, but her slow reading skills and the heaviness of her handwriting kept her back a year. She was marginally better at math, though often neglected to show her work doing long division. The youngest McClain boy was named Jonathan. He kept up an earnest attempt to make Verge show her work in division

115

and other mathematics. Though she never took his advice in arithmetic, she was pleased to have him read to her and thus kept up on all the English assignments she would otherwise have failed. So, Jonathan was judged by Naomi and Mama Clay and Judith to be a good influence. Ruth couldn't be bothered too much. She was consumed with the madness to which Tatters could be driven by her innocent glances, by the inconsequential questions she put to him, and by the simple words she uttered to other boys that could impact the adolescent heart even when they were not spoken in his presence. In fact, the others had judged Jonathan to be such a positive factor in the life of Verge that they made certain arrangements to have him as a tutor of sorts to the youngest Harbarger girl. The primary competitor for Jonathan's affections and attention was a boy of slightly older and more stalwart composition than was Jonathan. The older boy David was the son of a farmhand on the McClain farm and his father had brought him on to help and to learn a useful trade while the father was still able enough to teach him. This apprenticed farmhand was David and Jonathan saw in him the most respectable and imitable specimen of young adulthood Jonathan had had the privilege to attend. Moreover, David did not ignore him as the vast majority of the other McClain children did. Jonathan had a temperament that wore on his siblings. He demanded a certain amount of leeway, a certain forgiveness for his idiosyncrasies, which more often associated him with his sisters than with the fraternity raising him. Jonathan hated baiting his own hooks, or removing the fish he caught subsequently. He could muck a horses stall okay, but sucked his thumb loudly on some nights, and had a weak throw without an eye for catching a ball. At their young age, this made him fast friends with Verge, and Jonathan would spend many hours with her, reviewing their lessons and playing simple games of cards and jacks and pretending to the happy idyll they imagined all adults to enjoy. Sometimes, Jonathan would forget to come to their scheduled time together and Verge would learn later that he had been held up working with David, threshing or some other farm labor hated by Verge.

Like many women her age, Verge never understood men's work the way her mother, or even her sisters did. Verge, fragile and broken, had always been spared the bulk of work that normally fell to all children her age during those times. There were chores one rarely escaped, but Naomi had so fretted over Verge as to keep her distant from all the work of modernity. As she grew, the industrious properties of men's psyches never permeated Verge's awareness and she resented the bond that grew between David and her beau to the point that she could see in that friendship a nascent doom that would develop into a no less certain than untimely end.

Though they tolerated Jonathan in much the same way that they tolerated Verge, no one then living on the Russell tract had much love for the McClain clan in general as they all knew that the more prodigious farmers looked down on the folk of the hollows as living in a steadily outmoded and fast vanishing way of life, to which the machinery that everyday amplified the McClain's prestige were a testament. Jonathan himself was something to be abandoned and forgotten in the hollows and part of the reason the Marks brothers were none too kind to Jonathan was that his presence reminded them of this attitude held by the McClain's and the disdain they had for even those of their own kin who were unfortunate enough to fall outside the pail of their ample returns. Such an attitude amounted to an unforgivable callousness in the eyes of a matriarch like Mama Clay who made it her mission to never move a child out of her house if it could be helped. Needless to say, this was one mission at which Mama Clay was to fail, but her efforts in that direction were momentous and the results were that of a great and extended family of a wealth, perhaps lacking the luster of gold, but one still heaped high in the esteem of folks from all around the county.

Tatters was the first to move beyond the hollow, but not before he had finished school and secured Ruth as his wife, a courtship that lasted all the pair's happy teenage years. The thing about the mountains is that they can hide so much. This is one reason for the judgments made by those outside the mountains, even of other country folk like the McClains—who were honest agriculturalists through and through. It could hide the long blossoming of mountain girls and the dormant love of boys and the cool waters of a spring overrun with laurel where it runs from the mountains to a low field in the hollow where the hills obscure the growth of crops as well as of families. The move was not permanent but was pragmatic. Together with Ezra, Abe had made a plan for the development of the Russell tract's resources. It was decided early on that Wayne would become a partner with Abe and Ezra (thus allowing the Marks' to maintain a majority ownership within their family) in a small mining operation. When Jonathan became a regular presence around the hollow, Wayne decided the boy's small frame and willingness to please his elders was a great asset and made it known that he wished to bring the youth on and put him to work renovating the mine shafts. The men decided it better for Tatters to get work in town. They could divide their labors and raise the capital necessary for their business venture. All the work would be by their sweat and the women would be hard at work to raise crops enough for subsistence. So, Tatters, going on seventeen, finishing up his academic career with his usual nonchalant excellence, began making trips into town to spread his name around and find some work. He kept up his trapping and was much better; he never had to kill the animals he trapped any more. The knots he tied and his lay in the runs allowed for the animal to break their own neck when the snare was closed. There were many ways to contribute to the homestead.

Tatters and Ruth were on and off in those early days of their adulthood. Resentment of the expectation of their marriage would distort the natural beauty one saw in the other. It was easy to be angry with the patriarchal emphasis on their union but it was never easy, in the bosom of the mountain, to outgrow the obligation implied by the toil invested in their upbringing. Sometimes, they took it out on each other. Sometimes, Tatters looked for more than work in town. He looked for another body to offer an elusion from predestination.

At that time, Tatters would commute into St. Clairsville and bring the paper home with him in the evening. The Great Depression came into the hollow. Mama Clay worried over the pictures of breadlines, despondency. She looked at the small plots of crop and wondered whether the Dust Bowl could be the hollow—the rich uncultivated history of the land unknown to her, and the vast agriculturalists of Nebraska and Oklahoma were of a different breed than Mama Clay and the Markses who had been subsistence farmers only and were raised by industrial labor or forestry.

Verge watched these goings on with a measure of detachment. She was rarely included in planning and was accustomed to being incorporated in the work of the homestead in a circumspective manner adapted to frailty and incompetence. She knew Tatters was learning to play poker because he had taught her and the two played together frequently, betting acorns, pebbles, and trading between them the stranded seashells whose existence Tatters shared with Verge one drizzly afternoon when he grew tired of trying to explain the movements of the knight on the chessboard. Chess had seemed incomprehensible to Verge, especially the specious role of the Queen, and her mind seemed unable to focus on "strategy" and "logistics" as Tatters kept saying, though she had an intuitive head for the probabilities a deck of cards provided to observant players. Her mind wondered far less as she ticked off the list of remaining face cards or aces; obsessed with the revelation of the flop. In fact, so obsessed was she that Tatters began, secretly, to learn from Verge—who was mysteriously gifted an allowance any Monday that Tatters awoke with his pockets flush from a weekend of fortunate gambits.

Ruth was jealous of this affinity between Tatters and Verge, though Ruth, all through her teenage years, was hard to separate from her mother.

The death of Holofernes Harbarger had taken a special toll on the women he'd left behind. Naomi had been given a purposeful existence by her marriage to Holofernes. Even though the two had many secrets between them, the moonshine and its degenerative effects notwithstanding, they had loved each other in the hardness of living and that hardness had hardened their love which would rear up over Naomi's shoulder like a monolith she'd cut from the stone of the mountain herself. This monumental weight was obvious to Ruth. She would do what she could to assist her mother's burden but the mourning days of a widowed homemaker were singular and Ruth was distanced from her mother's sorrow by inexperience, happiness, and her virginity.

Even when Ruth knew that the relationship between Verge and Tatters was an innocent one, she knew at the same time that there were women in St. Clairsville where poker was played for money who weren't trading seashells in the innocent sun, and because of this she sometimes directed her insecurities at Verge. None of this was of particular interest to Judith. While Naomi would wear her mourning in black Judith withheld her own and kept a silent eye on the desperation of her older sister and their mother. In this silence, Judith cultivated an apprenticeship in womanhood under Mama Clay with both Margaret and the infant Harold Marks as resources for her tutelage. When Harold was slow to take to women, Mama Clay assessed an excessive attachment to Judith in the boy, who was heartbroken the day Judith finally left the hollow and frustrated all his youthful sexual energy in pining after a woman too much his senior to be interested in pubescent advances.

When Tatters was twenty-four years old war broke out across Europe and he announced his engagement to Ruth. Though correlated, the two events had no causal connection to one another beyond the eventuality that the newlyweds would be separated; a motif of that generation's tales of matrimony. Tatters waited to be drafted. He was too occupied with establishing their apartment in St. Clairsville and transitioning Ruth from her life in the hollow to one in town.

It had been a spring wedding. Everyone had come out on a Tuesday, the twenty-first of March, for a modest ceremony at the church and a day of picnicking and drinking a variety of moonshines, best of which was shared between the recipes of Ezra and the groom. Ruth had everything dressed in sun-faded yellows and soft lilac for sashes around the pinched waists of her smiling bridesmaids' buttercup-colored sundresses. Wayne was Tatter's best man and Ezra stood there beside little Harold, who was only ten that year. Judith still put a modicum of effort into looking after Harry and Margaret, though they mostly flew about of their own wills, free and happy bye and large. The ceremony had gone on without anyone to give Ruth away and so the constable offered his arm and was subsequently included in the only wedding photo. Whenever he would see the photograph, Tatters would always struggle to recall the constable's name. Little occurrences made up the day.

After the union had been made right before God, when the food and drink and merry were made in the wide yard of the church beneath the dappling of trees spread out across the lawn, Verge happened to be alone on a wooden bench at a wooden table covered over in linens when Judith and Ruth, her sisters, joined her in the shade of the tree. At first, the two older girls acted as if they hadn't noticed Verge was there; they had come to the table to be alone and were annoyed to find the youngest sister already seated. In any event, they went on as if they were alone.

"Have you settled it with Tatters?" asked Judith as Ruth fidgeted with a bit of lace floating in the breeze.

"I have."

"What's he say?"

"He's says we can afford the room, but you gotta take that job at the diner opening."

"How's Tatters know them anyways?"

"I told ya before, that Italian run a pushcart. Tatters done ate there everyday he went in town."

"Italian, huh?"

"Yeah, but Tatters says they're nice. He says there's all kind'a people in town. I think Ernest-o is his name," Ruth looked around preoccupied. The white folds of her dress made her disinterested.

Judith went on, "I can wait tables. I jus' want outta here."

Verge got up and stormed away. The glass she'd been drinking from was tipped over and rolled onto the glass.

"Heavens!"

"I'm glad she didn't break the glass," said Judith.

Verge went around looking for Jonathan. He wasn't in the yard and so Verge sat down by her mother, who was at a table with Mama Clay and Abe. Naomi turned and adjusted her daughter's hair away from her face. Verge leaned slightly away from her mother's grooming.

"What's wrong now, girl?"

"Nothin', Mama."

"Don't seem like nothin'."

123

"It's nothin', Mama," but Verge was visibly crying as she spoke.

"Tell Mama," Naomi said and embraced her.

"Judith's leavin' Mama."

Abe got up and walked away. Mama Clay sat on.

Naomi said, "Judith might take on some work for us, baby. We've been getting' on too long with too little since yer Daddy died. Judy's gonna be a big help ta us now that she's of age, you see?"

Verge nodded her head as she nestled into her mother's bosom. The women sat a moment in silence before Verge got up from her mother's lap and sat straight. Mama Clay offered a handkerchief which Verge accepted and used to roughly dab her cheeks.

The scene unfolded in the shade of the trees as the evening deepened. Drink was seeping into the minds of those in attendance. Abe surveyed the women seated beneath the trees as he sipped shine with Tatters, sharp in his borrowed suit, black and pressed. The two men exchanged fair swigs of the mountain liquor and talked about life.

"Verge is done upset yer puttin' Judith up."

Tatters took a long sip of whiskey, "I got my reasons."

"What's them?"

"Can't all these girls marry my brothers."

Abe shrugged.

"That girl don't want ta be in the holler no more. Can't say I fault her that."

"I reckin'."

"I reckin', Verge is good as married to that McClain boy, slow as he is, whether them two reckin' it or not."

"I ain't thought on it t'all."

"Hell you ain't," Tatters laughed.

Abe took a draw on his shine.

"Either way, Judy'll make a wage workin' fer them Italians an' send some on home until Verge ain't their mother's problem no more. Hell, maybe Judith'll marry up."

"We don't need no more investors."

Tatters just smiled.

"You never know what you're gonna need."

"Time'll tell," said the father.

"I gotta piss."

Tatters went off into the woods, away from the commotion of his wedding day. Dark was beginning to quicken its descent. In the cover of the woods the shadows came on more strongly and Tatters soon lost sight of the picnic grounds. It felt good to walk in the cool of the leaves and so he pressed on, ambivalent to the play of light around him, until he came to a fallen tree and decided there was as good a place as any to empty his bladder. In the quiet, Tatters removed himself from his pants and waited. As the day drew close and quiet, Tatters thought he heard something alone in the woods. It was a sound not unlike the snap of a twig, but more distinct, one of the guests smacking their lips over the pig roast. Then it was quiet again. Tatters relaxed and began to urinate. There was a muffled sound in the underbrush, but Tatters ignored it. He picked up the sounds of whispering and then Jonathan and David appeared out of nowhere being boisterous and full of camaraderie, their arms flung loosely over the shoulder of the other, David practically supporting Jonathan by the waist. They stopped short when they came upon Tatters, still loudly pissing into the brush. Though they acted as if they had expected to find Tatters there vulnerable as he was, the two were quick to put space in between them. Tatters was not embarrassed to be seen as he was, by the little light that remained. He took his time to finish the business he'd taken the walk for, gave a firm shake, and tucked himself away. Jonathan looked uneasy and glanced down and then up and then down again, not averting his eyes. David seemed to hide something behind his back.

David nodded, "Tatters."

"You boys found my pissin' place."

Jonathan snickered.

"Man's gotta have a place ta do his business."

"Indeed he does," said Tatters. "What business brings you out here?"

"Little too much a yer whiskey made Jon ill. He done got sick over yonder."

Jonathan held his stomach. "We had some business to settle up," he said.

"One way a puttin' it," David said.

"You thinkin' a comin' on at the mine?"

David let out a sigh of relief. "Yessir, if'n we don' git in the service."

"The service?" asked Tatters.

"We's joinin' up," said Jonathan.

David gave his partner a sharp elbow.

"It ain't exactly known yet, sir," said David. "We's got a few things ta put in order first."

"I'd say," Tatters was fixed on Jonathan.

"Don' worry, sir, I's—" but Jonathan wasn't anything as he began to vomit loudly with David looking on shocked, like he had never seen such a thing. Tatters left them to it, resolving to have a talk with Jonathan when there was less liquor involved between them.

When Tatters arrived back at the church, his older brother was talking with Abe. The two men leaned against the broad trunk of a tree sipping whiskey and nodding agreeably to one another. Tatters approached and said, "Jonathan's gonna be leavin' in a season or two," without a pause.

Abe asked, "How's that?"

"Thinks he's joinin' the military. Army I reckin'."

Abe was quiet.

"Figure he'd be askin' first," said Wayne.

"He's signin' up with David. Reckin' they's sharin' a backbone nowadays."

Wayne rubbed his chin and nodded. He looked across the small crowd to Verge. "Never you mind jus' now. Have a drink."

Some time passed without a word, the night full in bloom, and they all drank their whiskey under the wide green umbrella below the moon. Later, when people began to drift off in their own ways, Verge engaged Tatters in a distracted game of poker. Distracted because Ruth was anxious to get on the road; Ezra having promised to drive her and the bridegroom into town to their newly furnished apartments. In between the vexing insistence of Ruth, Verge had managed to put in, "Everybody's leavin' me, Tatters."

A little slurred, allowing Ruth to get the better of him, Tatters said sleepily, "Ain't nobody leavin' you. Me an' Ruth jus' right in town. S'Clairsville ain' far."

"I ain't meanin' yous."

"Well, Jonathan ain't fit for service no how."

"Jonathan?"

"Yeah," said Tatters, "he ain' a gonna make a month in th' military."

"Indeed he shan't," said Verge and played the remainder of her hand in silence.

Neither player was intent on the game and Tatters gave it up to be with his wife. Verge was distant when the gathering thronged about the loud truck with drunk Ezra behind the wheel and sent the newlyweds off to town and their honeymoon in a new home. Only now Verge knew Jonathan's idea without him knowing she knew. She saw David by the fire, part of a semi-circle of youths that surrounded Judith, who had a captive Harry at her side while she spun a story around the specters of the hollows and the sorrow of her patricide. Standing at a distance, Verge listened.

"...light from the lantern can be seen across the valley. If I stood up on that mountaintop I could see that lantern down in the hollow sure as you see me right here. And down yonder by that brown patch of earth, where ain't nothing but that big old tree growed up all twisted, down there across the road from my homestead you can see that light start up high in them mountains, out west where people went to die in the old days. When my

Daddy was still livin' an' I couldn't sleep at night I'd see it start way up there in the mountains. I ain't never seen, but I heard tell that there was a fire down in the belly a' that mountain and up where no one but them trackers and woodsmen go there spouts a flame comin' up like Hell itself! An them hellfires light up that lantern and start it off down the mountain born by who only the Devil knows. I ain't never seen nobody, but I seen that light comin' down the mountain fast enough to be on horseback and cross the train tracks down along the road and come alight in the boughs a' that tree."

The air was opaque, laden with Satan's shadow and the rustle of his spies in the thickets. Some of the children held their breaths. One asked, "Then what 'appens?"

"It vanishes," said Judith. "Up in that tree, it jus' disappears."

Those adolescence tried to play it cool, as they had heard was the way, but their glances were nervous if less chatty than the younger kids who distracted each other or prayed and felt a little more safe. Verge took account of David who seemed dull and slack-jawed in the firelight, his clothes rumpled and sloppy from drink. Still, it was that unkempt masculinity that drew Verge to linger on him. He was broad, and his neck was a bit long, but it drove sharply into a hard jaw that would be firm and commanding if it weren't so lubricated by liquor. In the shadows, Verge felt her hand wandering across the front of her dress and she took account of how David's full lips were pushed out enough to shine in the dull light. She began to understand why Jonathan loved David so. She became irritated with herself. How she had enflamed her loins. She turned away knowing only frustration in her bed and, as she stepped toward the tree under which she stood, a fit overcame her and she collapsed onto the ground without any commotion. She lay convulsing in solitude. When she came around, the party was over. Her family was all that was left, talking quietly and drinking around the fire. Nothing had been badly damaged in her fit, though she knew it was near impossible to hide the flecks of white dried in the corners of her mouth. She did her best, smoothed her dress, and joined the thinned crowd next to her sisters, sans the bride who was finally enjoying the body of her husband without shame.

Judith took brief purview of Verge and knew basically what had happened.

"You all right?" she asked.

"I'm fine," Verge said.

"You don' look so fine, girl."

Verge was dour.

"Look, I din'—"

"What din' you? You's don' even know what yer talkin' 'bout."

Judith was taken aback.

"You 'n yer stories. You don' even know."

"Verge, don' start," the girls had been speaking in hushed voices but Judith could see Mama Clay's eyes on them, heavy with sleep though the elders had become.

"It's Helizikinopo."

Mama Clay took notice. She touched Naomi's arm and brought her within earshot.

"What?" asked Judith quietly.

"See. You don' know. Sometimes I think even Daddy din' know nothin'."

"You talk crazy."

"I talk right. Jus' cause it's crazy to you don' mean it ain't the truth. I done seen a few things in these nineteen years."

Judith sort of smiled, but Verge kept on, saying, "An' I don' mean no damn lights either."

"Here now, girl," said Naomi. "What you goin' on about?"

"Ain't nothin'."

"Ta hell it ain't," said Mama Clay.

"Judith's tellin' tales ta scare them kids."

"Well, tale's tales," said Naomi.

"Not all of 'em," Mama Clay said. "I heard you. Helizikinopo. Them's old names from old times, child. I know you ain't seen no Algonquin in nineteen years."

"No ma'am."

"Then what'd you see?"

"I saw a fire that was down in the belly a the mountain. And it wants me to go down there to it."

"Hush, girl," said Naomi. "Fire don' want nothin'."

"I don' know, Mama! Why's you askin' me this?"

"Why's you gettin' on yer sister? What'd you see?"

"I told you. I saw a fire underground. But not just that. The fire's a light, an' I know a path up north, goin' up from where you come. They's buildin' on it, but the path is done there. Everyone thinks one thing but the case is always somethin' else. They ain't buildin' nothin' tain't there already."

"How you know all this, girl?"

"A woman shows me. A dark woman."

"Is that her?" asked Mama Clay.

"I don' know," said Verge. "Jus' leave the holler an' git it done with, Judy. I know I ain't never leavin'."

It never occurred to Tatters that he had given away Jonathan's secret to Verge. So involved in the new married life was he that soon everything but town living and work in the mills was distant and indistinct to Tatters. Ruth had become pregnant in the weeks following her wedding—her nurturing womb another barrier between the world of the living and Verge, who would never love her nephew who was named Howard. When, three years after Ruth's wedding, Jonathan proposed to Verge, everyone assumed it was part of some plan the young man had been seeding.

The way it finally happened was, Verge had been given to wandering off in a manner reminiscent of her father. She didn't wander to get drunk or to hide, but was out seeking, though she herself could not have told anyone what it was she looked for. Perhaps it was nothing, as she was wont to say. But perhaps not. By mid-July Ginny's Diner had opened in its permanent location and Judith was a waitress there, the first full time staff Ernesto Guiseppe could afford to hire. With Tatters, Ruth, and Judith all gone from the hollow within a summer, it was as if a tether had been severed and now Verge was left to drift. She had been disillusioned by Jonathan, who had made an honest attempt to enlist. In the summer of 193_, the U.S. army was turning people away, and both David and Jonathan were instructed to try the Civilian Conservation Corps for work under the New Deal. Disheartened, the pair had sought Ezra to show them the lay of the woods where Holofernes had done his forestry and they themselves began hauling timber, paying Ezra a modest "finder's fee" for a crash course in the industry. Abe's connection to the post-truck was still good as all the Marks' knew well that transportation out of the hollow was an expense essential to any business they hoped to run. What Verge could not understand was when Jonathan and David put up a cabin, to which Verge would refer always as "that shack," and began cohabitating as they moved their timber business into the black.

What Verge could not see was the capital Jonathan was able to put back in this manner, keen as he was still to enlist. Every Sunday, when Tatters visited his mother, he would bring in the papers. Jonathan made sure to check these to see how the war was on. In spite of all the opinions of the countryside, that the war was another of Europe's problems, Jonathan had a strong conviction, not just that the U.S. ought to get involved, but that the country was somehow destined to be involved. This fatalistic drive gave to Jonathan a single-pointedness of mind that few of his peers, save perhaps David, would understand. David was always singularly close to Jonathan.

With this development, Verge was isolated, and Naomi began to suffer from the absence of her daughters. She would feign illness for pity and wail on her loneliness into the night. If Verge displeased her mother, the older woman threatened to lay herself across the train tracks. So, Verge wandered alone, not so much afraid as just objective about her condition. Thus convinced of her lonesome nature, she failed to note Jonathan had presumed to follow her wanderings through the mountains, and had come to know a place where Verge often went and sat by a fallen ancient tree. It was there that he waited for her, one autumn night, in one of the few truly prescient acts Jonathan would ever commit in his entire life.

It was cold, such was the draw of the forest on Verge. She was in furs as she went along, her feet in rags and her father's old boots. Jonathan had bought himself a pea-coat and a pair of khaki trousers which he had proudly shown to David. He had spent the morning with Mama Clay and Naomi waiting for the hour when Verge would slip away, finished with the chores and bored and twenty-one years old. When she did at last, off went Jonathan, wishing he had Tatters' skills in the hunt. He headed her off nevertheless and patiently waited in the clearing, seated on the fallen tree where Verge often came. Jonathan would always recall how he could see his own breath as he waited there.

Eventually auburn haired Verge came into the clearing, unimpressed by the sudden appearance of her estranged beau. He smiled at her, to which she had no response.

The first thing Jonathan said was, "Roosevelt is going to help the Soviets. I read it in the papers."

"You an' Tatters an' them damn papers," Verge said.

"We're goin' ta war. After the Kearny an' Iceland. It'll happen soon."

"I don' care about no war."

"I'm goin'. You, care 'bout me?"

"I don' know, Jonathan. You seem busy. With David an' all."

"Marry me. Marry me, Verge Harbarger."

Verge couldn't respond. Nothing about her and Jonathan's relationship had been what she thought of as romantic. Yet there he looked plaintively, his arm stretched out, a ring clutched between his two fine fingers, ungloved, white in the cold and pressed hard against the ring. He seemed almost to thrust the thing at her, and she took a slight step back.

"Jonathan….I…"

"Please," he said. "I love you."

"I…I will. I will marry you."

He stood up an hugged her.

"Thank you," he said tenderly into her ear.

She relaxed in his arms and then he stepped back. Without hesitation, he moved in suddenly to kiss her and their gross inexperience blossomed as their lips crossed, Jonathan's cool tongue unconvincing as it prodded her mouth. When they broke away, Jonathan stepped back, muttered his goodbyes and took off into the trees. Verge stood dumbfounded, sinking into her thoughts on the trunk of the old tree.

The whole affair sprung on Verge as if it had been waiting for Jonathan to produce it from his hat. In December, the U.S. declared war on Japan and the Axis Powers. By February, Jonathan and David were in Georgia for Basic Training. When he returned in April, he and Verge were married on the McClain farm. Everything was rushed and chaotic and the McClain's treated Verge as an invalid, which suited her, since she had no interest in planning the strict and traditional wedding staged by the prim McClain matriarch. Tatters and Wayne were both absent. The brothers had been drafted in March and sent to Fort Meade. All

Jonathan could talk about on his wedding day was how the Japanese had taken the island of Bataan the day before and after the terse formalities of the day, Jonathan made to burn his wedding bed like the fields of Yenangyaung. Nothing about Verge's wedding had been so pleasant as the sunny March picnic her sister enjoyed. The war had charged everything with this earnestness and disproportionate passion and weight. David had openly wept throughout the ceremony and the McClain's had dressed up what had once been fieldhand's quarters to serve as the sanctuary of the couple's consummation. It was made clear to Verge, by her father McClain no less, that she was expected to submit to Jonathan; that she was to do what was necessary for him to finish the deed. This was advice Verge was singularly unprepared to take, her total ignorance of the subject compounding the vague disgust she felt toward the thought of a man like Jonathan writhing between her legs. That's just how she pictured him, writhing, nothing like the strong determination David delivered in her imagination. How he had wept, if only for her, Verge had thought.

No one stayed on after the reception, which was how the McClain's referred to the event following the ceremony. There was good food, little drink, and by night fall Verge and Jonathan were ushered off to sire McClain children, a duty Verge had not perceived as her husband had pleaded with her in the clearing of the hollow. When they were alone together, husband and wife, Verge had never been alone with a man. Certainly not at night, as it were. She knew she had to give herself over to him, but what that meant she couldn't be sure. Just when she thought she should fall faint, or supplicate herself in some way, Jonathan approached, fell to his knees and embraced her about the waist briefly before hiking her dress into the air and using one hand to tug her underpants down best he could. Startled, Verge fell backwards, onto a prepared bed, and Jonathan lunged forward to pleasure her with his mouth. The whole experience was, for Verge, terrifying; thus overwhelmed, she clamped her thighs about Jonathan who suckled at Verge's womanhood as if at a nipple. No coherent thought occurred to Verge as she was; certainly some new madness had overcome her—could she find pleasure in such depravity? There was nothing to satisfy Jonathan. Nothing had formerly prepared the girl for this and it suddenly became clear what she was expected to do. All at once the whole distinction between men and women crystallized with her husband fumbling out of his pants. Having frustrated himself, Jonathan used his hand and mashed himself against his wife, who was shocked to have consented to the act at all, disbelief at once with desire now stirring. She tried to help him. Even flaccid they were able to make a pitiful entry and thus enveloped Jonathan gradually began to swell. They just lay there shaking against one another, scared and unsure, asking that it all be okay. Then there was just...nothing. Jonathan lay back and the two were truly nude beside one another. Verge believed she could love her husband. She had been raised to want to love him in the very least.

The very next day, Jonathan, David, and Ezra were off to begin building a house. In the beginning the idea appealed to everything real that was maturing in Verge, but when the construction rushed on and David left for training and Jonathan left for training and

Verge was left with three simple rooms and an outhouse on the far side of the Russell tract, out in the mountains away from the road and the families, the whole tragedy solidified in Verge's mind. She had not gotten pregnant and she would not before Jonathan was in Africa fighting with David and the draft was more and more a subject of conversation. Everyone had been signed up. Out in her little shack time passed in a haze, dissipated on the mist that rose in the morning from the mountains. The time after Ruth and Tatters' wedding was blurred, soft around the edges. There was nothingness and Jonathan and the trauma of their wedding night— the alienation of Verge from her own being. Seeing Ruth with Tatters, how the couple loved one another, Verge knew there was no place for that in her own existence. Time would come when Ruth would move back to the hollow with Tatters and Howard. By then, Verge would have faded.

Though her house had only three rooms, it was sturdy and warm and somewhat modern. But her husband had barely laid his head down than he was gone, off to the War. Verge waited. From the hills she learned patience. They seldom wrote. By October, Jonathan and David were gone, headed for war on the eighth of November in Operation Torch. The first in a string of sparse letters spoke of weather disruptions and heavy fighting in the Moroccan town of Fedala, the target of Operation Brushwood. But that was a long way off. Wayne and Tatters had left for England on the fifth of October. Most of the men in the hollow were gone. Another letter from Jonathan would not arrive until August, from Messina, Italy. It read, in part:

"I think this is what passes for a vacation in wartime. I have a moment to write and I think I should. Do not worry that you are not pregnant. There will be time for that when we're back. David says we are invincible. After Fedala I was scared, but now, in Italy, I know nothing can stop us.

"The people here are friendly. I wonder what Ernesto would think. Ask Judy if you can. I hope you're getting out an visiting. I miss just visiting.

"Nothing is right here. There is killing. I know what war is and I know we did the right thing. But it seems senseless. I am homesick and that makes it worse. I miss you and think of you."

Verge knew this was why Jonathan did not write, because he could not find words for himself, because there was nothing to say. This was his great plan, what he wanted, and now he had it and would kill for it or be killed.

"They say they've got big plans for us," wrote Jonathan, "Maybe I'll see them Marks brothers over here before it's all done with."

Verge's response read, in its entirety:

"Jonathan,

"I miss and love you. Please take care of yourself. Watch after David. I await your return.

"Love,

"Verge"

It would be another year before Verge would hear from her husband again. Time passed. She over-wintered with the Markses and her mother. Everything was static. Judith brought news from town. The papers told about Jonathan's unit and an amphibious assault in Anzio, Italy. In the time after, Jonathan never spoke of Operation Shingle. It wasn't until June 194_ that the hollow learned David had been killed in Anzio. Wayne and Tatters wrote from Isigny-le-Buat in France.

"Dear Verge," wrote Jonathan. "David is dead. Hope is buried with him in Lazio."

On August the fifteenth Jonathan had been part of a landing in Normandy, France. He had been injured despite the light resistance his unit had encountered as they went ashore into a France whose liberation was quickening. He was awarded the Purple Heart and patched up before being sent back to the front in the Vosges Mountains.

While Jonathan convalesced, the women of the hollow were visited several times by company men who took counsel with Abe—Ezra had himself been sent to the Pacific Theater. The company men were ostensibly from Brown & Root. They talked big and impressive talk which aligned them patriotically with the Army Corps of Engineers, though they were far better dressed than any Army Engineer that Abe could imagine. He was skeptical.

When the men had first come around the hollow, Abe assumed it was his small mining operation that was of interest to them. This would have been the easier issue to confront since his partners were all off to war and even the most opportunistic capitalist would have been hard pressed to take advantage of war heroes who had stormed Normandy, bombarded Pacific Islands, and were counting on the earnings of their small endeavor to sustain them when the war was eventually over. But the men seemed not to be interested in coal. To impress Abe, they spoke at length of a unique engineering feat being planned by the company. Though vague, Abe came to understand it was some manner of oceanic oil operation, though how they would get oil from the sea was an utter mystery to a man with coal-dust under his nails.

"I ain't interested in sellin'," Abe had been clear from the first.

"We aren't interested in buyin'. But you got a good tract a land here," said one of the businessmen in a smooth Texas draw. "What we's lookin' for is a lease agreement on a piece a your land."

"Uh-huh. Well, look here Mr.—"

"Avrich. Mr. Avrich. But you can call me Tom."

"Alright. Tom. I'ma gonna talk this over with ma wife. You come back here with more than fancy words and we'll think on leasin'."

"You understand my terms, Mr. Marks?"

"Git out."

"Well, think on it. We'll be back."

Both Abe and Mama Clay were distracted. Their boys were off at war, none of the women had been properly schooled in the family's business, and Abe was getting on in age. He was neither as assertive nor as sharp as he had been. Years had past since he last bested Tatters at chess. That night, after the men from Root & Brown had left, Abe and Mama Clay lay in bed and talked.

"I wish them boys was home," said Abe.

"I don' wanna talk on that no more."

"Sorry. I jus'. I don' know."

"What's they want?" asked the wife.

"They wanna lease the land fer some project. Some kinda gas pipe or sumpthin'. I can't figure it."

"All them city houses got gas in 'em. Like that stove in Tatter's place. I'd love ta have me one a them. Heats the water an' ev'rythin'."

"The stove heats their water?"

"Well, no. But, its gas Tatters said."

"Hmph."

"The whole place is run on it."

"Sounds fixin' to 'splode ta me."

"Tsk."

"Hmm," Abe was thoughtful. "You'd really want one'a them fancy stoves?"

Mama Clay smiled, "I ain't young no more, Abe. An' nether is you. Our boys are gone. The war's on. Can't somethin' be easy fer once? Ain't you tired, Abe?"

Abe looked crossways at his wife, "That ain' like you."

"I've been thinkin'."

"Alright. I guess I best be thinkin' myself."

Mama Clay drew up close to her husband's side. He put his wide arm around her round shoulder and nestled her closer.

"Yer my man, an' I love you. What you decide, I'll support. We can sort it out with the boys after."

"I reckin'," Abe was silent.

When Mr. Avrich returned he was alone. He carried with him a briefcase and a brown cardboard tube, which Abe would soon discover held a map of the area containing the Russell tract. Root & Brown, it seemed, knew more about the land than the people living on it, or so Tom Avrich seemed to think. He spoke very authoritatively on all manner of things, but Abe mostly just nodded his head. When it was clear to Avrich that Abe had settled his mind in the interim since their last meeting, he moved to business.

"We want to lease a strip of your land comin' down through this pass here in the mountains. We got a few depots to hook up to, out in Accident, Oakford, and Leity. Maybe we can hook up to the East Tennessee and th—"

"So what's this ta me? What you offerin'?"

"Well, what's it worth ta ya?"

"Listen, you ain' taken nothin' from my land. You can clear what timber you need ta build yer pipe. But you lease the strip. I want…I want a flat fee. I don' wan' no percent jus' in case you Texas boys can' do yer deed."

Avrich leaned back in his chair, "What's a fair fee to ya?"

"That ain' it. I wan' yer gas run ta my house. An, I wan' a new stove fer my wife."

"Is that all?"

"Three, no…five hundred fer the land."

"Ok…five hundred a month, and—"

"Month?"

"Yes, Mr. Marks, we were assuming—"

"Right. Yeah, a month."

Avrich smiled. "I'll have the paperwork writ up."

The first thing Abe had done when he got a check from Root & Brown was to open a bank account for himself and his wife. Everything prior had been done in his son's names, or under the company name and Abe was proud to deposit that first check into his own account. It took some weeks for the whole process to get started, but when Abe showed Mama Clay the second deposit slip and the thousand dollars they now had to their name, she forgave him the sounds of machinery and blasting that drew ever nearer to the homestead but stayed conspicuously out of sight. Their boys were proud of their father and thought, with what little they could really discern from Brest, France, that life in the hollow could only get better. Abe bought some more land, the piece across the old road from the Russell tract, where the land had been left brown after a plantation house had been razed. Mama Clay hoped to convince Tatters and Ruth to move there when Tatters returned.

Verge could see the work being done from her home, though she never asked too much about it. The engineers at work on the pipeline hadn't figured Verge's abode into their plans, because it simply wasn't there when the surveyors had been wandering through the valleys hoping to find a clear enough pass to reach at least into Maryland, if not down into the Carolinas. When the Appalachians had yielded a satisfactory route for a north-flowing line, up from the South and from Texas and Louisiana, the prospectors at Root & Brown secured the funds necessary to buy or lease the lands they would need. The Marks' made out okay by their own standards. For a company flush with government money and a reputation for building battleships, the Russell tract was leased for a steal. Never mind the abundance of clauses which, to Abe, were incomprehensible and ensured that those in hollow would benefit from the lease, but not indefinitely. Abe had stipulated that he would never have to pay for the gas which drove his wife's new stove, a mere pittance if he could know the wealth of liquefied natural gas flowing through his land.

The boy Ruth had birthed, Howard, would be the only child had by Tatters and his wife. Howard was near three years old when his father had gone to war and when the men returned in the winter of 194_, Howard was six and afraid of his father, who had become like a stranger to the boy. By this time, not only did Mama Clay have herself a gas stove, but she and Naomi and Verge were all enjoying new mechanical washers that made laundry days into simple laundry mornings. These contraptions were the favorite innovation of the women of the hollow, even more so than the stove whose oven burned at such steady temperatures that even Mama Clay's pies were deemed to have been improved by the uniformity of science. Even the introduction of the telephone into the hollow paled in comparison to the laundry machine. The poles and wires that went up all around the pipeline were considered a sublet eye-sore.

The celebratory return of Tatters, Wayne, and Ezra was another obstacle for Verge, whose husband had returned many months prior but who had been so broken by war that his return was like an omen of some foreboding tragedy. Jonathan just sat in the corner with head in his hands, hung low between his knees only to be raised whenever a swig of whiskey might afford him respite from the dark visions that clouded his mind.

Jonathan had again been injured just outside Strasbourgh in November 194_, and this time he was sent home, a bronze star and two purple hearts as consolation for the loss of his friend and spirit. He languished alone with Verge for another year before the rest of the men returned. Screams broke their conjugal bed. Jonathan never again attempted to make love to his wife. In fact, he hardly spoke to her except to quietly thank her for performing the housework and preparing his meals. Abe thought to help the couple by affording them a small allowance, though this seemed only to further depress Jonathan who now saw both he and his wife as a pair of invalids who had been exiled to the far side of the hollow where the new gas pipeline emerged from the north valley and wound slightly away from the homesteads of the Russell tract before taking a decisive turn to the east.

Verge hated the pipeline. It was her home that had been most effected, though the path of the gas went around the actual house by a wide berth. What was most devastating to Verge was the ancient tree, where she went in solitude and thought, had been annihilated in the process and the place where Jonathan had made his proposal was now a mess of rock and soil where the pipeline was bolstered and hoisted up and over the parabolas of the lowlands. Still, she wandered, looking for alternative refuge, finding nothing that consoled her like the near monolithic decrepitude of that old place. Hardly anyone knew about it to begin with, and Verge never spoke about this secret sadness, but this loss was followed by the subsequent absence of Jonathan's peace of mind and her sorrow was compounded. Her tether already severed, Verge then found herself without even a compass to test the directionality of her drifting.

A madness crept into Jonathan when it was announced that Wayne would be married. It was not the marriage itself but the subject of Wayne's desire that aroused in Jonathan a distinct mania that gripped him in obsessive gloom. Wayne's bride would be a German. He had met and fallen in love with a German woman,

Elfriede Bayer, who had associated herself with the *Edelweißpiraten* and subsequently looked on Wayne as a savior and liberator of her people, which was in some ways true and not at all in others. Elfriede was diminutive, porcelaneous, and strong which earned her the nickname "Elf" since the dialect of the hollow was unkind to foreign diction. She arrived after some months of correspondence with Wayne and was met in the hollow with yet another celebration that drove Verge into reclusion. Jonathan hated Elf. The accent, the way she and Wayne occasionally spoke in broken German to one another, the blond locks of hair and pouted ruddy lips. Her very being affronted every sentiment of decency still left to the veteran and his ire spread easily to Wayne, whose bronze star turned green in the eyes of Jonathan whenever "*Ich liebe dich*" was heard on the air. Thus did the cottage built by Jonathan and David for Verge become a hermitage, suffuse with the growth of forest and tall grasses to obscure the world.

One night, Verge awoke alone in bed. She went through the three small rooms and found the front door open wide.

"Jonathan," she called.

Crickets, an owl, the lonesome whippoorwill. The sounds of the black silence of night. She went out. Without thinking she went the way of the hollow that led her to the place of Jonathan's abandoned forestry. Fallen timber lay rotting in the moonlight. She went on toward the shack where David had lived with her husband for a short time. It had fallen into disrepair, though it was occasionally used as a place for the men to stay on a hunt, far as it was from the old fort-house and farther still from the Marks' homestead. She stood silhouetted in the doorway. There lay

Jonathan, his big toe hooked into the trigger guard of his shotgun. There remained a wisp of smoke on the air. Slight was the smell of cooked flesh. The shotgun had kicked back and was angled almost toward Verge. The barrels had been in Jonathan's mouth when it discharged. The blast split his skull in twain above the jaw. The spray of blood against the wall still ran to the floor in grotesque ribbons like a shredded veil. Verge slammed the door and went home. She told no one what she'd seen.

Jonathan's suicide coincided with the first real snow of the year. It had hardly been a week, none of the other residents of the hollow had heard from the couple and it was left to the young Margaret, lover of the telephone, to call on Verge and make sure the snow was not more than the tiny shack could bear. The phone rang for some time before Verge picked up the receiver and answered with a cold silence.

"Aunt Verge?" said Margaret.

"She's not here."

"Um…"

"She's gone girl. Leave her be."

"Aunt…Verge?"

"The woman has come. I can see her. She there, in the doorway. She can see. She has seen."

"Aunt Verge, you's scarin' me…"

"Don't be afraid child, death is not come for you. It is the end of…"

Margaret slammed down the receiver. "Mama," she called out, "Somethin's *wrong* with Aunt Verge."

Off went Harry and Wayne into the snow. They got to the little house. The door was open, the rooms, empty.

Verge had seen her there. The men had looked all around and had followed a trail of footprints to the pipeline where they had become muddled and indistinct and gave no clear indication of where they led. The men never saw as Verge did. No one saw quite as Verge did. She had seen the woman there, finally, clearly, not some faint light or apparition, but the real body of the dark woman of her dreams. She had spent the days after Jonathan's suicide conversing with the dark woman in a language unknown by man. She had at last received the invitation and followed it down into the deep of the mountains, away from the road, away from stoves and laundry machines and the train tracks that had claimed her father. She followed it away from the mine and forestry and the gun. She followed it into darkness and through that shadow into light. She followed the pipeline through the desolation of her ancient tree and went barefoot through the snow into the heart of the hills and lost sight of all her familiar, tiny life. She went down unto a slab of rock embedded on the floor of the dell and pressed her face against the cold stone whispering, "Helizikinopo" into the hard earth as the snow came down all around her. The clouds broke apart and the snow descended like shattered glass, piercing her skin and sinking into her heart beneath the frozen moon. Away from all that had happened so fast, away from all that she could not understand, away from the life that had been made for her by others, where others' happiness danced around the fire of her sorrow, separate, indistinct, weary, Verge McClain laid down and died.

PART TWO:

From the Distance of Time

A STAKE IN THE LAND

"Don't nobody get that much land by any means legal," this was the reasoned opinion Irvin J. Russell expressed to just about anyone who came into William Wittacre's Wares. But Irvin J. Russell was a young man still, with his shopkeeper's apron on and standing behind the counter with his hands together as a woman stands, demure and waiting on indifferent men who only want to get what they came for and leave.

"Them people down in the holler didn' go down there to have nothin' to do with the law. They's done gone down there to get themselves plum away from law an' all the hassle that law done bring with it." This repudiation was oft repeated and usually receive considerably well by Irvin, excepting this one instance in which the remark, so spoken, was uttered by Irvin's good friend and cousin, Thomas, an orphan that saw in Irvin, if not a father, then the possibility of an older brother who would stand fast to him, even if he held his hands together as a woman would, which posture is perhaps why Thomas occasionally saw a bit of a mother in him as well. The pre-adolescent energy of Thomas in addition to the affection that the boy held for Irvin, would usually allow Irvin to pique the boy's interest with any minor provocation. The parroted indifference of his protégé of eleven years was too much for the young soul of Irvin to bear and he buckled at the slightest pang of revenge calling him to teach a valuable lesson. And there were many lessons Thomas was due to learn, it is true.

"You don't even talk like that," Irvin said from spite.

"I do too. Sometimes," said the other.

"Ain't nobody ever heard you say nothin' like that at nothin' I said."

"Well, it's true ain't it. Ol' Merritt don' want nothin' 'cept be left alone."

Irvin folded his arms across his chest and looked over the counter at Thomas. "Who told you that?" he asked, moving from behind the counter with a splayed straw broom bound by rough twine to a branch from the wiry oak out back of the store. Sweeping the dirt suffuse throughout the shop was a means of appearing disinterested but was something done so rarely that Thomas could not but notice the peculiarity of Irvin's movements.

"Ol' Merritt done told me hisself."

At that Irvin stopped sweeping and looked full at Thomas, his mind seizing on an idea that would become the theme of his lesson. Of course, he had no clear lesson plan, that could be formulated over time—for he was as certain as anything that there was something he could get on Ol' Merritt that, no matter how minor or seemingly insignificant, could be twisted before the eyes of an eleven year old to resemble the most fantastic chimera ever to roam these parts of Appalachia. There was some detail in Merritt's past that Irvin could exploit on a lark, of that he was sure.

Proceeding on a whim, Irvin said, "I reckon then you have no interest in all that money Ol' Merritt's done got laid up on his property somewhere. Hiddin', you know. Buried, who knows? Ain't nobody been lucky enough to set eyes on it yet. An' live, I guess."

Thomas' eyes widened visibly. The verisimilitude of hidden wealth took hold in his growing but still feral mind, and he, the orphan, tainted by the adult knowledge gained through living without adults to guard him from that knowledge, he could see the change in fortune that would open before him if only his small hands could lay themselves on a secret fortune culled from the ground.

"How you know anything 'bout that?" asked Thomas, feral in the same manner that a wild fox is feral, wily and skeptical lest the trap be sprung. But traps do spring on prey, occasionally, even wily prey, and especially wily prey that knows it's wily in the way that people possessed of talent are adept at recounting their abilities.

Donning the airs of knowledge, Irvin stood close to Thomas and lowered himself to the youngster's ear so that their faces were side by side in the empty store, the shafts of sunlight revealing the jagged pattern from Irvin's sweeping etched across the dust of the knotted, unpolished floor. "I don' reckon I ought tell you anything," Irvin said in a mock whisper that feigned conspiracy. "But I'll tell you 'cause maybe I got a similar mind as you, that is to say we might have a mind to the same intent if you follow me, I done heard somethin' about it when Mr. Wittacre hisself was down here talking with an associate of his I ain't seen in these parts." Thomas held his breath for a moment and exhaled subtly when he realized what he was doing.

Irvin straighten up again. "We can talk on it later."

"But I wan—"

"Don' matter none what you want, I'm the one that done went an' got this all figured out. You jus' let the whole' thing to me."

Thomas relented. Irvin knew what he was doing. There was Thomas, the orphan, alone in the world but for Irvin, who was the second oldest of seven children, with another sibling on the way, and here is Irvin out in the world all on his lonesome too, working for Mr. Wittacre for extra money now that his youngest brother's of age to work the plow and one field hand can be spared to fetch other means of sustenance for the family and maybe set aside a portion for himself if he's prudent. Plus, Irvin's mother knew he wouldn't meet a wife on the farm. Their oldest had been lucky and found a proper wife from the neighboring farm, but a family can't just swap children with the neighbors, half of whom weren't fit enough for Irvin's mother to want to share one child with, let alone seven soon to be eight.

*   *   *

Ol' Merritt could have come from Beowulf, displaced mariner of the North threshing the waving grain cast rippling before him in the dust-moted sunlight of autumn. He was considered old to be threshing grain, and went by his surname. He rode a donkey too old to be ridden out of the hollow and the distance into town was considerable at the time, considering he had a hundred and fifty acres to himself, on which he lived in the hollow, away from the road to town and away from the town, which was becoming considerable itself and considerable trouble as far as Merritt was concerned. Old as he was threshing grain he remembered a younger man sympathetic to the Regulator Movement but unwilling to stay in the Carolina's long enough for someone to bother to ask him about his taxes. No, he was come into North Carolina knowing he was to go north, that there was still a frontier where he could be buried like a tick and nurture himself on the raw earth that gave a hard but forgetful life. Hard, because it was you alone against all the earth, forgetful because you forgot how hard it was before and this new hardness is the bread and butter you crave; the salt mineral piquant drowned finally in the sweet warm fat of the land.

Drown and forgotten, that life across the sea that ended after only eight years. Eight years, just he and his Pa and his Ma's body. Seafaring was a dangerous lot at times. Sometimes, threshing grain, he remembered burying that swollen corpse that was his mother, and his father cursing the ground they stood on, never settling for its cold comfort and pushing them north and neglecting the Regulators and the tidewater aristocrats who sought to get wealthy off the sweat of other men's brows and even neglecting the moonshiners further north who would give old General Washington a run for his money as they would anyone else that stuck their old false teeth into the great back-wood economy of the frontier. They settled and they got land. By God they got land by the acre until there was enough land around them and the great

157

rolling mountain behind them and they built up their ramshackle fort house with the help of a ragged boy they found in the woods on the property. They were able to buy up about twenty acres at that time, all on the savings brought from the Old Country, what had been left over from their journey, and the earnings they'd made through trapping along the trail northward. The soil, they were told, was a bit sandy, and half their original acreage lay draped across the stony foothills of the mountain, reaching up a fair five to seven acres onto the undulated crests of the mountain ridge itself. For that rocky terrain they got a deal of five and a half cents an acre. The better stuff out on the lowland cost them eight cents, so Pa Merritt had taken the whole lot for a dollar and forty-two and a half cents. He kept a whole ten-dollar bill to himself.

The boy was a Native and he kept his sister hidden in a thicket by night and within hear shot by day while he helped the father and his son, now some fourteen years, work on the house that would eventually shelter the four of them at meal times, the father and son at night. The Natives would sleep outside on their own after the fashion of their parents, or whoever it was that had brought them up and since passed into the West or the Valley of Death.

The Merritts didn't have all their property, not by the time the house was settled and young Merritt, soon to be Ol' Merritt and the only one, watched his Pa disappear in front of him, rifle and all, down a fissure in the earth covered over by dead leaves, the skeletal remains of their fallen branches, and a bough of laurel drooping languidly among the underbrush. They had been running their coon hounds along the bottom of the hollow when the dogs picked up a scent and run them up into the mountains until the trees climbed onto rocky outcrops and swung out into the wind high overhead as the ground below became craggy and uneven with the piling of rocks upon the ages. Merritt's Pa had let out a whoop when the hound had treed something up ahead and went rushing toward his quarry unaware until it was too late that he was being swallowed whole by the mountain, never to come alive again from the earthy bosom he had settled into without another glimpse at what lay beyond. His legs had been mangled worse than anything, but he bled out from a gash in his forehead that revealed a long, thin hole punched clear through the skull. There hadn't been much blood to speak of, because when Ol' Merritt had collected his wits and fetched the Indian boy to lower into the fissure to retrieve the body, a rich black dust and a fine brittle gravel, black and anthracitic, encrusted the bodies that emerged from below.

Three days later, Ol' Merritt was in town going over surveyor's maps at the small, three-room courthouse.

*   *   *

Irvin and Thomas had separate apartments above the store. Their lodgings were not symmetrical and Irvin enjoyed the space afforded one who works for their bread and needs the room a man needs for the various vices that occupy the waking hours he spends away from work and the attentiveness work affords. Thomas was provided lodging more or less on the charity of Mr. William Wittacre, the town's patriarch after a certain manner, the owner of a sizeable plantation called *Terra Angelica* by its proprietors and "the plantation" by everyone else. It employed a range of hands from around the town, supported a small collective of sharecroppers, and sent the town's only slaves into the fields, the tall, gaunt, exotic Negroes and the burnished, straight-haired Indians who would slave on the land that was theirs before they would leave it for the west and flee from the only crust of earth that had yielded them bread in their lifetimes. The Wittacre's were lenient with their Indian slaves whose local nativity bore with it the usefulness associated with familiarity. This and the fact of the Indians' own inherent restlessness made it clear that the leash ought be let slack from time to time for the reward of fresh venison, furs, and the reconnaissance of the tracker's blood. The Negroes were not useful in this way, dark exiles that they were, brought down in their station by the weight of distance that made them stare wide eyed at everything strange and pass in strangeness as dumb among people who had only ever been the Masters of others sold by their own blood once upon a time in Africa, or what the white men called Africa—the word itself already solidifying the Negro's alienation in this New World that lost its newness day by day as it was pulled by the tides toward Europe; if not pulled physically there, then at least distorted and reshaped as Europeans were washed in upon the tides and tried to patch their homes back together on fresh land.

In truth, most people considered Thomas little better than those Indian slaves, abandoned as he was by all kin save Irvin, who as a cousin of some removal, looked on Thomas as a kind of ward. Thomas would never have seen himself in this manner, and rightfully so. It is a dark mark on the human soul when one is finally beaten down so as to see oneself as a rightful slave and darker still is the mark on the slave that sees himself deserving of enslavement. One found this attitude, occasionally, among the Negroes, particularly the house-Negroes that were comfortable rocking little white babies by a fireplace. The field Negroes were still able to see a bit of Master in themselves, reclining as they often did beneath the expansive Appalachian sky, draped in the dappled sheen of stars that called to mind some unbounded part of the soul still nascent in the gut that rumbled forth a threat to return to the breast if ever a real chance came into view among the celestial bodies reeling through the night.

Whether or not people saw it in him, Thomas had plenty to make him feel better than a slave and so he rarely suffered from his low station. He was, after all and in many ways, still a child though one forced into maturity by circumstance. He felt himself quite fortunate to be the benefactor of such a landlord as could afford him a whole spare room above the shop and a superintendent such as Irvin to boot. There was little else a boy of Thomas' age needed besides space to roam and a trusted eye to keep him from trouble. In freedom it was all the easier for Thomas to see in Irvin such respectability, a symptom of a childish naïveté that shielded his eyes from the inexperience of the outwardly priggish shopkeeper; an inexperience that led to grandiose fantasies concerning the alleged past of certain quiet men of the hollow.

They were together in Irvin's apartments, each on one sparse chair, white with chipped paint and grey beneath, a loose wooden support that warped slightly with the shifting weight of the body it held. Thomas' was asking questions after his fashion. Irvin was responding after his.

"Who was it Mr. Wittacre was talkin' to Irvin?"

"I told you, I ain't never seen 'im before."

"You reckon he's new to town?"

"I reckon he ain't *from* town. Haven't seen 'im since."

"When was it you seen 'im?"

"Must'a been two, three weeks ago."

"That long?! Why ain't you told me?"

"I reckon I was fixin' on a plan."

"A plan Irvin?"

"Yeah, Thom, a plan."

"We gonna get us that money?"

"I got anythin' to do with it, yeah, Thom, we'll get us some money." *One way or another*, Irvin thought reclining in his modest cot. "Get on to bed, Thom. We can jaw on about this in the mornin'."

"I can't sleep, Irvin."

"You better sleep, we'll be up half the night tomorrow."

"Why's that Irvin? What we gonna do? You gotta plan?"

"Tomorrow, Thom. Tomorrow. Goodnight."

"But Irv—"

"Get outta here, dammit! Tomorrow!" Irvin chased Thomas off with the back of his hand and settled into bed only after he heard the latches click on both of the two doors separating the two rooms.

* * *

Everyone saw it as the queerest thing when Ol' Merritt came riding into town, barely seventeen and with that Indian girl all fixed up to be a bride. The boy's name had been Catecahassa and it turned out the girl was his half sister. Her name was Nanuxse and

162

her brother claimed she was the granddaughter of Shemenetu, Big Snake, a warrior chief whose sister, Helizikinopo Snake, still haunted the groves of the Appalachian lowlands. Ol' Merritt just called the Indian woman "Nan." Catecahassa said his English name was "Black Hoof," which Ol' Merritt knew had a dangerous ring to it among the frontiersmen but let the association fall by the wayside as he'd known the boy to be no threat and since he now had a mind to be kin with the squatters given his own kith and kin had all passed beyond the veil of this world as soon as they had made themselves at home there.

Judge Everett looked down from his bench, or at least from the podium the town passed off for a bench without even smoothing out the edges too much or gilding the rough, deeply gouged lines ornamenting the paneled frontispiece. His effusive black eyebrows arched and bushed prominently above the iron stare of the judge as he looked down the crooked aquiline nose that gave him a raptorial look. He said, "You even of age to marry of your own accord, boy?"

Ol' Merritt looked up, just seventeen years old, his bride, already five years his senior, standing stoically by his side in nothing but a sackcloth morning gown she kept in a wicker trunk hid deep under an outcropping of rock in the hollow. He looked up, unblinking, and said, "Sir, your honor, I buried my Ma in North Carolina when I was nine years old. I buried my Pa down in the Holler yesterday. It's just me an' them Indian folks that were squattin' on the land when we bought it. One of thems is right here. I reckon I gots to be old enough to marry on my own accord 'cause I got no one left in this world that can marry me off."

The judged narrowed his downward gaze. "Your Pa's dead you say?"

"Yessir, your honor, sir, which makes the land mine. He done registered his will. You go fetch Mr. Parsons and he'll tell you."

The judge grumbled and shook his head and held up his palm, "That won't be necessary, son. That Indian woman there a citizen or you aimin' to make her one?"

Merritt took a folded nub of paper from his overalls, unfolded it into the creased brown square he couldn't read and presented it to the judge. The old man took it and held it in his steely gaze. "Seems to be in order. Hell I ain't to keep a boy from his Indian woman, Pa dead as he is and all." The judge groaned and grunted and got out from behind the podium and walked out of the courthouse onto the porch and took a look around the town square, small as it was in that time, with only the smithy, the church, and the general store looking on. Black Hoof was waiting on the stoop and a few locals loitered on the porch of William Wittacre's Wares. The judge waved and called a few of the men over from the general store. He looked at Black Hoof, said, "Get in there an' give witness, boy," then went back into the courthouse and pronounced Ol' Merritt and Nan husband and wife.

When Merritt exited the courthouse with his sackcloth bride, William Wittacre had appeared in the square on his white horse, dappled in butterscotch and the sun sifting through the oak leaves that whispered above his head. Wittacre watched as Merritt helped his bride onto the donkey, which he led with Black Hoof by his side past the sweating horse and Wittacre looking down at them with a scowl. The next day, Wittacre was in the courthouse, locked in the tiny room that housed the town's cartographic catalogue, making sure that each piece of the map fit a deed filed somewhere in the courthouse's three bare rooms.

*   *   *

The town had grown considerable since Ol' Merritt's wedding day when it counted barely three hundred residents out of the 4,000 or so in the county. There were maybe nine hundred fifty-two people living in the town presently. Just about eleven percent of the entire county, which remained rural and frontier-minded even though the frontier had moved on west, pushing further each year into the Louisiana Purchase and leaving the 8,564 county residents to think themselves pioneers on their own small mountainsides. Out of these 8,564 there were about seven hundred ninety-five slaves in the county, and only thirty-five men of commerce, among which was counted Mr. Wittacre, and he allowed himself to be counted again amongst the 1,675 county residents who were freely engaged in agriculture.

The town was on a bend in the Algonquin River and Everett's Creek branched from the river, flowing from the mountains southeastward to the river toward the sea. Everett's Creek formed the boundary to Ol' Merritt's land on the southwest side where it ran out of the mountains and wrapped around the far west corner of Merritt's southern border before leaving the property line to stretch out toward the Algonquin. Merritt had to trust the surveyors on north, east, and the rest of his southern border. No one would ever think to contest his mountainous western lines. It was that fertile rolling grassland in the south and east that was ever the concern of Ol' Merritt, especially seeing as he never got around to clearing more than five, maybe seven acres of it, and he'd certainly never worked any more than six. Even when his boys were right there at home and the girls in the hollow could mend their field clothes, the Merritt's never saw more than eight acres yielding crop, half that grain and corn and whatever harvest would see lay a few more dollar bills up over top of that old wrinkled ten note that lay hidden on the crossbeam of the old fort house. It was one thing in the early days when he had hunted the mountain acres from midnight to dawn and left maybe five acres go wild along the creek. But in later days when it was more eighty-nine or ninety-three acres gone wild clear down to the Algonquin, less than a leisurely two hour ride from town, that the anxiety Merritt felt about his property lines became sharpened into paranoia and every other day or two he'd take his old donkey around by the creek and down and back north checking for signs of misdoings on borderlands of his holdings.

It was there on the borderlands, where the creek ran rushing from the mountain in a gleaming white frothed flow, the tributary of a hundred streams and these a hundred rivulets gathered from the cumulonimbi, that Irvin had arranged to met with Thomas and begin their lessons. The water was in his ears as he sat, squatting among the water dense phragmites sprouting in tufts from the pebbled beaches at the creek's edge. He squatted at the top of an embankment just before the tree-line where the clearing of the Everett's land stopped on the creek's southwest shore and a donkey trail stood cleared between the creek on one side, and on the other side, further on down the bend, a wooden corral fence made of rough hewn interlacing logs went on down out of sight into the east, beyond the density of forest that stood un-cleared for thirty-six years now. The sun was going down over the mountain and cut across the folded ridge of pines that filtered out all but a golden light spreading across the valley in which Merritt's land unfolded from the heaving ground onto a yellow bed of flax and oats. Irvin looked around chewing listlessly on a long blade of grass. He stayed mostly out of sight. For now he remained on a steep incline about the bank on Everett's side of the creek. Some sound drifted up the creek from on down, toward town. Voices, two distinct voices. Loud, carrying on the light breeze out of the east and echoing up the creek's sheer patina. They twittered on in a high timbre, they're voices husky with the breath of failed whisper, shrill as the spoken words were produced. Irvin stayed low, below the reeds. Then the voices stopped. Elevating his head, glancing downstream, then to the south, then back around west, Irvin scanned the lowlands. The dry grasses rustled shortly behind him and slit open where Thomas stepped out followed by a wiry but elegant girl in a baby blue cotton dress pinched at her waist by the linen apron that covered her front.

She looked right at Irvin and said, "Irvin J. Russell what you bring this poor fool out here for? Ain't no money buried on no Ol' man's land no where up here not no how!"

Irvin rolled his eyes and said, "Esther why you done followed him out here? It's damn two hours back to town if it's anything and its well on six o'clock now! We'd be jus' fine out here, I got a lantern out from the shop and everythin'. Esther, can't you jus' leave well enough alone!"

"I said she ought not come out here, I did say that."

167

"Thomas!" Esther and Irvin said at once.

Irvin went on: "Dammit boy, you done gone an' told *her* everythin' an' now the money we dig up, an' believe me it'll be *us* that dig it up when the diggin's done, is gonna get split *three* ways instead a jus' two like before! Get it?"

Thomas dug his toes into the sandy soil.

"Never you mind Mr. Russell. Bringin' him out here. Ought to be shamed of yourself. That's for sure. Run him all the way out here. What for? Ain't no money buried out here. That's for sure," said the feminine other.

"Fine, maybe we won't find it. Maybe it ain't out here exactly, but we gotta start somewheres, so since you're here, help us look," Irvin went below the reeds and brought up the canvas duffle he stuffed with supplies enough to make him look serious, but not enough to weigh very much.

"Irvin Russell, there ain't no money *nowhere* out here!"

Irvin walked on ahead of them, crossing at a ford onto Merritt's land and driving them on into the twilight below the near forty year stand of growth and trees that were reaching into maturity along the muddier side of Everett's Creek. They got to where the land opened and the creek wound along to the river and the tree line broke away from the creek to follow Merritt's rambling corral fence along the southern boundary of his lot. It was there on the bend that Thomas stopped dead and stared in his feral manner into a break in the trees that fed a tiny rutted stream into the creek's spreading bed. Without much indication, the orphan broke off into the woods on his own. Esther gasped and followed with Irvin trotting along behind them, the bag on his shoulder.

Within the glen it was becoming visibly darker. The sun was completing its long slow dive into the mountains and the golden sheen that imbued the air with a sacred quality—holding motes of dust suspended in their serene downward spiral—was being displaced by the deep plum shadow of twilight that sunk lazily into the atmosphere to mingle with the murmuring effervescence of the creek. Esther moved forward into the trees with greater trepidation. Thomas was rushing ahead along the edge of the brook, which glimmered with the last rays of daylight. Irvin stayed back, holding the duffle and keeping close to Esther, who was walking slowly ahead now, occasionally calling out to Thomas and urging him to slow down and stay close. It was then that Thomas stopped suddenly. Ahead in the failing light his hand went up to beckon the others closer.

He was standing over a bit of disturbed earth not even fifty yards into the stand of trees. They couldn't tell, but there were perhaps another sixty or seventy yards of trees ahead, Irvin had guessed at maybe a hundred or so acres of growth from the creek to the other side of Ol' Merritt's property. He had no way of knowing exactly where on his plot the old man cleared for his crops. A best guess put cultivated fields off the road, closer to the hollow but out east enough for the soil to be good, even if all the land in that valley boasted sizeable rocks and a gritty, sandy quality. Instinctively, Irvin knelt down and prepared the small lantern he'd brought, striking the flint in the hollow of Esther's hands and raising the lantern as he stood to illuminate a sphere of yellow light in the deepening veil of forest night.

"I'm a gonna dig here a bit," said Thomas from where he knelt in the dust.

"Careful, that brook runs all over here," said Esther.

"Girl, what does that matter any? Ain't like he gonna fall into it diggin' in the dirt there!" said Irvin.

But no sooner had Irvin spoke then Thomas was proclaiming, "There's a hole in here! I mean, it's holler underneath!"

The other two rushed over and leaned above Thomas with the lantern, peering into where the boy had been digging to see a moist exposure fresh with rivulets of mountain water irrigating the hidden world of grubs and worms running wet and in secret below the parched surface that bore the scars of man's disturbance.

"Someone's dug here," said Thomas, pushing deeper and widening his search parameter.

"Irvin, you done made this boy crazy! There ain't money hidden out here, you got that poor orphan on a fools' errand out here an' its dark an' darker by the minute. Mama says I shouldn't be out here in the holler after night!" Esther was becoming agitated as night grew thicker about them and Thomas grew more and more excited over the story Irvin had fed him and evidence of which was now being compiled beneath his mud encrusted fingernails.

"I hit on somethin'!" Thomas said, ecstatically throwing clumps of mud and shod behind him. At this, Irvin helped as Esther looked on from under a furrowed brow.

Eventually Thomas came up clutching something and ran to the open brook where he drove his hand under the water again and again until it came up gleaming and white from the icy cold.

"What is it?" Esther asked as she approached.

Thomas doubled back on Esther, passing her by on his way into the yellow sphere that was by then their only light. The sun was gone behind the mountain and only the lantern, thick with oil and smoking slightly, gave them light beyond the fast dying illumination of the fireflies that danced among the nestles in the thicket nearby and flashed like fading candle-light on the wheat-tops of the field beyond the trees. When Esther returned to the lantern light, she saw that Thomas cradled in his palm a worn and decrepit wooden stake, eaten away on one side by the water and left hard, calcified, and grey where the wood had been given over to the mineral grit of the ground in which it was buried. The top portion of the wooden shaft remained intact and imbedded in the petrified remnants of the pointed end, and there on the flat beaten wood left over remained the sparse cracked traces of a bold red paint refusing to fade away in the shod sepulcher by the brook.

"What'd somebody bury an ol' stake for?"

"Property. Someone one done staked a claim out here that someone else don' wan' staked." Irvin paused a moment, thinking, then said, "This here's a clue."

"I reckon," said Thomas dreamily.

"Clue to what? So it's an ol' stake in the ground, how do we know it was dug up or just left there? It's likely Ol' Merritt's Daddy's claim. What'd you know about claims anyhow?"

"Look, ain't nobody just bury no stakes without reason to an' them reasons usually ain't legal ones, especially out in the holler back when the war was still on or just finished an' law hadn't exactly settled out in these parts, you see girl?"

"Maybe it marks where the money's at! Maybe there's more stakes and them's clues on where the stash is!" Thomas was wide-eyed in the lantern light.

"Shush!" said Esther and put her hand to Irvin's lips as well.

They must not have been far from the southern tree line because as Esther indicated, Irvin turned to look over his shoulder and saw the broken path of another lantern as it cut across the field out yonder. It moved at a plodding pace, bouncing lazily over the wheat-tops as if carried on the back of a weary ass.

"Get down!" said Irvin, hastily snuffing his own lantern as he ducked low into the glen.

They all figured it was Ol' Merritt on his donkey. But the clear path it made across the field was toward a huge and sprawling oak tree that stood conspicuously amid the wide clearing and bore its age on the vast and exposed limbs that twisted and climbed among its moon-bright foliage. They lay in silence watching the faint glow of the lantern approach the hulking tree.

Esther raised herself up, whispering, "What's he at down there?" as the low flicker of a campfire emerged from the shadow of the oak.

The crickets seemed to roar in the urgent silence as all the youth leaned forward toward the slow drift of embers on the air, unaware of the movements of the hollow behind them. For a moment, they all held their breaths. A long shriek, shrill and terrible reverberated out of the depths of the hollow. Esther reeled about; frozen where she stood before the gaping blackness she had forgotten behind her. The fireflies fell dark as the shrieking high-pitched howl went off again against the night and the trees shivered their leaves to the ground in the north where a thunder raged from the hollow. Thomas fell to the ground clutching the stake. A sharp ring broke the spell of night as Irvin unsheathed the machete still shrouded in the canvas duffle bag. Esther had barely begun to move when off to their right the ground shuddered beneath the pounding of phantom hooves in the darkness, and the brilliant light of yet a third lantern emanated out of the hollow and floated charging toward the tree.

Now it was Esther who cried out: "God! God, God, oh God!" she cried. "It's her! Helizikinopo!"

Irvin clutched her shoulders, staring wildly into her stricken eyes, "What you yellin' on girl! Who? Be quiet now!"

Esther regained an ounce of composure and dropped low to the ground beside Thomas, still petrified with the stake in his grasp. She spoke in a whisper, trembling as if cold from exposure, "Mama told me I shouldn't be out here. Mama said. She'll eat us! They's eat children!"

Irvin stood straight, gazing out of the grove into the field. It was on the edge of the trees that he saw the man. Lean and gaunt, the figure looked out from the forest toward the oak tree now full in the light of the third lantern. Irvin thought they had gone by unnoticed until he saw that figure there a little ways off. He thought they still might make it without being seen until the figure turned and gave Irvin a knowing glance before returning to the tree in the distance and the lantern light that seem to climb the heights of the tree and disappear into the sky above it. Irvin followed the figure's gaze, the face finally revealed in the far off glow of the campfire and the third lantern that was quickly closed above the massive oak, which stood black against the cloak of dusk pierced through by the hard points of starlight that highlighted the total blackness now enclosing them.

*   *   *

William Wittacre had stood, not far off, at the mouth of the hollow, his dappled horse shifting in the dust as Ol' Merritt approached from the mountain, wet with sweat and labor, his hoe slung with familiarity over the broad, tanned shoulder. Nan stayed away from the other white man; she stood some distance by the tree line, watching with one hand on her round protruding belly as her husband went to meet Wittacre. When they were within comfortable earshot, the two men began to speak easily with one another.

Wittacre began, saying, "Mornin' son, reckon I ought thank you for takin' the time to see me today."

"Reckon I ought thank you for comin' out here to see me, I'm the one want to speak as it were," said the other.

"Judge says you got somethin' might interest a man like myself?"

"Judge might be right. That's left to see I suppose."

"Awright. Let's see it then."

Ol' Merritt strode over to Wittacre as he took a square of brown paper from his overalls. He unfolded a worn piece of paper from within the folds of brown paper, explaining as he walked, "I figure maybe you've been workin' some land that might belong to me, an' I'd have you stop, if that'd be fine by you." Wittacre took the paper with some force, looking at the crudely drawn lines demarking what seemed to be outdated property lines.

"I knew you was buyin' up property out here but it'd been better if you'd come to me about my own land before you went jawin' off to the judge about it."

"I ain't jaw with the judge on nothin'. I done my own diggin' with the help of Parsons though he don't know what it is I'm a lookin' for."

"Merritt, I reckon *I* don't know what you're lookin' for. What you want with this anyhow? A lot of this land's up on the mountain. I got no use for mountain land, I'd sell that to you cheap—take maybe, nine cents an acre for it."

"My Pa done bought my mountain land for five and a half cents an acre."

"Inflation. Your Pa was profiteerin' off the war, see?"

"I'da reckoned a man like you'd be itchin' to get rid of that land. I want the cursed bit there you see?"

Wittacre shifted in his saddle. "Where'd you get an idea like that? Why'd I buy up any cursed land? You're talkin' nonsense, boy. How old're you anyways? What was the old judge doin' marrying you when he should'a been askin' why you weren't off fightin' the war."

"Well sir, I'm about twenty-four I reckon. The judge done asked what he wanted to know I guess, though I was a boy when the war was on and I mostly just walked north from the Carolinas with my Pa. Been married these past seven years now and got me a young 'in down in the holler and another on the way. Figured I need to be getting' a bit more land for my kin."

"What kin? You got plenty and this ain't the way a man goes about getting' no more."

"Maybe you could tell how a man goes about getting' land. See you've a fair share yourself and you're workin' a fair share more still."

"What kin you got, boy? Babes, your whole lot, crying mouths an' an Indian nigger besides. I ain't takin' a thing from you and your slaves."

"I got no slaves on my land," said Merritt.

"That so?" said Wittacre. "I reckon then if I go down to the courthouse and I fetch your Daddy's will I won't find that Indian nigger figured in with your Daddy's estate, land and all, huh? Reckon you didn't own that wife neither before you married her. Now what, you'll put some quadroon chile out to the field?"

"Be that as it may, I got no slaves on this land. Black Hoof is free to go as he pleases."

"That remains to be seen," Wittacre smiled.

"Either way, I don't reckon you've been workin' no land with red stakes drove in on it."

Wittacre shifted in his saddle again and the horse shifted with him. He eyed the map and saw for the first time the red marks put roughly down on the soiled paper and saw at last the dated stamp from some city clerk capable of making a copy of the document he now crumbled and handed forcibly back to Merritt.

"Don't worry on that none," Merritt said smoothing the paper out best he could and fitting it back into the square of brown paper he kept in a coffee can atop the crossbeam. "This here's a copy. I done went down state last year. Seen to me some business in the capital. Seen some folks down in the ports. Got me a copy of this made."

"Dammit Merritt, what're you playin' at? Are you blackmailin' me, boy? I don't know what that Parsons told you but you watch him. Mark my words that's a Jew in Protestant's clothes and there's no crookeder Jew than one not fit to keep with his own and wander out here to peddle poison on the frontier."

"Tsk, now, sir! I've done traveled with Parsons far enough and he's done proved honorable enough for me by far. I'm just pointin' out the obvious to you. Don't you figure that the judge's Daddy done kept hisself to the far side of that creek for a reason? Now the judge don't know nothin' about this and he don't have to ever hear tell of no red stakes. He'd not want his good name tarnished by association with no land poacher. I don't even care where you hid 'em, 'cause it's enough to know they're hid somewhere, and a whole lot of 'em too from what I can figure from the records."

Wittacre grit his teeth and brought the horse full around to look at Merritt. "What'll it be then, boy?" he asked.

"I'll take that mountain land at *four* cents an acre. I'll pay you a fair ten cents for the rest I want. You see it here," Merritt held out the map again.

Wittacre pulled heavy on he reigns and drove his horse away from Merritt and his damned hollow. "I know what you want, boy. I'll get it drawn up tomorrow. You have the cash, you bring it to the courthouse in three days and I'll have the paperwork waitin' for

177

you, signed to boot. But I don't want to see you again, boy. Not then, not ever. You keep clear of me boy, and see if you can at least work the land that's good for it."

"I reckon you let me worry 'bout what's worth workin' an' not."

And that was the last words Ol' Merritt exchanged with William Wittacre for nigh on forty years. Ol' Merritt got the land off Wittacre and then some as Wittacre was cut off from the pastures that he worked but didn't own by law. It was these that Ol' Merritt was happy to keep clear all round about the ancient oak that stood rooted at their center.

*   *   *

They were truly children now. Even Irvin, who at nineteen thought himself a man and man enough to look after Esther, thirteen, and his prodigy, Thomas, the petrified eleven year old clutching the stake desperately in his grasp. They were running. Children running away from the dark figure that menaced Irvin's vision and leapt from each rock, dropped down from the night nestled in each treetop and carried an axe or some blood-stained Indian hatchet that would leave slivered shavings of rock embedded in his clavicle when the final blow was struck. Such a blow never fell but drove the children on across the pasture that had lost its golden pastoral glow and was now ravaged by the dancing light of Satan's dark church. They ran on until they came abruptly into a clearing among the tall grasses and were thrust headlong into the shadows behind four men seated casually around the fire beneath the expansive creeping oak spread high overhead. The air was tense as the children held their breath, but the men were relaxed, reclining, and sipping shine as the flames were kindled in the thick cloudy glass wherein dwelled the caramel colored liquor.

Thomas was beginning to come to his senses. "Who's they?" he asked pointing, his voice tiny in the night and barely audible in the clearing, suddenly enlivened by the meeting, not of a cannibal witches coven, but of the rough hewn businessmen on the threshold of the west, staking their contracts on winnings from the vaults of the mountain.

Irvin was prepared to answer, but the grass behind them was dashed apart and the figure from the glen stepped forth into the pale distant light of the fire. "They ain't your concern children, get home."

The bodies were frozen. They stared wildly at the figure, reduced to babbling infancy in the middle of a story of which they themselves were authors. One of the men by the fire turned and saw the rigid night kneeling by the grain. "Catecahassa, what'ch you got back there?"

"No mind. Children too far from home."

"They's hungry? We got corn grits an' beans. That'n looks old enough for whiskey if he wants it."

Irvin looked at Black Hoof.

"No," Black Hoof said. "Go home."

"What's goin' on?" asked Thomas, now resuscitated by the slow evaporation of a haunting's misty veil.

"Go home." There had been something urgent in Black Hoof's eyes as he had spoken to the children, a strong desire to see them gone lay there and a vague anticipation of an event not yet come, the sight of which was forbidden the young interlopers who's youth was better served by ignorance of the workings of the hollow.

Silence passed among them and by and by there came from the direction of the road a light striding forth with the urgent bobble of a foxtrot bringing a rider on horseback closer to the oak by the minute. Black Hoof narrowed his gaze, tired and concerned and full of grit and foreboding as he moved toward the children and scooped both Thomas and Esther bodily into the air and hauled them into the night whisked toss of crackling grain.

"Follow me," he said to Irvin, disappearing into the density of growing wheat.

The men around the fire looked on indiscriminately as the four others disappeared, no more than the faint phantom mimicry of interlopers feigning importance and wrapped in the enigma of their own hidden narratives which were obscure to the sensibilities of mining prospectors invited from afar, drunk on the shine of the hollow given gladly and in partnership. They returned to their talk as the light from the approaching horse broke its course and plunged headlong after the trail left by the carried children and Irvin lagging behind. The horse was quick to close the ground behind the backs of the prospectors and Black Horse soon knew it was Wittacre that took aim in the indeterminate lamplight. The shot cracked like a whip against the back of the mountain and rung from the deep of the hollow as the tense necks of the wild strained in the direction of the gun's reverberation and the horses started up wild-eyed in the firelight and the talk of men ceased in the cessation of the steel thunderclap's affect. In the instant the whip was cracked Thomas cried out and leapt stiff under Black Hoof's arm. He whimpered vaguely as the rigidity of his limbs went softly slack in the crook of his bearer's elbow.

They were on the edge of the wood when Black Hoof relented and brought Thomas and Esther to the ground. Esther convulsed in tears. Thomas lay quietly, occasionally moaning and tossing his head about in a dim and painful sleep. Irvin came suddenly upon them, breathing heavily. The driving hoof-falls that bore Wittacre onward clamored ever closer. Wittacre's dappled horse broke in a leap from the field and drew up quickly beside the others, huddling under the darkness of the trees. Dismounting on his approach, Wittacre saw Thomas' condition straight away and took immediately to beating Black Hoof about the head and shoulder's with the butt of his pistol. Irvin called out and made an abortive effort to impede Wittacre's attack. Wittacre routed Irvin's charge with the back of his hand and growled at the boy to "Keep out of this." He returned to Black Hoof who was at that time pinned by the neck beneath Wittacre's riding boot. Cursing, Wittacre took aim and fired with a certain nonchalance. He fired twice, and though little remained of Catecahassa the blood-mad rider stepped back and coldly fired a third shot into the lifeless form.

Upon the retort of the third shot, Ol' Merritt strode out from the tree line. With his rifle he shot Wittacre's prize horse dead on the spot. Then, he scooped the whimpering Thomas from the ground and took off into the wood.

"That sonuvabitch!" Wittacre spat as he plunged into the thicket after Merritt.

As the flight of the two men faded into the pitch night, Irvin sat in the crowning quiet. His breathing resided to normalcy in his chest and the silence resounded now in the hollow. Reaching out to his left, Irvin took Esther's hand and the two wept.

Merritt pushed on and on into the hollow and rose at last into the lowlands of the mountain. He blindly leapt forward along a rutted path on which he'd long run his coonhounds. The mountain laurel brushed heavily against his shoulders, making a soft hiss as they passed over Thomas' back. Merritt carried Thomas slung over his shoulder like a sack and relied on his innate familiarity with the flat cracked rut of the path to guide him between the trees. Eventually he could feel the ferns pass beneath his feet and tremble at the rough passage of his calves among the underbrush and he knew nearby was a thick patch of moss on which he could lay Thomas. But it was only for a moment. The sounds of Wittacre's pursuit closed in upon them.

Hurriedly, Merritt tore at his clothes and fashioned a roughshod tourniquet around the wound he'd located in Thomas' upper thigh, just below the buttocks. The wound was to the outside of his leg and had entered from behind, before finding its way clear through the other side without so much as nicking an artery. Thomas was safe from bleeding out, but he was in shock and would no doubt feel significant pain when he came to. As he tightened the knot, Merritt scanned the trees overhead and slowly recognized the place to which he'd come.

Esther's cries could not be heard in the deep of the forest. She and Irvin had dissolved from the world of Wittacre's hunt, but their voices carried across the pasture to the prospector's campfire, and the children were soon discovered on the edge of the glen. Irvin sat motionless as Esther wailed.

"What'ch you children doin' here?"

Two prospectors had come to assess the need of the crier.

"Weren't there three of y'uns?" asked one.

"Com'on now. Where's yer brother?" asked the other.

Irvin looked up. "He's not my brother. He's been shot. Ol' Merritt run off with him into the woods," he said.

The prospector looked at each other.

"I don' know what kinda craziness is goin' on out here in this holler, but we needs ta git you children home now," said one.

"If we gits ya ta the road, can ya tells us where yer home lies?" asked the other.

"Yes," said Irvin.

Esther sniffled and collected herself. She smiled finally at one prospector, then again to the other.

Wittacre had left the children alone in the dark. He'd grabbed the lantern from his fallen horse when he went after Merritt. The lantern's light danced among the trees, throwing wild shadows across the knotted pine and gnarled twisted arms of the oak and sycamores that leapt up before Wittacre's charge. His face was maddened in the lamplight. The crash of Merritt's flight had been heard clearly ahead but the cacophony had stopped suddenly and Wittacre's own discord had obscured the sounds of Merritt's activities. Wittacre moved on more cautiously, the ground turning rapidly from soft downy mosses to cragged rocks piling one upon the other. He was moving noticeably up just then, when a crisp crack like a broken twig brought him around to face the east.

Merritt could see his prey's face as he turned. Perched in the strong nook of a tree, Merritt took the shot at Wittacre's illuminated face. The shot echoed long as it rolled abundantly among the folds of the hollow, sending forth a burst of nocturnal birds and scattering the bats gliding through the canopy. But Merritt's aim was off and the bullet seared the flesh of Wittacre's shoulder. Though not a fatal shot, the force of receiving the wound took Wittacre off his feet and carried him bodily into an outcropping of rock. It was dark and the world was shadows that swallowed Wittacre whole. He was there, bleeding in the moon light and then he threw up the lantern and disappeared with it into the earth. The sound of broken glass issued up from beneath the ground, reverberating with a cold cavernous echo. Then there was an amber light within a fissure of the rocks and Wittacre screamed. His scream was unceasing and curdled the moon beneath the rolling boil of clouds. Merritt dropped from the tree, checked Thomas lying covered in dry leaves, and ran to the spot where Wittacre had vanished.

A fire raged in the belly of the earth and pinpoints of light began to pierce the loose scales of rock that covered the mountainside. A rumble shook the hillside like a cough and Merritt knew it was over then. He could still hear Wittacre scraping his way up the cleft of rock and so Merritt gave his arm to the flames and lifted the charred figure of Wittacre from the furnace made in the stone vault. The fire had spread quickly from the lantern, and Wittacre was burned all over. Bits of charred black rock lay encrusted in his flesh and clinging in embers to his clothes, or the tattered remnant of his riding boots. His hair was gone, and the blistered flesh of his scalp glistened when the moon arose from the cloud.

"Why didn't you let me die?"

"You ain't that big'a bastard. Not yet anyways. Plus I figure you gotta live with what you done."

"Thomas…is he…"

"No, he'll live. But he's my boy now. I'll see the judge first thing."

"Kill me."

"Let's git goin'."

The prospectors left early the next morning without signing a thing. Smoke drifted in lonesome wisps from the mountain. Wittacre sat on his porch in the evening, shrouded in white, his face hidden from then on behind a white veil of bandages and gauze. Irvin watched from the porch of William Wittacre's Wares as Ol' Merritt crossed the square and entered the courthouse. He reported Catecahassa dead and signed an affidavit ascribing the death to accident. He sign some forms for the adoption of Thomas and returned to the hollow.

The land was worked and the stakes were forgotten. Sometimes, at night, Helizikinopo cried out in grief for her slain grandson. On these nights, Nan slept closer to Ol' Merritt's side. Thomas walked with a cane, an orphan and half a cripple. But his wound had mixed with the earth and saw deeply into the mountain and knew that one day, eventually, the fire must burn out. All fires burn out, but none burn quite so fiercely as that fire he knew dwelt within the land.

THINGS IN BROWN PAPER

Irvin J. Russell, Jr. was sitting by the window at the old oak table given him by his father, notched and knotted by years of worry and war when his daughter Thea came meekly into the dining room and said, "There's a package arrived for you, Papa." He raised his head from a scar in the wood made by a woman who had sat awake by candlelight running the blade of a knife around a knot and toward the edge of the table. The gray and wiry thatch of Irvin's beard separated as he forced a shallow smile at his youngest child and asked, "Who sent it?" from a distance much farther than the table at which he sat.

Thea stood in the doorway holding hands with herself behind her back, one leg fidgeting to and fro on its toes. She was mournfully beautiful with her eyes downcast, away from her father and the sun shafting through the windows across their modest dining room and onto the hardwood floors her brothers had just recently restored. Briefly, Thea caught the eyes of her own reflection in the sheen of the buffered floors and looked away from one phantom to another specter that had once been her Papa yet still sat across the room at the table.

"It's from Sears-Roebuck," she said quietly.

Irvin's heart leapt a little inside his chest. The faintest beads of perspiration spread across his forehead and his half-toothed smile again broke involuntarily through his beard to show the momentary elation the old man felt. As it passed he thanked his daughter but she was gone, shuffling nervously through the living room and out the front door onto the porch where her older sister was mending their brother's work clothes and their mother hung laundry on a line beside the house.

Irvin turned away from the empty doorway, if he could, from his empty life. Every year he could feel the distance between him and his children growing greater and greater. The girls especially suffered under the weight of their father's invalidity and spite. The war had ended twenty-seven years ago. Irvin had gone off to war like any respectable Southern landowner, leaving his wife and five children behind. The oldest son, too proud to listen to his old man, wishing to prove himself in his youthful vivacity, had left for the front while his father was still away and had died hopelessly holding ground against a cavalry charge that decimated his whole battalion.

When Irvin imagined his eldest dying he sought vainly for a glint of honor and valor in the charge, the last stand. He could see so vividly his own battles. The chorus of bullets singing through the air; the bass rumble of cannon relays accentuated by the plumes of white smoke that puffed into the air and mingled with the lazy clouds that paid no mind to the carnage men wrought below them. He knew too well the terrible crescendo of hoof beats against the packed earth and the battle cry of young men willing to kill and die and leave this place soaked red beneath them. Sometimes he saw his son with the company standard, basking in the dying light as those hoof beats drew near. Proud, erect, and defiant his son stared down the western wind and fell to wounds uncounted, so strong was he that life refused to leave him until his legs were useless. Other times Irvin knew that his son carried no standard and that he had fallen back fighting. Loading his rifle, picking up the ready weapons of the dead and wounded and firing back into the cavalry charge, firing back at his fate too willful to submit himself to it. Glory for his family, for his home.

Irvin pounded the table and nearly wept when, as it inevitably happens, he realized the futility of his dreams and the tragic waste his son had made of his life. *Damn the war*, he would think, instinctively clutching his knee; his pants hung empty and knotted where the rest of his leg should be. He leaned back and took a breath. On the bureau just inside the dining room door there was a rectangular box, the size of a brick, wrapped in brown paper, tied with a length of twine. Thea must have sat it there when she'd come in. Even from across the room the tag could be seen sticking up, personalized for him, Irvin J. Russell, Jr.

A sudden inspiration made Irvin twist himself around in an excruciating display and drag his crutch from its place against the wall behind him. His hand warmed passing through a shaft of sunlight and felt cool in the shadow beneath the window sill, wrapped around a wooden and inadequate substitute. Drooping yellow flowers and wild lilac bounced in their vase when Irvin struggled and scraped against the table to get up. Once upright, he felt a bit forward with the crutch, put his weight down, took a pained, awkward step to meet it, and proceeded in such a fashion across the dining room. At the bureau he passed his callused fingertips over the smooth, cool brown paper that kept his little secrets. He held himself up on his crutch and dared laugh just a little to show himself he was tickled by something. That a message from this world could still get through.

Picking up the six ounce box, which cradled easily in his palm, Irvin began to step-drag-step through the living room, past his worn, tired rocker and toward the open front door where his wife tended to sheets and children's clothing. Thea ran about the yard with dandelions trailing from her hair which was braided but coming loose and flying in wisps behind her. She fluttered across Irvin's vision to the ramshackle plank fence that sagged between the posts from years of supporting the weather's burden.

*   *   *

Thomas had grown into a formidable craftsman. Hindered by injury, the trades he developed were ones in which he could be stationary. People in town were fond of his furniture, especially the rocking-chairs for which he achieved a local celebrity. He had stayed on with Ol' Merritt until the old man died. It was then that the two Merritt sons took over the land but never split it up. It was not in Nan Merritt's way to have many children, though she produced two sons and a girl for Ol' Merritt before they were done. The girl, Theodosia Rose, had been born soon after the adoption of Thomas into the Merritt clan. The older brother was named Henrik after Ol' Merritt's father. The youngest son received the name of Nan's slain brother and marked the fire that burned in the mountain, Catecahassa Rowtag Merritt. Nan impressed upon her children that this fire was a flame kindled by the greed of men who had come to native lands to exploit what the stones had kept hidden from the hands of those who were blinded by something less than ambition. Thomas himself would listen to Nan as she spoke, so even in her voice and calm—that ancient maternal authority something that needed no coercion but persuaded by the sheer tone one attributes to the lesson learned from the clarity of its truth.

Ol' Merritt had been threshing wheat when death came upon him. The event happened and was not an event for Ol' Merritt though it reverberated throughout the hollow in subtle ways that were at first indiscernible but grew in exponential bursts of consequence.

The day had been as any before it, at least those that followed the purchase of land from William Wittacre. The great plans of the Merritt clan had been foiled by happenstance and the crack in the earth that had claimed the father consumed the enemy as well as the opportunity for the wealth promised to any immigrant who desired to make their new home in America. They had awakened with the dawn, eaten their simple breakfast, hitched the animals, and off went Ol' Merritt into the fields where his age seldom showed. It was well before the War Between the States and the shadows of that conflict remained far away from the edge of the hollow, just distant rumors carried by Irvin into the recluse of the mountains. Ol' Merritt, seventy-one and still threshing, had no mind to the workings of the country beyond his homestead and the family he raised there. The sky was wide and open above him and the minds of men were closed and sleepy despite all the commotion and whooping of the Great Awakening revivals that were true spectacles in a grand old fashion. He worked his land, the mountain to his back, until the stillness crept across the field and Ol' Merritt let his scythe drop to the ground. A wind stirred up and the old man took a last account of the heavens as the feeling left his arm and that invisible knife found his breast. Henrik would tell of the smile gracing his father's face as he fell backward, his body received by the cultivation it had wrought and laid gently down onto the golden bed to take the final rest. Thus was the third body placed in the old cemetery deep in the valley, wreathed about a tree not unlike the one that had been saved in the fields. They were like two ancient fateful sisters holding sentry on the ends of the tract; one where the living raised the life they lived and one where those living passed on into death and were raised no more from their beds. The place was sacred to Nan, and she kept it in her own way.

Thomas was twenty-six years old at that time, married to Esther whose parents had abandoned her to the hollow, believing her bewitched by the Native magic everyone in town believed to rule the workings of the land. It was thought that Wittacre had been cursed to live on eternally, himself eighty-three when Ol' Merritt passed on and still living in bandages, deformed by fire and rage and kept alive by contempt and determination. Thomas would watch the plantation from the field, knowing that there reclined the phantom of a man, his dogs at his feet and useless to him, as his two daughters watched over him. When it grew cool, Thomas' old wound would ache.

It was growing cool when Thomas finally had the gumption to speak with Nan on the matter. She was the elder, and rocked gently in one of Thomas' best chairs on the porch of the old fort-house. Thomas drew a chair up beside her.

"It's been 'bout a fortnight nigh Ol' Merritt done passed on."

"It has chile."

"I'm worried on Wittacre o'er yonder."

"Don' worry on him."

"He's got an eye on you an' yours. He ain't like you, Nan. Man like that got hate in his heart. My leg reminds me often."

Nan sighed, her breathing lightly labored, a slight rattle in her chest.

"I'm sorry ta trouble you," Thomas got up to leave.

"Stay on, chile."

He sat back down.

"We's family but we ain't, you understand my meanin'?"

"Ma'am, I reckon I do."

"You reckon, or you do?"

"I reckon."

"Then you don'. My husband done loved you like his own, you know that."

"That I do," Thomas took out a pipe from his overalls and began to pack it with tobacco.

"Well then, you an' the younger Black Hoof, an' Theodosia, an' Henrik, you's all kin."

Thomas struck a match, produced from the same pocket, and drew on the pipe until the dry leaves glowed and gave the sweet scent of their smoke.

"We all done put our blood into this ground, we all done ate what the land give and 'cause we ate it it makes us. We's all the same here, through an' through, I speak the truth."

Thomas puffed gently and rocked in his chair.

"Let that Wittacre hate. Let him live a thousand years off that hate. Let his spirit lay in waste. Don' you worry on him none."

*   *   *

Irvin Jr. inhaled deeply. The land he now knew had a different smell. This nostalgia of scent was one of the most painful memories he could then conjure. Her face was gone. Sometimes, Irvin believed if he could just smell that smell again, if just the redolence of the land that bore his name would find its way back to him he might be able to reclaim that noble visage whose absence haunted his waking and sleeping hours with a quiet sadness equaled only by the death of his son.

He stood leaning heavily on his crutch, just watching the remaining children and his wife do their chores. He looked at the fence he'd built in the fashion of Ol' Merritt, a copy of that fence that ran along the creek between the land he longed for and that of the Everett's, pretending to remember the child's game that had finally made his father a man at nineteen.

Momentarily, he called out to his wife, "Hannah! Hey, there, Hannah!"

She finished hanging the garments she was working with and took heed of her husband's call. Holding her dress up so as not to tread on it, she crossed the yard to Irvin standing on the porch.

"Yes?"

"You seen Abraham?"

"He done gone in ta town this mornin'."

"Has he?'

"That's what he said."

Irvin said no more, leaving his wife to stand there so that he could seat himself in the old rocking chair brought with them from the hollow. After a time, Hannah asked, "Is that it?"

"Huh?" grunted Irvin.

"Is that all?"

"Yeah...yeah, that's all woman."

"I'll git back ta my work then."

"Fine, fine."

She turned to leave him there, but he stopped her to say, "Thank you."

"Well," she said, "yer welcome."

As his wife returned to the laundry, Irvin looked wistfully at the sagging fence. Thinking of how he longed to repair it, he nearly wept but instead felt foolish and blushed.

*   *   *

Esther had grown into a woman of grace and beauty. She was tall and thin, which made for a lanky awkward adolescence. But Thomas had seen in her all along the potential for womanhood and the strength that existed in spite of the terrified little girl who had cried on and on in the hollow the night they had

195

trespassed on the business of the land and found themselves drawn irrevocably into the web of living spun by those who had invested their very being in the place. She had begun her move into the hollow by nursing Thomas. The whole affair had been, in part, her fault as she reckoned it, though Irvin carried the debt he owed Thomas for the rest of his days. At the very least it had brought Esther and Thomas together and led Thomas to a purposeful vocation at which he excelled. Since Ol' Merritt had died, the joy that normally presided over Thomas in his work had been depleted and this metamorphosis was the cause of Esther's worry.

Thomas was soaking the length of a tree branch in a long trough for shaping when Esther had approached him. The words of Nan were still loud in his ears—a few days had little power over the matriarch.

"You ain't been yerself, Thom," she said, breaking his somnambulance.

He looked wearily at her, still bent toward the trough of water where he watched the wood soak up the cold water and soften in the shade.

"Now ain't that'a way ta be. Lordy, Thom you ain't changed none since you done got drug out here."

The man smiled.

"There. That's a start at least."

"What'chu come out here ta bother me fer?"

"I din' come out here ta bother you none a'tall! Back he goes, ain't that'a way ta be."

Thomas straighten back against the chair and looked fondly on his wife standing with her arms crossed; a slight breeze gently rippled her dress.

"Alright then," he said.

"You ain't been yerself, Thom."

"I'm worried."

"Well I can see as much as that! You think I come down in ta the holler an' done nursed you up and ta health just to be ignernt of when you's is worried an' when ya ain't? Out with it, c'mon now!"

"I'm worried on Wittacre."

"Nan done told you—"

"Dammit, woman, I knowed what Nan done said. But Nan ain't got ta live in the holler on another thirty years. We's gots'ta live on."

Esther dropped her guarded stance and came to kneel beside Thomas and he raised the wood up to test the give and replaced it in the water.

"Baby, ain't that man gonna do us no harm."

No words could say what Thomas' eyes did just then. He rubbed his hand over the scar on his thigh.

"Ain't jus' the old man Wittacre. He got them daughters married up right to prospectors and managers down state and that brother'a his is some kinda banker if I reckon it rightly. Them kinda men's got weapons that ain't guns but will cut a man down sure as he stands there. They cut out the very ground a man's got ta stand on."

Esther stood back up and crossed her arms.

"Well, I was raised up that you judge not."

"Well, we be judged, woman," and with that rebuke from her husband, Esther had left him in a huff.

*   *   *

Irvin Jr. sat on the porch rocking in the sun. His daughters were through with their daily chores and pranced about the yard carelessly, falling where they may, unhindered by the weight their father bore and the decision that wore on his mind as the runners of his old rocking chair wore ruts into the planks of the porch that were smoothed from constant pressure and shone in the sunlight. In the kitchen the brown paper package waited for him and he returned often to it in his mind as he drafted a letter that he must sit to write before the morrow. Never had he been a man of letters or great learning and this allowed him to agonize in a peculiar way over the words that were really so plain and simple in their meaning. He rocked and stroked his beard and watched the girls with their arms outstretched attempting to take off and leave him finally to his fate. They could just barely be discerned in the slant of the sun that left a golden lace of living flesh haloed around the opaque density of their inner core wherein no fathomable detail could be read in the mystifying light falling as it was all around, illuminating the mountains behind the house, in the distant east that refused the forgetfulness of Irvin's memory and cast him in exile upon the shores of a strange tide he knew would never reverse and thereby return him to the place for which he pined.

As he sat and rocked and thought about what words to use, Irvin saw Abe come finally over the horizon, a deer killed and field dressed and slung over the young man's shoulders. Old now, sentimental, Irvin was nearly overcome by emotion—envy, wrath—at the sight of the sixteen year old, his ward these past eighteen months and fresh from the North of Europe, so similar to the figure of legend told him by his father. Though there existed no relation between them, something in Abraham stirred in the junior Russell the long dormant phantom of the woman whose face he could not conjure, but whose voice lived in his ears even so many years later.

*   *   *

William Wittacre slept in a grand bed ornamented with four gilded posts and draped by fine tapestries that were light and silken still from the summer months. He had not yet heard that Ol' Merritt had passed away; news from the hollow was scarce and well guarded. A black nurse watched after Wittacre since his daughters had married. She had eased his troubled sleep with herbal remedies and ointments that left rich mint aromas thick in the old man's boudoir. The nurse had just left Wittacre for the night. She had been gone a few minutes when a low sound in the room's shadows disturbed the old man from his torpor.

"Who? Who's there?" he said. He breathed heavily afterward, not from any fright or excitement but simply because age charged a heavy toll for him to speak.

Nothing. A groan left Wittacre as he tried to settle back into sleep. Then, another sound.

"Damn!" moaned Wittacre. "I know someone's there. I know…"

"I am here," said Nan, emerging slowly from the shadows, silent as she was old, covered in the skins and furs in the style of her people, a splay of feather abundantly arranged on the silver crown of her head.

Wittacre cried out but his voice was lost in his chest, dead before it was born into the blackness of that night. The dark woman came to his bedside and quietly sat down.

"Hush, now," she said, "I ain't take this trouble to hurt you."

Wittacre was not immediately satisfied but a few moments with Nan seated solemnly with her eyes closed was enough to bring a tentative calm to Wittacre's demeanor.

"I needs ta settle up with you. Times is comin' where the business a' these hills is gonna come down to younger folks than us. What're we leavin' 'em? Pity and sorrow? What?"

Wittacre gurgled with laughter under his shrouds. Nan was taken aback.

"You think you understand so much, woman. You don' know *shit*."

Nan sighed. "I suppose you ain't never changed in all these years."

"I hate you and yer half-breed kin if'n that's what yer on about," his weak voice came alive when he gave sound to his rage.

"Well I din' come here ta ask you ta like us. I came here 'cause my husband is dead and the grudge you bare him be dead with him."

Again, Wittacre would have laughed had not the gurgling in his chest prevented him from doing so. He hacked and coughed instead, a deformed grin exposed from beneath the bandages that hid him from sight.

"You don' git it, do you woman? I'm the oldest a *fifteen* children born over twenty years! You kept that old fool'a yers ta yer ways, but them ways is dead, deader'n that grudge I got agin' you and yers. My youngest brother's the only one livin' in these parts, but he ain' gonna let you red-skinned poachers off, especially now that Ol' Merritt is dead. Ha! You shouldn't never've come here!" and he was given over to fits of coughing, spittle and drool running down his scarred chin.

Nan was visibly disheartened. Wittacre convulsed minutely with glee.

Nan said, "I was hopin' this could all end with us."

"I ain't dead yet woman."

"Nor I," the woman said with pride. "But we will be, mark me, an' before this year is out. You know it sure as I do."

"That's the thing we've always understood. Time. 'Cept I aim ta make it my weapon. Them children a yers ain't known that fire…"

Nan looked on in disbelief. The emotion Wittacre exuded was foreign to her.

"You tell them tales about fire an' greed—*my* greed—you see? But it's mine still, an' you's is jus' tellin' stories," the coughing cut him short.

"I don' wish ill on you, but I warn you now, leave this thing be—forget your anger and die in peace or languish and be consumed by it."

Wittacre shrugged, and waited for the scratching in his throat to subside. He looked around. Nan saw his effort and brought the glass of water from the bedside table to the sick man's lips. He drank slowly and rested his head back onto the down pillow when he had finished. Nan returned the glass to the table.

"What's the difference woman? I'm dead and dead. Either way, ain't gonna matter to me none. It's yer kin gonna have to worry on it. One thing you people never understood was the value of wealth. Ain't jus' ta pile up and hide. Money means action, an' actions got consequences."

"We need no money to act."

"But to defend…" coughing, painful, Wittacre winced beneath his white wrappings.

Nan got up from the bed and stood beside Wittacre.

"Then, you ought have this."

She withdrew from her robes a small box, wrapped in brown paper and tied with a length of rough twine. Setting the box by the bedside, she began to withdraw from the room when a sound from Wittacre stopped her. He had not the strength to speak, and so he beckoned the dark woman closer with his feeble hand, shaking as he held it toward her in the dark.

She came close as Wittacre said, "I will live through my hate for you…"

Nan stood straight and backed away from the bed as the sound of shattered glass suddenly pierced the silence. Water ran across the floorboards and the nurse stood stark, wide-eyed, shaking at the sight of Nan, bedecked in feathers and furs, looking mournfully at the nurse. The servant screamed and when she next took account of the room, Nan was gone.

*   *   *

Painfully, the junior Russell made his way to the shed where Abe was preparing the deer he'd killed. The older man watched with interest as Abe went to work, thoroughly cleaning where the field admitted only to gutting and the removal of the throat and upper vitals. As it was, the deer was suspended from the ceiling of the shed with its front legs tied up behind the head, a stick kept the hind legs apart as Abe carefully cleaned the rest of the cavity, splashing cold creek water into the opened body so that it may hang and cure before butchering. It had been years since Irvin himself had been capable of this work. He watched, nostalgic, quietly alone.

"You know," said Irvin after a time, "if'n you bring them guts back, I know a fella down the road a spell that might make us up some fiddle strings, or a few fer that old flat-top box you picked up."

Abe kept working as he said, "Nah, tain't worth the trouble. 'Sides, them deer guts ain't as good fer instruments."

"Oh?"

"Gotta round up some a them stray cats o'er at the Johnson's place if'n you want good strings fer them guitars an' such."

Irvin nodded and stroked his beard, "I think yer a little confused 'bout yer terms there."

"How's that?"

"Catgut ain't from no cats, boy," laughed Irvin. "You git yer catgut from sheep or cow sure as it comes from some barn cat."

"Still," mused Abe, "Sheep 'n cow ain't no deer."

"No, no tain't."

Irvin watched as Abe worked on a few more minutes.

Then he said, "I din' really come out here to talk about no deer. Ain't much interested in no fiddle strings either."

"Well, I'm about done here. We can talk soon as I warsh up."

"Good. Do that."

Irvin watched as Abe threw a few more cups of cold water into the deer carcass and left it there, going away to the little creek to wash his hands and splash the chill moisture onto his face and the back of his neck. Irvin went back to the porch on his own, waiting there in his rocker for the return of Abe. Still, he mulled the words he would use over in his mind.

When Abe came to sit beside Irvin on the porch, the old Civil War vet said to him, "You know, Abe, I was nigh on thirty when I went off to war. An here I am, damn near sixty, good as a ghost to my family. Mind you I sired two more kids as an invalid, though I don' think Hannah will ever forgive me fer leavin' like I done. She was never a strong supporter of the War."

Abe produced a pipe, then another, and packed the two for the both of them, even lighting Irvin's for him before passing the smoking corncob to his elder.

"Thank ye," Irvin said. "I din't come from these parts, jus' like you din' either. I come from a little ways north and back east, into them mountains. Maybe if'n I'd a stayed on back there, I wouldn' a never got caught in that damn War. But it din' happen that way, and, to be honest, I ain't gonna tell you exactly what did happen, 'cause I jus' don' know it all. I was young, you see? Hell, maybe it's all jus' stories anyway," Irvin was getting ahead of himself. He tried to take account of the little facts he had on hand.

"What I mean is, this here's my home now, an' my children's home. I don' reckon we'll ever head back east."

Abe was getting listless, "So, you reckon I ought go back there?"

Irvin deflated a little. He had crafted his next words so carefully.

"Yes," he said, "I reckon I think you ought."

"I ain't got nothin' in this world, an' nothin' for me back east far as I can tell."

"Well," said Russell, "That might not be the whole of the truth."

*   *   *

The day after Nan's visit with Wittacre, Irvin J. Russell came into the hollow with his young son, Irvin, Jr. The uncertain truce between Wittacre and the hollow had spared Irvin from ill consequence and he remained at William Wittacre's Wares, now more vital to the business' operation than ever before. Given his injuries, Wittacre was left unable to manage the store as he once did. As Irvin grew, so too his responsibilities grew until he ran nearly every aspect of the store and the townsfolk came to see the place as his even though he never took ownership of the little building and its contents. He still lived in the rooms above the store, now with a wife and child, the numbers of their brood kept low due to the quiet rise of a moderately urban life. It was this slow urbanization that Irvin went to the hollow to escape. Not a permanent escape, but a retreat from the many people that inhabited the shop and the town square and the various small venues of public space that, year by year, became increasingly abundant throughout St. Clairsville. Irvin, Jr. came often to the hollow with his father. It was a happy retreat for the small boy as well, though he was somewhat shy and had never brought himself to come near Ol' Merritt when the man had lived.

The day was just such an idyll retreat for the father and son Russell. Though it was true, Irvin senior went because he had heard of Ol' Merritt's death, the demeanor of the hollow was well known and the natural occurrence of an old man's death would not wrack the place as some tragedy. Irvin expected Nan would share some choice stories regarding her late husband; in homage and celebration of his singularity.

It was early in the afternoon when Irvin arrived to find the Merritts had broke for a spell and gathered on the small shaded porch of the old fort-house to tide themselves on bread and butter, to talk and while away an hour or two, to sneak a sip or two of moonshine, and to sit quietly in each others' company. Irvin kept a horse out back of the store and it was to his son's great delight that they had ridden the old mare into the hollow. A day trip such as this was not so common and like all rare occurrences it awoke the young boy early in the morning; a fact for which the father Russell would be thankful. Happily they saddled up, leaving for the hollow by half past eight. In this manner they could take their time, walking some of the way so that little Irvin could play, exercise his childhood curiosity, and otherwise wear himself out for a good night's sleep.

They were walking the horse down the last bit of road when Nan saw them turn into the path leading into the hollow. She could just make them out from where she sat on the porch and they were quickly obscured as they descended into the tall grass. Black Hoof did not see the Russells at first, then spotted their trail from the motes and dust they sent up as they passed through.

"Get some water," said Nan. "Let Thom know we've company."

Catecahassa went off as he was told; his movements in the image of his slain uncle.

As the Russells drew near, the child broke away and came running to the porch and to Nan specifically, who braced her old bones to receive the boy as he leapt into her lap. Little Irvin was restrained in his manner and withheld his full exuberance at the last, stopping awkwardly before the old woman and climbing in a haphazard fashion onto her thighs.

"Howdy," said Irvin, Sr. as he drew up and directed the horse into a patch of lawn where a familiar trough of water was ready.

Black Hoof presently returned with cold water from the creek, which both guests drank with thanks. When the travelers were satisfied, everyone exchanged greetings and Irvin proposed to share some news while his son went about to play.

"I'm sorry about Ol' Merritt."

"I thank ye, but tain't nothin' ta be sorry over. My husband was an old man; and sometimes old men die. 'Specially in the autumn sun when they's threshin' instead'a lettin' that work ta the young."

"Well, be that as it may, he'll be missed."

"Sorely he will. Sorely."

"I got some interestin' news on a different note."

"How's that?"

"I think Wittacre's a fixin' ta sell the store."

"Is he now?"

"I reckon'. His brother, that young'un that lived down state, he's been around with a bankin' fellow, goes by Avrich, and I believe his brother is done married up ta one of Wittacre's daughters."

"Is them's the only family that git talked about in town?"

"Jus' seemed like things you might wanna know s'all."

Nan was reserved. More than anything, she was tired. Perhaps this talk worked on her nerves more than it ought.

"Well, besides all that, I gotta move if that store gets sold. Unless I get sold with it, I suppose," Irvin chuckled at this and Nan smiled a bit herself.

"I figure yer as much a part'a that store as the porch is," said Black Hoof.

"You's so quiet I fergit yer sittn' there," said Irvin.

Black Hoof shrugged.

"Where's that sister a yers?"

"Chasin' that son 'a yers," replied Black Hoof with a wave of his hand off to where the little Russell ran wide circles around Theodosia whose black hair was ashine in the sun.

"How old you now?"

"'Bout twenty-two."

"Twenty-two! Boy, you better get up outta this holler an—"

Irvin was made quiet by Nan's light hand on his knee. She had sat up straight and looked out over the land. Away along the road could be seen a wagon weighed down by a canvas-covered load. A small team of horses shifted and whinnied as they wait.

Someone came down the path toward the house. Nan sat back in her chair.

"Who th' hell'dya think that is?"

Black Hoof looked away, grinning. A younger woman in arm with a gentlemen just noticeably older appeared in view. As the couple came within earshot of the porch they quickened their pace as the woman appeared determined to make some point of her earnestness. As they approached, the Merritts began to make overtures of welcome, but the couple would have none of it and as soon as they stood before the porch and its occupants, the woman began to deliver her pent up angers upon those who would hear her.

"What'd you do to him? Huh? Devil! What'd you do ta my Daddy?!" she said stamping her feet; her arms straight and white-knuckled at her side.

Nan, to whom these vitriols were addressed, sat quietly and the storm raged on behind her adversary's eyes.

"Ain't you got mind enough ta speak?"

"Now here, what's all this?" Irvin thought to ask but the glance he received killed his words even as they left his mouth.

"Ain't none yer business shop-keep. Mind you, you won't even be that fer long."

"Maddy," said Nan.

"Oh, my name sounds awful on yer black tongue. What'd you do ta my Daddy?"

"Me an yer Daddy had words was all."

"Well he ain't got words no more! None for me and none for that poor Negress you done scared ta death with yer magic; comin' an' goin' in the night ta steal my Daddy's tongue!"

The man who had accompanied the woman made some move to comfort her or at least blunt the fury of her retorts but she shook him off with a stubborn reflex in her shoulders and stamped even closer to the porch, her one foot resting firmly on the stoop.

"Me an' my 'usband's goin' down ta Texas. I ain't got a mind to bother with you all no more. But reckon my words, you git what you deserve. I knowed you ain't got Jesus! Ain't no love for you in this world, I can see that!"

"Hey now, them's sound like threats ta me," again Irvin spoke up, but he was silenced immediately by Maddy Wittacre's rage.

"I ain't never come down to no holler and I ain't a'comin' back. My sister's done gone down state an' there's plenty a servant's ta watch my Daddy."

"Yes, run child, run from the death of your fa—"

"You shut up! Jus' shut yer mouth. Witch!"

Nan got up from her chair after some labor. Maddy and her companion took a step back. The man, supposedly Avrich, but no one at that time was certain, was then as far away from the old fort-house as he could get without scorn. Slowly, Nan came down from the porch followed by her son, Black Hoof. The old woman stood nearly face to face with the younger one, her eyes a cold reflective calm, tempered through her age to see across a distance of time. Something about the rage wavering in Maddy's eyes was fearful; an ancient fear that arose not from the calculation of ages but from the primal place were death hides from daily sight and springs upon consciousness unaware, thereby gripping a person with the paralyzing knowledge that they stand always before the gun—if not the gun of their enemies, then the spiritual gun of time whose strike was less a searing explosive terminus and more the swift then slow bleed of the sacrificial knife. Maddy now stood before the gun-blade; Nan was resolute under its stroke.

"I knowed what you done," said Maddy.

"You knows what yer Daddy done told you."

"My Daddy was the truth."

"He ain't dead yet."

"But all you is. You's all dead sure as I stand."

Nan was tired of words. She stooped low and gathered the earth in her palm. She worked the dirt through both hands and stepped to Maddy with a deliberate motion. Without word of warning, Nan ran both palms down either side of Maddy's face; the soil sticking to her white powdered skin in smooth brown lines the shape of Nan's fingers.

"You will never wash this soil from your face," Nan intoned as she stepped away.

Maddy gasped. She fumbled backwards, nearly fell, and was supported by her husband. What came from her mouth was muffled, a subdued shriek, and she turned swiftly and disappeared up the trail. The man lingered for a moment, taking account of the hollow. Nan waved her hand in a slow semi-circle before her, and the man went away, striding with dignity feigned over too rapid a pace.

Black Hoof was chuckling to himself once the Merritts were all alone again with Irvin. Nan looked to her son, turned away from the road, and returned to her chair on the porch. Black Hoof stood half on the steps and looked at his mother while he shook his head.

"Why you do that ta them folks?"

"Let them wallow in their ignorance. Their own fear will consume them."

"If'n it don' consume us first," Irvin said at last.

"They'll always be afraid; afraid of what they might lose."

"Ain't you?"

"I ain't never owned nothin'."

"Ownin' ain't all ta losin'."

"Be it as it may; I have a favor ta ask a' you, Irvin."

As his father spoke with Nan, the woman carved from burnished wood who lived as an idol in his mind, the junior Russell watched from the side of the porch where Theodosia gently held his shoulder.

*   *   *

It was night. The whole of the Russell household was asleep in bed save for Irvin Jr. and Abe who sat with a single candle lit between them; a night conspiracy brewed over glasses of bourbon whiskey and pipe-smoke.

"This is what I wanted you ta have," said Irvin, sliding a package wrapped in brown paper across the table to young Abe. The box was about the size of a brick, if slightly larger all around.

"Yer medicine?"

"No. Somethin' my medicine can't fix."

212

Abe took the box and laid his fingers upon the twine that bound it.

"Don't open it till you aim ta use it," said Irvin.

Abe hesitated. "Use it?"

Irvin smile. "Ain't nothin' but paper really. Least, that's what I's told. But if'n ya want it, it's the rights to some land. There's one other claim out there, though I doubt it'll ever be claimed."

Abe nodded.

"I guess all this seems odd to you."

"Sir, I ain't been around too long, but I been around enough to see a thing or two. I might not know what I'm a talkin' about, but you knows enough ta have yer reasons."

Irvin seemed satisfied. "Abe, I told ya all I knowed, but I reckon most of it don' make a lick a sense ta you no matter no how."

"Sense enough. People's been doin' likewise since people a been doin'."

Irvin nodded and smiled until he winced a bit; the pain ever residing in the place where his leg should be. Abe held the box for a moment before replacing it on the table.

"It ain't right," he said. "Yer kids ought have this."

Irvin shook his head, "Their home's here now. They never knowed them parts and got no rights to it."

"What rights I got?"

"All the rights that's in that box and that's all the rights there is, save the one that's missin'. But if'n that other claim ever come up, you'll find it split, fair an' square."

Abe was quiet.

Irvin went on, "Listen, I can't go back. Nor my kin. I'm done an' an old man now. When I left that place, an' mind you I still *smell* it, when I left it I was a boy no bigger 'n yer leg. The rights was really give ta my Daddy, though I don' think he wanted them."

"Why'd he take 'em then?"

Irvin looked in pain, "Somethin' happened. I don' full know what. He *had* ta take 'em."

"Some one he knowed call in a favor?"

"No, I don' think. My Daddy never owed nobody nothin' far as I know. Or it was paid."

"Still, why should I take this?"

"Are ya dumb boy? Why question this. Good bit a land jus' falls right in yer lap? Yer too young ta think this much on it."

"I'm thinkin' you's scared. I reckon I need reason ta take something another man's afraid of don' I?"

Irvin had no response to this. He didn't know—so much of his life was some vague transition from one state to the next; no different than anyone else except he could never settle and once he did he was up rooted by the War and crippled and left to learn how to live all over again though this bout was more like learning to die. Something in Abe was so much like the mythic Ol' Merritt recurred the thought on Irvin's mind; a thought repeated alongside the unopened package he had received that morning from Sears-Roebuck. One package contained the future; the other, the past. Both wrapped inconspicuously and setting about the house ubiquitous as fate.

"What is it, then?" asked Abe. "What're you scared of?"

"I can't hardly say," said Irvin. "All's I know is them hill's got memory longer'n man can reckon."

*   *   *

Black Hoof was awaken from a deep sleep by screams that ran a haunted course around the hollow. It was Nan and she screamed to wake the wakeful. When Black Hoof found her, she was standing on the porch pointing out across the fields to the old oak tree sprawled across the grasses. Henrik was hung from a prominent branch, his flaccid body black against the moon cresting the horizon. A band of men appeared along the road, unknown, silhouetted on horseback, rifles rested against their shoulders. The visitation had been an alibi. Now the slaughter. The men charged down the hollow.

Nan had swiftly regained her composure, no time then to mourn her eldest son hung from the tree. She looked at Catecehassa and said, "I din' think they would come this soon."

"I prayed they'd not come t'all."

"Git yer sister and send her to town. She knows what to do. Give her that box yer Daddy kept in brown paper. It's in there on the cross-beam on top a them dollars. Leave the money."

Black Hoof moved without a word, collecting the rifle inclined inside the door as he went, removed a chair from the dinning table and used it to reach the box on the cross-beam. Theodosia was already awake and dim lights could be seen moving about the quarters where Thomas lived with Esther. No lights could be seen in the fort-house; the horses were moving in on Thomas and Esther.

Nan had slipped off into the night fueled by instinctive tendencies and the last flare of life that comes before the long kindled flame is extinguished. Once in the underbrush, she crawled in the dirt for a bit, moving forward and gathering what camouflage the ground gave to her searching hands.

Meanwhile Black Hoof had collected Theodosia who had understood the moment she learned Henrik was dead. Swallowing her tears, she took the box and fled straight away toward the town, crossing away from the hollow, toward the creek and the Everett's land in the hopes that her neighbor's interest in his own property would protect her from murder by strangers. The interlopers, whoever they were, were being waylaid by a resolute Black Hoof who had gone without hesitation to the home of Thomas and Esther in order to repel the attack. Theodosia would remember her brother's face the rest of her days as he sent her away from their home on that last eve.

"Take these papers ta Irvin. Mama done made the arrangements with him," Black Hoof had said.

Theodosia was all calm surface, but a panic gripped her just beneath and her hands shook as she took the box.

"This ain't all a' it?" she had asked. "This ain't everythin' we got?"

"It ain't everything," Black Hoof said, glancing nervously back toward the path, toward Thomas and the danger that drew ever more near.

"What's happened ta the rest?"

Black Hoof took a final look back, "Jus' trust Mama."

He kissed her forehead, told her he loved her, and drove her into the woods, away from the last stand.

When Black Hoof arrived at Thomas and Esther's he found Esther loading what rifles they had as Thomas dug about an old cupboard for his pistols. Black Hoof was ready with his gun and took up position by the window to see where his enemies lay. They were bearing down into the hollow with some speed until Esther spat, came running up next to Black Hoof and fired a rifle out of the window. Her aim was off, the shot went wide, but startled the horses causing one to throw its rider into the field.

"Woo-aa!" she hollered, saying, "Them bastards ain't a takin' my homestead!"

"Git down!" demanded Thomas. "Dammit, woman, jus' reload that rifle."

The pace of the attackers slowed somewhat after the first shot, but they were near then, and Black Hoof let them have one from his pistol. The first volley came immediately after Black Hoof's pistol-shot as four horsemen opened fire almost simultaneously, imbedding lead balls into the wood of Thomas' small shack. Black Hoof fired again and struck one of the horses, which fell over, nearly on top of its rider. As the attackers reloaded, one fired off a few pistol shots, two of which entered the house and sent a plume of flour into the air as it struck a sack of goods stacked in one corner.

"Damn!" cried Thomas. "What is this?"

"I ain't sure yet," said Black Hoof with calm, taking another shot through the window before ducking down again to avoid a second volley.

At this relay, Esther cried out and fell, clutching her arm. Thomas went to her quickly and discovered it was just a graze; a little blood stained her dress and an area of her bicep looked burned.

"I'm fine, I'm fine," she insisted. "Damn!"

"What's happenin'?" called Black Hoof, hunched over, pushing a ball down into the tilted breech before snapping it back into place and raising up to fire.

"I dropped the flint a' this'n!" said Esther.

"Nevermind," Thomas went off, his Kentucky rifle loaded, and took position opposite of Black Hoof just as a lantern was thrown into the cottage from outside. It burst upon the floor and the flames leapt across the boards as the oil splashed and ran about.

Esther immediately dropped the rifle again. She had opened the jaw of the firing mechanism and was attempting to screw a new flint into place when the fire lit up. At that time she dropped what she was doing and, taking up a empty knapsack that happened to be nearby, flung herself bodily onto the flames.

"Dammit, woman," said Thomas.

Esther flailed and beat the flames and reduced their number somewhat before Thomas yelled at her, "The rifle, woman, the rifle."

She had time to give him the eye before crawling back, took up the muzzle-loader again, and finished screwing the flint into place, double checking it against the frizzen. She had no time to measure out powder, so she just poured what she could manage into the muzzle, stuffed the ball into place best she could and ran with the long rifle to Thomas, who had taken to firing his pistol into the night. Their assailants were on top of them now and had taken up some cover. Nonetheless, with Thomas occupied shooting his pistol, Esther took aim and fired at one of the invaders. The powder she had administered was too much and the gun roared and flashed and threw her to the ground. Yet the velocity of the shot became such that, though her aim was poor, the ball struck one attacker in the shoulder, passing clear through him, exploding out the back of his torso with a spray of blood and the remnants of his scapula. Though not dead, he was debilitated.

"How many?" yelled Esther, taking cover again.

"Don' know. Five? Maybe six," said Black Hoof.

There was a slight break in the firing from outside and Black Hoof stepped forward, leveled a pistol and fired, this time hitting his mark square in the forehead, killing him without ceremony and sending his body backward over a log to spill his brain into the dirt. Emboldened by the kill, Black Hoof took aim for a second shot, fired, but was off target this time and struck an assailant in the hip, putting him on the ground. Bloodthirsty, Black Hoof made to fire a third time, but had been too long exposed and was himself struck suddenly in the chest, to the left side, just above the clavicle. Without much fuss, he went down and rolled back against the wall with his hand pressed tightly against the wound. From where he sat, he could see that the fire had not been extinguished and was flaring again, catching hold of a chair and some of the supplies opposite of where the gunfight was taking place.

"Esther," said Thomas, "you need ta take Catechassa and git out."

Esther's eyes were wet and she struggled to reload a muzzle loader. She threw the gun down in frustration and took up Black Hoof's Harpers Ferry instead, and was quicker to load the pivoting chamber breech.

"Give me that!" said Thomas. "Take them long rifles an' git outta here! Take him an' go!"

Esther began to cry, nodded her head, and acquiesced. Another volley resounded in the hollow and a series of balls made loud packing sounds against the side of the cottage. Black Hoof winced and called out. One of the balls had just barely penetrated the wall and made a shallow flesh wound in his lower back. Esther went to him, drug him from the wall, and began tearing the hem of her dress to bind the wound in his chest. Thomas fired the Harpers Ferry, dropped it, took up a Kentucky rifle, and fired it, the second time hitting a then unwounded attacker in the center of his chest. The volume of powder in the Kentucky had been less on that shot and the ball imbedded in its victim's chest, burning where it lay just before his aorta. Esther had about finished binding Black Hoof and the fire was really sweeping up, licking the ceiling and spreading still across the floor.

"Can you walk?" Esther cried to Black Hoof.

He didn't give a verbal response but instead made his best effort to rise himself before being helped to his feet by the wife of his dear friend. On his feet, Black Hoof's head swam and the ball in his chest was a red coal that seared his insides and sent a burning sensation well into his neck and shoulder. He made awful sounds of pain but managed to move forward with Esther's help in spite of the fire that was raging in his chest. Black Hoof still clutched his pistol, which Esther stopped by the door to let him reload. Esther clutched one Kentucky rifle under her arm and reached to take the second from Thomas as he knelt down to reload the Harpers Ferry.

"That'n ain't loaded," Thomas cautioned.

"This'n here is," Esther said, motioning with the rifle she pressed against her side with her injured arm.

Thomas stopped what he was doing, took care that he was far enough from the window, and kissed Esther deeply as she stood there.

"I love you," he said.

"I love you," she said.

Then Esther turned with Black Hoof and fled into the night.

One of the attacking party called out as Esther and Black Hoof fled. Another assailant, still uninjured, began to pursue them, along with the man who had been badly hurt in the shoulder—his rage maddening him and making him blind the pain that each step brought to his barely attached arm. The attacker who had been shot in the hip was regrouping alongside the assassin with a bolt of lead just centimeters from his heart.

Thomas took one last account of his home and went outside as quickly as he could, still hobbled by the old injury that plagued him throughout his life. He went around the opposite way, letting Esther and Black Hoof lead the two assailants on. They were some ways away as Thomas took careful aim. He was fearful of hitting his wife and friend and so took a painful kneeling position, leveled his sight, muttered a prayer, and squeezed the trigger. The gun recoiled, the ball flew, and the attacker already badly injured fell, his spine having been severed by Thomas' shot. Thomas made to reload quickly, but he was exposed now and was shot in the side. He fell over took out his pistol and fired all six shots in rapid succession, missing with all shot but one, which struck the apparent, and until then uninjured, leader of the posse in the thigh. The posse leader made an angry curse as he pawed at his hit leg. Seeing the injury was clean and that the ball had passed clear through without fatal damage, the posse leader limped over to Thomas who lay on the ground, speedily feeding bullets into the open chambers of his pistol. The posse leader feebly kicked at Thomas' pistol, still managing to disarm his victim, before pulling his own revolver and shooting Thomas three times in the chest. Sputtering blood, Thomas died beneath the hollow moon.

The uninjured invader returned shortly and reported that Esther and Black Hoof had also been killed. He was instructed to bury the bodies in a predetermined location deep in the hollow. The posse leader gathered his injured cohorts, gave them instruction on searching the remaining property, and went about quickly dressing his own leg-wound before painfully mounting his horse and riding off in the direction of Wittacre's Wares. The remaining marauders stayed in the hollow, loaded the bodies onto horseback and took them into the deep of the wood, where they plotted graves in the vicinity of an aged white oak. The man with the chest wound died and he and the other two slain attackers were buried along with the others whose homestead had been so violently disrupted. All said, the gunfight had lasted only about nine minutes, but the grave-digging went on into the night. It was nearing dawn when the bandits emerged from the hollow and raked over the smoldering coals where Esther and Thomas' cottage had burned to the ground. They hesitated, as off in the distance, they saw not the sunrise, but the flickering orange glow of fire far off, across the road.

Meanwhile, Theodosia had succeeded in reaching town. She put a fair distance between herself and the old fort-house before she heard the gunshots break out and echo around the darkened landscape. She thought of her mother and wept a little then, the relays of rifle-fire urging her forward like the sting of a whip. She had gone at once to Wittacre's Wares, exhausted, sweating, dirty. She scrambled onto the back porch where the door lead directly up to the apartments above. With both fists she began to pound on the door, accompanying the frantic fist-falls with a hoarse and terrified call for Irvin. After a short time, the door opened and Irvin stood there, himself armed with a rifle.

"What on earth's the matter, girl?"

"They's come…" she said gasping. "They's come inta th' holler ta kill us!"

"Who has?" Irvin was suddenly urgent taking Theodosia firmly by the shoulders and bringing her inside and up the stairs.

Theodosia began regaining her senses and looked around, frightened. "Where's your wife?"

"She ain't here. That's why me an' the boy come ta see y'all. She off visiting her Mama over the next mountain."

Theodosia seemed relieved until she remembered Irvin, Jr. She quickly withdrew the box, wrapped in brown paper, and placed it in Irvin's hands. He knew immediately what transpired. Nan's foresight had paid off. Irvin had misjudged the grudges that are born on the edges of civilization; he had made a deadly miscalculation in his advice to the Merritt clan. He looked with pity on young Theodosia Rose.

"What will you do?" he asked.

She wiped the tears away from her cheeks.

"I don' know. I can't go back to the holler," she sobbed, "They's gonna kill me sure as I stand…"

Irivn took her in his arms and tried to comfort her.

"Look," he said, "we can git ya ta the other mountain, ta my wife's kin. From there ye can git away."

Theodosia cried and shook her head, "I jus' don' know no other life than down in th' holler. What am I gonna do?"

"It's all right, we'll see yer safe."

She continued to cry for a spell then gradually settled. Irvin calmed her, took her upstairs, and asked if there was anything she could use. Theodosia was not talkative, and so Irvin just stoked the low embers in the wood stove, kindled a flame, put the cast-iron kettle on to boil, and went downstairs to the shop to fetch some tea. The night wore on and the pair sat in silence, slowly drinking their tea. Then, suddenly, Theodosia appeared on edge again.

"What's that?" she said sharply.

Irvin listened and he heard foot steps, slow, deliberate, near the back porch."

"Stay here," Irvin said and went quietly out of his small kitchen and down the stairs to the back door.

He waited, listening, for the foot falls to circle the house and approach the back stoop. There was a pause, then a foot on the stair. The stranger, as Irvin assumed it was, hesitated before trying the door. Whoever it was must have found the door to be weak, because the next Irvin knew, it was flung inwards with great force, tearing the lock off the wall and loosening the hinges from their moorings. Irvin was back far enough not to be hit by the door, but he immediately saw the pistol in the intruder's hand and dashed back up the stairs with the stranger in pursuit. When he got to the kitchen, Irvin saw that his son had been awakened by the commotion and was upset; Theodosia comforted him in refuge behind the door to the bedroom. Irvin was not as quick to the gun as the people of the hollow and so he waited for the intruder at the top of the stairs, positioning himself at an angle that hid him from sight.

In no time, the pursuant was at the top of the stairs, but before Theodosia was spotted Irvin intervened. A scuffle ensued in which both men vied for control of the pistol. Irvin's attacker had a mind to shoot Irvin; the gun went off just beside his face. Little Irvin screamed as the shot rang out, which spurred the father to fight harder and push the intruder back into the hall toward the stairs. The fighting men broke their grapple and in the instant the intruder took aim Irvin leapt forward, spearing his assailant in the midsection. Both men tumbled, but Irvin managed to stay on top as they flailed and crashed down the stairs. At the bottom, laying halfway out the door, neither men moved. Slowly, Irvin came to and with little consideration, took up the pistol and cracked the unconscious attacker's jaw with it. Then, he returned to Theodosia and his son in the kitchen.

"What's 'appened?" asked Theodosia.

"I ain't sure, but we're leavin'."

Irvin, Jr. visibly shaken, was kept calm by the hand of Theodosia. The two were left alone for a moment, then the father Irvin returned with a sack of clothes. He busied himself in the kitchen.

Tossing a knapsack to Theodosia, Irvin said, "Run down ta the store and take whatever you need."

The girl nodded.

"We'll head ta ma wife's folks. Then we can figure a way ta keep you safe."

As Theodosia went downstairs, Irvin turned to his son, "Don' you worry none. We's gonna be fine, jus' fine."

It was thus that Theodosia made her escape from the vengeance of Wittacre and the Russell's themselves came upon the verge of exile. They avoided the road and stuck to trails out of sight and mind. Timid and scared, Theodosia looked with a sad heart toward the orange glow that grew on the very periphery of the hollows.

William Wittacre lay in his four-post bed. The box that Nan had given him sat unopened on the bedside table. He could hear the guns resounding in the distance. He smiled secretly to himself. The nurse came in.

"Is ev'rting good, sir?"

"Fine. Fine," replied Wittacre, his voice still labored. Those were the first words he had spoken since the visitation.

Nodding, the nurse retreated. Once the door was closed, she fled the main house to her quarters. Something about the old man scared her, and she had found any reason to neglect her duties since seeing the Native woman in the room where her Master slept. It was ill omens. Now those omens took form in the gunfight that burst the quiet of night from a distance.

Chuckling at the African's superstitious fears, Wittacre made the extreme effort of leaning over and retrieving the box from the table. Previously, he had looked at the offering with disdain, but now that his enemies lay in ruin a hateful nostalgia overcame him. He was curious to see what the dead woman had left him. His hands shook and were weak, but he eventually took firm hold of the twine and untied it. He tore back the brown paper and opened the box. An audible sound escaped him. Within the box, nestled on a mound of shredded newspaper, was a knife hewn from stone; handle and blade one solid piece, the edge a jagged row of serration made razor sharp by determined fashion. The part serving as a handle was wrapped in leather. A string of beads and small tuff of feathers hung from the handle's end. He took up the weapon and admired it. Then, he laughed aloud.

"I'm glad it brings you joy."

Wittacre made a startled cry and dropped the knife.

"I was hopin' you'd find it to yer likin'."

"Wha—b.."

"Hush, now. I know. You expect me dead."

Wittacre struggled to move, to rise, to do anything to get his hands on the woman that stood at the foot of his bed. A light flared up as she struck a match and lit a lantern, taken from Wittacre's own storehouse. She came around the side of the bed and sat the lantern on the bedside table. Wittacre had forgotten everything but his rage. He spat and grunted in his effort to go at Nan. She put out her wrinkled hand.

227

"Calm. Calm. It's over now. Be at peace."

There were no words. Nothing to give the moment a final meaning. Nothing to define the relationship of the two world-weary souls that faced each other there, in the finality of time. Nan made a motion, looked up to the sky beyond the ceiling, and with the swiftness of a much younger woman, swept up the stone knife, turned it in her hand, and plunged it into Wittacre's chest. The old man let out an awful moan and the blood ran. He sputtered and cursed and the blood filled his mouth. Nan mounted the bed, pulled back the knife, and struck again, deeply into the side of Wittacre's neck. Blood sprayed up in a high arc as she withdrew and her visage became marked with red. Then, Nanuxse, warrior, smashed the lantern over herself. The flames leapt up and she was consumed along with Wittacre, the gilded bed, and the whole of the plantation house. At last, the fire within the mountain had come home to burn until extinguished by the dawn.

*   *   *

Abe had gone and taken the box with him. Irvin, Jr. was glad to be done with it. He had gone about the house in the night, taking account of all that seemed so distant from him in daylight. He was tired and his last thoughts before retiring were of Abe and the medicine that waited for him in the kitchen.

Though Abe was a young man of little experience, he had seen the fear in Russell's eyes when he spoke of the land.

"I went up there once before the war was on, and once agin' I went up jus' after, when my wound was still tender," Russell had explained. "But I ain' been back since, an' I reckin' it's comin' on twenty-five years since I been there. I can't go back…"

Abe had little to say. The young man could see the emotion welling within the old invalid and felt embarrassed for the both of them; unable to bring himself to lay bare the concerns with which he had been infected.

"Don' open it till you plan on a' usin' it," Irvin had repeated again as Abe prepared to leave. "An' there'll be another. Someday, you might find 'im or he'll find you."

Abe had turned to ride off, back northwards and east into the mountains. Irvin stopped him as he left.

"Thank you," said Irvin.

"Fer what?" asked Abe.

"Jus'…jus' take care. Git on now." And Abe had, riding off with the clothes on his back, the little box of papers, a Harpers Ferry rifle, and a few dollars given him by Russell.

The old man leaned heavily on his crutch with one hand resting on the box containing his medicine as he recalled the tall figure of Abe on horseback riding off on his odyssey back to the place lost with Russell's leg in a distant past—where even memory began to fail him in his escape from the present life he maintained among his family. Irvin took up the box and made his way back to the table. His path was lit by a single candle wavering as he walked clutching both the candlestick and box awkwardly in one hand. He reached the table and sat down his things, taking care to find the chair with the familiar scar running across the table to his breast. He sighed. Touching upon the personalized little tag, Irvin unbound the box and slid it from its brown paper wrapping. Within was a corked vial resting on some wood shavings and a wad of cotton protecting a glass syringe held in the jaws of a stainless steel frame and plunger. It was that old fashioned morphine, delivered by Sears-Roebuck to ease his suffering years. He perspired and pushed the needle through the cork to draw it full. He flicked the syringe, watching the tiny bubbles' clumsy effervescence. A slight depression and the yellow tinged liquid spurt shortly from the needle. With an easy pain the needle slid into his vain. Breathing his last, Irvin J. Russell, Jr. pressed the plunger home. Care subsided, the world was washed clean, and the last of a long metamorphosis was finished.

DUTY

Tatters had been long-involved in heavy combat throughout Normandy. It was somewhere near Saint-Lô, or perhaps after, during the push toward the Rur...it was all beginning to run together. Those years in Europe were a rage of blood and killing and dying. Sometimes, he almost believed he had never killed anyone over there; but then the days and nights would intrude on him in the endless multitude of their number—so vast seemed the lengths of battle he saw that he could never bring himself to say some of the numbers aloud: 242 days of combat. No, just then, he recognized it. Brest, an operation called "Cobra". They had been engaged in the hedge-rows though this was less surprising at that time than it had been. But despite the sick familiarity adrenaline had gained, Tatters had never possessed nerves steeled enough to stand against the fortified pillboxes and landlocked naval cannons used by the Germans to defend the city.

When the hedge-rows were abandoned, the fighting went house to house, sometimes among civilians too frightened to fight or flee, sometimes amongst those determined to fight. They had gone through a house, a skinny row house three stories tall with food still on the table where the owners had left it when they evacuated or were forced out by the German occupiers. Tatters had shooed the flies away and eaten some bread. Under a hard yellow crust, the butter was soft and unspoiled. He had been halfway through the chunk of bread he'd torn when he saw it, just outside in the street. A *Panzerkampfwagen* Tiger *Ausf.* E stood in a modest square, a roadblock in effect, it's squad backed up by the famous *Fallschirmjäger*. Everyone had dropped quietly to the ground; the acceleration began in the chest and the *amant adrenaline* embraced her lover in a savage grip. Tatters became paralyzed. But another was in action. Tatters saw him move across the kitchen, to the window. The Germans began to chatter; they were on edge scoping the streets. Gears within the tank engaged and the cannon swiveled. It seemed to Tatters the house was in range. Who was it by the window? David? No, David wasn't…David died in Italy.

But it was. He stood by the window and lobbed a grenade. It bounced and rolled against the tank's tread. The 8.8 cm *Kanpfwagenkanone* 36/L56 erupted in the instant David's grenade came to rest against the Tiger's paw. But David wasn't there? He died in Anzio, yet there he was, in Brest, throwing his grenade synchronized with the roar of the cannon. He turned to Tatters, he always turned to Tatters, standing in the window, enframed in that very last instant as the pale green curtains billowed in daisies around him and the Pzgr. 39 armor piercing, capped, ballistic cap with explosive filler came through the window. David looked at Tatters and smiled and though it seemed surreal and impossible Tatters could see the shell coming through the window. It struck David square in the chest as anyone with their senses dove for cover. Tatters could not bring himself to look away and David's body became a red cloud, a crimson nimbus bearing a mist of gore across the tortured landscape. Tatters could always feel the warmth on his face and then he woke up suddenly, shocked to be at home, in his St. Clairsville apartment, napping on the sofa. He would sit half up in a shock and look around. His son, Howard had been standing at his side. The boy stepped back afraid, his trembling eyes fixed on his father. Tatters reached out; Howard shifted subtly away. The child retreated down the hallway to his room. Tatters sat on the couch and hung his head.

He left the apartment to get a drink, to play a round of poker with Ezra. At home, Tatters ate dinner in silence. Ruth made small talk with Howard. Tatters went to bed and David watched him sleep—just looking at him in those moments before exploding. Tatters woke up, the sheets sticking to him, his pulse rapid. He showered and went to work. Ruth and Mama Clay worried. They said he should think about moving back to the hollow, that he should think of home. Abe had bought more land, the big plot across the road. But the steel mills were paying and the hard labor and the heat made him forget all the endless days of war.

*   *   *

The rider had set out from the plains on horseback. He had only a vague perception of his destination though he carried in his heart a map committed to his memory with the aid of legend and the history of his family birthright. He carried little. Armed with pistol, long rifle, and dagger, the rider trapped his food or foraged. Seldom he hunted, for he always took more than he could consume and willing traders were more rare than paying customers.

He was still a young man, though hard; that's how people described him, especially women who knew his age by his soft lips though knew his chest and heart and hands were hard. He was fully a man at seventeen, on his own, crossing the plains back to the east and the mountains. He took his time because he was dark and handsome and could be with many women as he traveled through the little outpost towns and villages that dotted the countryside along his route.

It was a route he'd never traveled. He always found it odd a road on which he'd never been could be so familiar by the landmarks told him back west, at the time he was given the box. As a child, they had called him Shemenetu, but he was to give up the name he was given in his return to the ancestral lands. He no longer resembled his namesake. Without a name, homeless for a time, he wandered in an easterly direction, taking work where few questions were asked. A woman had made a fine companion for a duration, but eventually she, like his name, would be gone. Still he thought of her—vaguely reminiscent of a woman on the periphery of his memory where those he never met yet whose lives live in the stories he'd been told in the days before he set out. Someone like his mother, dead when he was twelve; his father dead before then. This woman had been good company and her name had been Apollonia. She had been dark, like him, but Italian with thick wavy hair and the remains of an accent still on her ruddy lips. Like one time Shemenetu she was a being in transit and was mysterious about it, though he came to know she had run away. They passed through the Ohio Valley together, until coming to the mountains and turning south to the Monongahela. There she left him, saying only that she wept to be reminded of the Bonamico, winding amid the Aspromonte. At the time, he was too young to know what secrets were held by rivers that babbled but never spoke a word to the mountains on which they used the knife of time to carve their valleys.

*   *   *

Tatters had been furloughed from the mills. On the morning of his third week of unemployment, he began to think of the three acres his father had purchased across the road from his homestead. He began to think in general about his father and a phone call he had received shortly after his furlough caused his thinking to be shadowed by concern.

"Ye'low," said Tatters when he answered.

"Tatters?" came through the receiver.

"Yeah, this's 'im. Who's this?"

"It's yer Daddy."

"Alright, what'dya need?"

"Well, son, it's Verge."

"What about her?"

"She's missin'."

"Missin'?"

"I reckon that's what I said."

"How ya mean?"

235

"I mean, Margaret done called her up, an' Verge…well, you know how she is. Margaret says she was actin' funny like."

"Funny how?"

"I dunno, but she scared Margaret an' we's gone up there an' she's gone. We can't figure where she went."

"When's this?"

"I don' know…maybe, comin' up on…three days?"

"Three days? An' yer jus' now a' callin'?"

"Well, I don' know. I thought maybe she'd come back."

"Where's Ezra?"

"He been in town."

"In town? Hell, I ain't seen 'im."

"Could ya maybe help us look fer Verge?"

"Hell," said Tatters, "I sure as shit ain't got nothin' else ta do. Maybe we can talk on that land some."

"I'd like that," said Abe, his voice shaped by age and work.

The call had come in the morning, Howard was off to school already, Ruth busied herself about the house. Tatters took leave of the apartment and headed into the hollow to join the search for Verge. Ruth was glad to have the day to herself and made arrangements for Judith to pick Howard up from school, maybe take the boy to the movies.

Judith had a notion to take Howard to *Fun and Fancy Free*, but the boy was insistent and convinced his aunt that *Adventure Island* with Rhonda Fleming and Rory Calhoun would be more entertainment and so it was an afternoon of marooned seafarers and British, self-made dictators of the south seas.

When they had emerged from the darkened theater, Howard feigned at swashbuckling down the sidewalk as Judith watched him smiling. A low rumble broke in the distance and Howard stopped and stared off across the busy street into the mountains never far away.

"Sounds like thunder," said Judith. "We's best be gettin' on home, 'fore another snowstorm comes."

Howard jumped, laughing, and took off ahead of her down the street.

"Hey, now, hold yer horses!" she called after and trotted a few paces herself before she was caught up to the boy who resumes his imaginary fight against a jowly English tyrant.

As they came to an intersection, sirens could be heard winding up in the cold air from blocks away. The firehouse was not far from where they stood, and Judith bade Howard to wait there for a chance to see the engine rush by, blaring its harsh song on the afternoon air. Howard was enthused. Like most boys his age, he loved the big trucks and the ladders running along the side and the loud sirens blasting across the town. He liked to hear his father describe all the Army equipment and often wore the olive greens and oversized camouflage jacket from the closet he was not supposed to open. Only, he did not like it when his father fell silent while describing the M3 Half-tracks and the M8 Greyhounds and the M4 tractors and the M18 Hellcats and sat there in his silence with a tear visible in his eye before he got up and walked away somewhere only to come back dry-eyed but a little drunk. Howard thought of these things while he waited anxiously for the fire-engine to come wailing by, its sound already growing on the

237

breeze, reaching at last that crescendo as it went flying by with stalwart men clinging where they could.

"Boy, wasn't that exciting?" asked Judith.

"Sure was!" said Howard.

And on they went, pleased with themselves and the day.

They were distracted with each other as they walked along the avenues, stopping to get some candies at the five-and-ten cent store. Judith got a Coke and shared with Howard, who seemed unable to get enough from the smooth-rimmed glass bottle and smacked his lips each time they withdrew.

"It's that good is it?" Judith teased her nephew.

"Sure is!"

"Is that yer favorite phrase now?"

Howard nearly said "sure is!" but stopped himself and laughed instead and his aunt laughed with him until they turned the corner and saw the fire-engine outside Ruth and Tatter's apartment building. Thick black smoke billowed from the back of the block and from the windows in the upper story.

"Mama!" cried Howard as he took off at a sprint toward the blaze.

"Howard! Stop!" Judith repeated again and again as she followed.

As they neared, Ruth emerged from the ground floor, her head wrapped in a soaked cloth, water streaking her blackened face. She carried a charred broom that she used to beat the flames and sat a bundle of things in a pillowcase on the sidewalk before turning and rushing back into her home. The firemen occupied and paid no mind to the frantic Ruth, smeared with soot as she was and running to and fro with armfuls of cookery and Howard's toys. The boy broke away from his aunt's grip and went sprinting to where his mother had disappeared into the apartment house, staring into the stairwell where wisps of black smoke streamed from the corners of the doorway. When Ruth reemerged, she had a few last possessions in one hand and Tatters' three rifles slung over her shoulder. She looked dolefully at her son who began to cry.

Judith came running up, exasperated. Ruth was black with soot.

"Lordy…" said Judith. Then after a silent pause, "You'uns can stay with me. My place's small but—"

Ruth cut her sister off with a glance. "No," she said, "I reckon it's time ta go back home."

*   *   *

For a long time, the one who was Shemenetu and soon to be no one would think of Apollonia. They had had a long and final conversation one night by a small fire on the wide plain before the mountains. The crescent moon had hooked the mountain curtain and was drawing its shadow across a deepening eve when Apollonia broke into the nocturnal chorus of crickets and cicada chirping allegretto in the woven arbor chamber.

"Time is come I must go."

The young traveler had expected this. He had himself taken leave of many young women in a similar way, though he had begun to believe he might never depart from the dark fullness of Apollonia.

"Why?" he asked.

"Because, you are a man with an end."

He was silent.

"You carry burdens. I see it when you ride. Your hand goes often to something you carry by your breast."

He looked toward his vest. In the shadows, only he could see the vague trace of the box inside the vest.

"Even now, it takes you from me…"

"Tell me to leave it. I'll leave it for you."

"No," she said.

He had no reply.

"It is your duty," she said.

There was no denying the things she had said to him.

"You must go to where you have been heading. I do not think I can follow you there. I do not think anyone can…"

The traveler lowered his head.

"You are a lonely man. Even with me now, I see it when you look at me…sadness…"

"Ask me to be done with it and I will be happy."

"You cannot be happy. You will not leave it be, even for me. Especially for me. You will not stop for no woman, even a young and pretty woman who would bare you many children."

He laid back onto the grass and looked up into the vault of the cosmos. He did not ask it of Apollonia, but asked aloud into a void, "When will I be free of it?"

She sighed and lay down beside him, her arm draping languidly across him, her head resting on his chest. "You will never be free," she confided. "It is not in your nature to be free."

"Some men are free men…"

"And some men have been slaves…"

"Forever?"

"No, not forever."

"Tonight?"

"Tonight we are slaves to one another, for one last night. Tomorrow, I will be gone, and you must continue on. It is—"

"—my duty…"

*   *   *

After the fire, Tatters had found a welcome reprieve in the construction of a new house on the land freshly acquired by Abe. The building of the house came as a general distraction. In searching for Verge, they had found Jonathan's body. The McClain's had been severe in their reaction to their son's suicide and were not inclined to give him a proper, Christian burial; a fact that had sent Mama Clay into a rage of contempt and maternal pride. She had rallied those in the hollow to respect the memory of their lost kin and had made all of the arrangements to bury Jonathan as she would any other member of the family. Naomi was lost in sorrow. She, along with everyone else, assumed the worse for Verge and Jonathan's memorial was a memorial for Verge as well, though there was no body to consign to rest in the ground of the hollow.

Tatters was happy to be distracted from all of this sadness. He knew it was his duty to look after the homestead and his family, but the war and the fire and the death of the two McClain kin had disrupted his slow returning sense of normality. He was hopeful for his brother Wayne and Elf. The two had used some capital from the mining business and invested in an old general store in St.

Clairsville. It had formerly been known as Wittacre's Wares, but had stood ancient and vacant for many years. Wayne worked long hours to reinstate the old quaint homeliness of the place and turn it into a hardware store with a garage out back where he and Tatters could busy themselves learning the ins and outs of transmission and exhaust work through a haphazard process of trial, error, and success. The youngest Marks boy, Harry, was not so interested in cars and the like, and though he had given up on his youthful infatuation with Judith, he still plied her to ingratiate him with Ernesto Guiseppe in the hopes of one day acquiring Ginny's Diner for himself, thus further cementing the Marks' growing reputation as young men about town.

Such were the foci of Tatters during that time of unrest and the turning of a new, post-war era. What began as distractions soon took over and evolved into the fullness of real life. The only lingering unhappiness hanging over Tatters at that time was is estrangement from Ezra.

The war had fractured the relationship between these two business partners. Whereas Tatters and Wayne had served together and were therefore bonded twice over by brotherhood and battle, Ezra had been sent off to the Pacific. This literal distance, and certain untold events of which Ezra would never speak, had displaced a once central familiarity.

The disjunction between Tatters and his friend became untenable one day when Margaret came into the newly finished kitchen of Tatters' growing home. She sat down at the table across from her brother as he ate some reheated pot-pie. Tatters looked up from his lunch to see the worry on Margaret's young face.

"You need ta go an' see Daddy," she said to him.

"Why's that now."

"He ain't right, Tatters. He's worried on somethin' but I can't figger it."

"He's always worried on somethin'. Daddy's gettin' old an' old men ain't got naught to do but worry."

"I know...but this is differt somehow."

"What'chu think me talkin' is gonna help?"

"I dunno. You's always been close ta Daddy's all."

Tatters put down his fork and thought on that statement. He thought of the moonshine at his wedding, of the beating and the three dollars he'd got trapping and the time Abe struck Mama Clay in the kitchen at the old homestead before Margaret was born.

"You know what it's about a'tall?" he asked his sister.

"I think it's business, but I's never let in on all that, you know," there was a trace of contempt in Margaret's voice as she spoke of the family's business. She was smart and able-bodied, but as a woman had been kept a domestic animal in the household where the men went out into the world on errands of capital.

"I know..." said Tatters. "I can go talk to him."

"Thanks. I hate ta see'im all worked up over something and know there's not a thing I can do about it."

Tatters nodded and went back to his pot-pie. Margaret remained there with him and the two shared the afternoon in silence. The sun was bright and yellow in the sky. After a while, Tatters decided to put off what work he had planned for the day and follow Margaret across the road and to their father's house where he might discover what it was that that caused his sister such concern. Abe sat in the shade of the porch. He was getting heavy in his old age and his hands rested on his round and protruding belly as he rocked to and fro. He smiled thinly as Tatters approached. Margaret went on inside and her brother took a seat beside their father.

"I'm sorry about yer apartment in town. It's a real shame," said Abe, almost at once.

Tatters made no response. His father had needlessly apologized for the fire that claimed the St. Clairsville apartment almost every time he had seen Tatters since. Things were better in the hollow anyway.

Then, abruptly, Abe asked, "You seen Ezra?"

"No, I ain't see 'im."

Abe sighed. "I wish he'd come around."

"Why's that?"

"Oh, I don' know...just wish he would."

"There somethin' you need ta tell 'im?"

Abe was quiet.

"There somethin' you need ta tell me?"

Abe looked at his son, then away into the brightness of the sun. He leaned forward and took a beaten wad of paper from his pant's pocket. He unfolded the several pages, looked at them, looked at Tatters, and handed the documents over.

"What's this?" asked Tatters.

"Taxes. On our land an' the mines."

"So? We's paid our taxes."

"Not these'ins we ain't."

"How's that?"

"Well, I don' rightly know. But, if'n I'ma readin' them right, there ain't been taxes paid on this land since 186_."

"So?"

"So they's figured that I had the deed to the place. So I owe them taxes. Almost sixty years worth. It's everything we got."

Tatters bit his lip.

"How long you knowed this, Pa?"

Abe shook his head. His eyes glassed over. "I knowed 'bout a fortnight or so. I jus'…it was so soon after Verge an' all. I din' know what ta do."

"How long?"

"Does it matter, son? We ain't ever gonna git that much. We're finished here," Abe looked away again and wiped his eyes. Looking distant, he said, "Lord, I thought all'a this was over."

Tatters got up and left his father sitting there. He strode across the road, got into his truck, and headed into town.

*   *   *

Apollonia was gone, just as he'd expected. She had been a woman of her word. Those words would remain with the rider as he rode on. He repeated them over and over in his mind as he drew nearer to his final destination. There were no more distractions. No more women and games of poker in the outposts and trading stations. Just the way back east and the mountains. He thought a lot as he rode. He recalled the words of other women, of his grandmother in particular—what she had told him about his name and its history and where he'd come from even before he was born; about where he was eventually to return.

His mother had died of pneumonia, so he had lived with his ancient grandmother until the beginning of his odyssey. She had been forced to flee from his ancestral lands before the Civil War, when she was just a girl. That girl had grown up on the run into a formidable woman and even in elderly decrepitude remained a font of eternal authority passed down along all the women of her lineage. Something in the order of her words kept those who listened enthralled before her without question.

"It was I who called you Shemenetu," she had said. "This was the name of my great-grandfather, your great-great-great-grandfather, Big Snake, the warrior-chief. I had never known the man, but his spirit dwelt in my mother, Nanuxse, and the hollow in which I was born and to which you must return in my stead. Listen now and I will tell to you the story of your kin and of your duty to them. The box you now possess contains the stakes from the land, the deed, my Testimony, and a writ from Congress declaring your inalienable rights to the land. But you must know this history, because there are those who would take your birthright from you and have killed those in the past that stood in their way.

"They were one family, Wittacre, and they married into the Avrich clan. This union has brought together the two forces that would dispossess you—property and law. The Wittacre's were landowners back in the times before the Civil War. The two daughters of that hateful man had married men called Avrich who were a banker and lawyer respectively. I cannot know for sure what became of them, but I know at least that they went down to Texas, and I can be near certain they've started certain business ventures with aims not known to their partners. Ah, who knows the hearts of men anyway? And what these men hid behind their eyes was further buried by paper and contracts and money. I know my own mother would disapprove, but I'd just as soon you killed them as gave them a chance to have our land. Regardless, I can't tell you what became of them, but I do know that their ultimate fate is a fire that dwells in the mountain—not the fires of Hell, but a fire that rages in the earth, a real fire waiting to be rekindled in the deep. Remember this! Do not forget the fire.

"The last person I knew who had the land, Russell, he was able to start up a small mine there, but it was abandoned and lost in the war. He can no longer return there, being an invalid, or so I've been told. I have not seen him in many, many years. This man Russell's father, Irvin senior, he saved my life. It is thanks to him you now live. Never forget this debt. Remember to be grateful.

"When you depart here, you must give up your name, Shemenetu, and take up a name to dwell among the people of the hollow. Your return will be like the Scribe of the Old Testament who returned with the Word and the Life. In that box is my word and the means to your own life. There will be another, and you must befriend this man. I know not who he is, or if he'll ever make it back to that place, but if he should present himself, you ought not question his honor. If he has the rights, honor them, and so too will yours be honored.

"There is one last thing that I would give to you, but it must remain hidden. If someone were to discover such a thing in your possession it would mean a great danger to you and your journey home. I cannot tell what circumstances you will find upon your return. We were cast out with great violence. My mother and brothers all were murdered by the agents of Wittacre. It was a different time, but I doubt the hatred has yet died in them.

"Now, go, return to the land I had to flee. I will miss you and love you always. Do not forget your old grandmother, Theadoshia Rose...and remember the fire that burns in the mountain..."

*   *   *

The Brass Cactus was an old juke-joint across from the rail-yard on the south side of St. Clairsville. It had a certain reputation for gambling, drinking, and loose women. Tatters had won many a hand of poker in that dingy place, but when his truck pulled up outside on the day he had learned of the unpaid taxes, gambling was the furthest thing from his mind. The door swung open and no one paid Tatters any mind as he walked in, approached the bar and inquired with the tender regarding Ezra.

"He's upstars," said the bartender. "Better knock first," he added with a knowing wink.

Tatters said nothing and left the barroom, dark even in the bright of the afternoon. He went outside, around the corner of the building, and upstairs to an arrangement of small and seedy apartments kept mostly for the purpose of prostitution, though the city turned a blind eye to the tenets who never paid their own rent. Tatters knew the number wherein Ezra would be found; with a fat Italian woman, pock-marked and smoky. Tatters had seen Ezra sad and drunk with his face buried in the woman's full breasts. He expected to find his friend thus on that day, but the scene that greeted him was almost worse than Ezra's near invalidity.

Tatters opened the door to find no one about. He called out for Ezra, received no response, and went farther into the quarters.

He could smell the musk of bodies within and followed the odor to the bedroom where Ezra lay entwined, himself a sweaty mass. The room wreaked, not as much of sex as of booze and a stale smokiness from the night before. Ezra still had a shirt on, flannel, buttoned sloppily and hanging off his half naked body. Tatters grabbed him up by the collar and slapped him hard across the face. The woman woke up before Ezra did and demanded in a flaccid voice that Tatters explain himself.

"Shut up," said Tatters, striking Ezra again in the face.

Finally, Ezra began to come to, but was still drunk.

"That ain't her," he slurred. "That ain't her…"

"What the hell you goin' on about?" shouted Tatters. "Dammit! Git up! We's goin' back to the holler. Now!"

Ezra tried to stand but couldn't. He got sick on the floor. Tatters stepped back in disgust.

"What the hell happened to you?"

"That…that ain't her. She's gone. Left me. Oh, oh Rose! Rose *hic* Rose! My Mama *hic* died and that ain't her! She gone gone *hic* gone!"

"Shit," said Tatters.

The sober man slung the drunk one over his shoulder and dropped a few dollars at the hooker's feet. The bill fluttered to rest like dirty leaves against the rose tattoo on her ankle.

"Clean this mess up," said Tatters, and left down the stairs with Ezra sluggishly slung over one shoulder.

Once again out of doors, Tatters threw Ezra into the empty bed of the truck, climbed in the cab, and took off toward Wayne's hardware store being none too cautious of the potholes along the route. Elf was sweeping off the front stoop when Tatters pulled up to the curb. He hopped deftly from the driver's seat to pull Ezra, dazed and moaning, from the bed of the truck, half naked with a dried bit of vomit still clinging to the stubble on his chin.

"Ach!" exclaimed Elf, "Vhat is dee matter here, eh? Vhat's dis boy doingk?"

"This boy's doin' drunk, Elf. Git Wayne."

"Ach," sighed Elf as she turned and went inside to fetch her husband.

Tatters practically dragged Ezra around to the garage where a oversized blue barrel collected rain water beneath a spout at one end of the roof's gutter. Without hesitation, Tatters plunged Ezra head first into the barrel and let him soak a few seconds before withdrawing him again into the sunlight. Ezra spat and gagged and choked a bit before catching his breath. Tatters wasted no time instigating another sobering baptismal in the rain water. When Wayne emerged from the store he saw Tatters with both arms wrapped around the waist of an inverted Ezra, the poor drunkard's bare ass bobbing helplessly in the air.

"Jesus, Tatters!" hollered Wayne. "What the hell's goin' on here?"

"Wayne, you talked to Daddy recently?"

"No I ain't. Damn Tatters! Will you put that poor feller down?"

Tatters obliged and dropped Ezra to the pavement.

"You got a pair'a pants for this fool?"

Wayne nodded, then said, "What's this about Pa."

"We got trouble from the taxman."

"Shit. So you need this fool cleaned up an' sober I reckin'?"

"I reckin'."

Wayne was about to call for Elf when she came around waving a pair of pants in the air.

"Give dees to dat poor man," she said, thrusting the pants out to Tatters. Wayne took her aside and they spoke quietly in German to one another. Tatters looked down on Ezra in disgust, throwing the pants down hard at his crotch.

Tatters knelt beside Ezra, who was slowly regaining some sense.

"Can you hear me?"

"Ah, uh, yeah, yeah I hear you. That jus'…that jus' wadn't her…"

"You listen here: I don' care who it was or wasn't. You lie down with dogs, you wake up with fleas, git me? Now the money man's gonna come an' take all what you pay that whore with, you understand that? Git yer shit together an' head down ta that holler before dark, or so help me Ezra I'm gonna beat the tar outta you an' leave you out ta dry."

"Git…git my…" Ezra stopped, as if suddenly aware of some long buried fact. He looked back at Tatters with a hardness in his eyes that cut through the drink and fracture of war. "How'd you know about that?"

Tatters, not sure any longer what he knew, returned Ezra's hard gaze and froze him in it.

"Git goin'."

Ezra got up, pants in one hand, and took off walking out of sight of the Marks brothers.

*　　　　　*　　　　　*

The rider had grown weary. His thoughts wore heavy on his mind and mountains loomed all around him with their hidden histories etched in undecipherable runes across the bark of trees and in the decoupage of leaves laid out slick and damp all around; their various colors giving the impression of inscription alive on the ground. Then there was the smell. The rich fecundity rose all about in an aroma that was inescapable, effusive, and total. It penetrated through the smell of the horse and the unwashed clothes and the desire to forget. It penetrated deep into a memory that was not his but beckoned to him from the mouth of his hundred-year-old grandmother; the rose of her name given over to the odoriferous land in the days after his departure.

He had gone far since the morning Apollonia left him. Many days had passed since she left and nearly five years since he last spoke to his grandmother. After the long trek and many detours he would finally arrive.

Coming out of the west, the rider followed a deep cut in the mountains and came down into a long row of hollows along the wide bank of a cold creek that had been described to him many times. He left the banks of the creek in a valley of three hills to search out a certain tree he was told would mark the west end of the land to which he returned. There were moments when he felt stupid as he went from tree to tree, guessing at which one stood as the landmark to his legacy.

When he at last came upon the tree, there was no mistaking the wooden monolith that seemed cut from the bedrock of the hills themselves and spread itself wide in the center of the cleft of the world. The experience of his memory was welling up within him at the moment of convergence and it seemed as if time was shifting around him where he stood; rearranging itself to place him at a distance of time unperceived until then, once long ago when strangers brought his kin from their homestead to bury them at the terminus of thought. He walked away from the tree, to the south. Within a few minutes he came upon the graves.

Standing among them, he read aloud the names cut crudely in haste upon a stone. Just one giant slab of rock inlaid on the land, cold and deep as the mines hidden ahead. They were there, all together, listed: "Thomas and Esther Merritt; Henrik Merritt; Black Hoof Merrit." Another list bore the names of their murderers— Avrich and Wittacre. A few yards away were proper graves, Ol' Merritt and the first Catacehassa, Nanuxse's brother, and under stone worn down by time, Ol' Merritt's father lay at rest. This was the place he sought. The fog of memory moved in from the hilltops, descended in smooth wisps from the trees. The rider spent the night among the dead before moving on in the morning.

The next day he followed the valley to where he thought he would find the old fort-house. He didn't know, for his grandmother hadn't known, if it had been burned or if it still stood. He was pleased to learn the place still stood, but was surprised to see a wisp of smoke rising from the chimney in the growing autumn cool. The rider dismounted and walked his horse along the trail where the trees grew in sparse numbers and a road had been cleared for some time. The land was less thick in the area where the house stood, pruned for many reasons, the rumble of a train echoing through the valleys in the north, on the backside of a hillock where the fort-house stood. He came around and approached the house with care. A young girl picked honeysuckle and blushed when he approached. He hailed the girl in a friendly manner, but she took off into the house from which her father momentarily appeared.

"He there," said the father, "what's yer business?"

"I've none. I've been on the road for some time and am looking for work or a place to stay."

"Eh? Work? I dunno 'bout no work. I might have a bite ta eat fer ya. An' some quality shine if'n you can pay. Then we'll talk on puttin' you up fer the night."

"Can I git some water fer my horse?"

The father looked back into the house and then again at the traveler.

"Yeah," he said as he left the porch, "you can water yer hoss."

The man's wife appeared in the doorway with the little girl by her side. They watched as the father crossed the yard and came to the traveler and his horse to extend a strong, dirty hand in greeting to the stranger.

"I'm sorry ta keep ya outta the house fer the time. I got a wife there and three girls singin' the Gospel. I don' know you. An' I figger I don' care to 'til I got reason ta keep ya around."

"Hmph," said the traveler. "That's fair enough. Best keep yer girls safe there. Can't blame you on that account."

"Well, see here, I'm Harbarger. Holofernes Harbarger, known all 'round these parts."

"Can't say anyone knows me, an' fer that you can be yer own judge," said the traveler.

Holofernes eyed him curiously.. "Well then, stranger," he said, "you got yerself a name?"

There was a longish pause that made Holofernes a bit uneasy. In that moment of silence, the traveler thought back to his lost name, to Shemenetu, to his grandmother, to the Old Testament Scribe returning from exile with the Words inscribed on parchment.

"Well?" said Holofernes.

"Ezra," said the traveler. "Ma name's Ezra."

*   *   *

Night was coming to the hollow and Tatters sat at a table in his mother's kitchen with the woman herself and Naomi who had grown wan and frail in the long days since the passing of her daughter into mystery. Ezra had not yet made it back from St. Clairsville, and it was for him that Tatters waited. Mama Clay reached across the table to give her son's hand a firm squeeze.

"I'm sorry you gotta take the lead on this. Yer Daddy has a time makin' out all them papers," said the woman to her boy.

"I know, Mama. It ain't a bother."

"The whole world's a bother," said Naomi.

"Well, be that as it may, yer Daddy done told me the lot of it."

"There ain't too much ta tell. These fellers here," Tatters indicated a letterhead to his mother, "Wittacre, Avrich, an' Locke, they's leveragin' that pipeline agin' us. Suppose they knew that from the start. They's representin' the 'interests' of Brown 'n Root, whatever that means. What it means ta me is, Pa got run out on'a line whiles we was off ta war."

"Ain't no end to the sufferin'a this world. Ain't no end," said Naomi.

"Well, be that as it may, them at Brown n' Root don' own no land here. They pays us ta keep that pipeline runnin' through here," said Mama Clay.

"Well, Mama, that's true, an' then it ain't either. See this is all comin' down ta back taxes. Way back taxes. Damn near back ta the Civil War. An' we ain't got that kinda money. All'a ours is tied up in things, assets I guess they call it. Wayne's store, the mines, the new land Daddy bought. We can't come up with the sum they's askin' fer down at the IRS. But them'ins at Brown 'n Root can come up with that sum, least that's the claim a' Wittacre, Avrich, n' Locke."

"I see," said Mama Clay.

"I wish I couldn't," said Tatters. "These Wittacre folks is claiming a 'substantial interest' in the land cause of the pipeline and the sublease on the phone 'n 'lectric wires strung up an' down the holler here. So, they's offer ta pay them taxes, but that amounts ta buyin' us out. Then, we're at their mercy. I doubt we'd be let stay on."

Mama Clay shook her head.

"Ain't no end 'a the sufferin'," said Naomi.

Abe came into the doorway. He assumed a defeated look upon seeing Tatters seated there with all of the papers in front of him.

"I'm sorry, son."

Tatters had nothing to say.

Just then the door opened. It was Ezra. He entered the kitchen a changed man. The drunkard from that afternoon was gone in a wash of sobriety and though Ezra looked tired and wild-haired, a fire burned in his eyes that shone with a fierce clarity of purpose and reason. Without a word, he revealed a box wrapped in brown paper and bound in rough twine. Tatters' eyes widened as the box touched down upon the table. His mind reeled and raced back to that day when he fled into the woods and Abe had guarded a box near identical to the one now before him. Tatters looked at Ezra, who returned the stare. Abe came forward to lean on the table, his own eyes going from the box, to Mama Clay, to the box.

"Where'd you git that?" asked Tatters.

"It's you," said Abe. "My God, after all these years! It's *you*!"

"I reckon it is," said Ezra. He reached down and undid the twine. The box opened, and therein lay the red stake, the claims on the land, the Testimony of Theadoshia Rose, a writ from the Congress—old and browned and smelling of an uncounted age.

"What's the meanin' a' this?" Tatters was bewildered and still struggling to sort out the profound significance of what transpired before his very eyes.

"I got a duty to do," with that, Ezra took an old leather pouch from his breast pocket and turned it upside down above the papers spread out on the table. From the overturned pouch came a shower of gold coin. They bounced and piled upon the letterhead from Wittacre, Avrich, & Locke. Real gold, pure gold coin minted long ago, before the Civil War, before the World War that had nearly destroyed Ezra's mind, that had ruined Verge and Jonathan.

"There's plenty there fer them taxes," said Ezra. "If I'm ta honor you like I ought, this belongs to us all."

The following day, Ezra led Tatters down along the pipeline into the mountain deep. He traced the long trail of memory back to where the tree once stood, that spot now desecrated and obliterated beneath the march of a technological age. Away to the south, farther from the pipeline, still preserved from modernity by seclusion, they found the stone slab with the names that would not be forgotten. There too, on that stone, they found at last the bones of Verge McClain.

Ezra scratched his head, "I never reckoned she'd come out here. She couldn't 'a known…"

"Don' you reckon what Verge could and couldn'ta known. There ain't been many like her born in these parts, an' thankfully there ain't many more like ta be born."

"Is this gonna save us, Tatters?"

"Fer a time, I reckon it will."

Ezra nodded his head and knelt down beside what remained of Verge McClain.

"Why'd you wait, Ezra? Why all this time?"

Ezra couldn't respond right away. He had a ponderous stature as he rose from where he knelt on the stone and said, "Tatters, for a long time, I jus' wanted to forget. My life, hell, you knowed. My Mama was too old to bear children an' I done ruined her. She wasn't never well and I was barely twelve when she died. My Daddy had been dead on six years when Mama passed. An' my grandmother, my god, I can hardly count how old she was, an' wise, Tatters. She knowed so much, like the whole world was poured in her head, you know? It was too much. I got set out on the road as a pup. You don' quite know ta be out in the world half a kid. Maybe sixteen, hardly a man, still hard, an' world-weary when you should be tender an' soft. When I came upon Holofernes and them girls, I jus' about give up. Then yer Daddy showed up an' by God he had the damn rights! I thought all my prayers were answered right there. Then the war was on, an' you know…well…"

Tatters paced a bit and looked into the sun. "Yeah," he said, "I know."

After a time, Tatters returned to Ezra's side and said to him, "I done looked over them papers you had. That writ from Congress, there's something strange there…"

"Well, that alone should secure our rights here, mine at least. But I've come to believe we're kin in a way."

Tatters took those words in, "Now, I might not a'know what I'ma talkin' about," he began, "but that Treaty with the Wyandots, there's a name there, an' I knowed no one but Mama paid much mind, but Verge was, I dunno, obsessed with it. What I can't figger is how she even knowed. Was Helizikinopo, or somethin' similar."

"That was the name of my great-great-great-grandmother," said Ezra. "She was married to Shemenetu, Big Snake. From what my grandmother told me, it was from them that the land was poached by the Wittacres. I can't believe that Verge ever knew nothing about that."

"Holofernes thought she was possessed…"

"Holofernes was a drunken fool—like me."

"Like hell you are," said Tatters.

"Well," said Ezra, "that remains to be seen."

From that day on, Ezra took the married name of his great-grandmother, and was known until his death as Ezra Merritt. But he knew that nothing had changed; that, though they may continue to work the land, slowly the tract would be passed on and on into an unknown future. Such is as it always had been. Though, in a strange way, he never again doubted the veracity of his duties to that place, to the Marks family, to the memory of Verge McClain. Sometimes, in the early morning fog, while Ezra sat perched in a tree-stand hunting with Tatters, the two would see far up in the mountains a light that came from the fire within the earth. Whether it was the moonshine in their eyes or the play of the slow rising sun across the landscape, they could trace the path of that light down through the hollows until it came to rest among the houses they had built for themselves on the land passed down at last to them. Tatters would often tell his son Howard about that fire, and eventually, Ezra too would tell his children of the fire that burned in the mountain so that they might remember its light all throughout the sometimes dark passage of time.

ABOUT THE AUTHOR

Donovan Irven was born in Cumberland, Maryland, a small working class town in the Appalachians. He is currently enrolled in the interdisciplinary Ph.D. program in Philosophy and Literature at Purdue University; he studied philosophy, history, and creative writing at Frostburg State University, and received his Master's Degree in Philosophy from West Chester University of Pennsylvania. An APPA Certified Philosophical Counselor, Irven resides in West Lafayette, Indiana where he writes and practices philosophy. You can follow him on Twitter @DonovanIrven, and contact him through Facebook, or his blog, *In the Time of Ethics* [http://inthetimeofethics.blogspot.com/]. *Things in Brown Paper* is Irven's second novel.